Books by Sara Driscoll

FBI K-9s

Lone Wolf

Before It's Too Late

Storm Rising

No Man's Land

Leave No Trace

Under Pressure

Still Waters

That Others May Live

Summit's Edge

NYPD Negotiators

Exit Strategy

Shot Caller

Lockdown

Standalones

Echoes of Memory

SUM
EL

AN FBI K-9 NOVEL

SUMMIT'S EDGE

SARA DRISCOLL

KENSINGTON
PUBLISHING CORP.

kensingtonbooks.com

KENSINGTON BOOKS are published by

Kensington Publishing Corp.
900 Third Avenue
New York, NY 10022

All Kensington titles, imprints and distributed lines are available at special quantity discounts for bulk purchases for sales promotion, premiums, fund-raising, educational or institutional use.

Special book excerpts or customized printings can also be created to fit specific needs. For details, write or phone the office of the Kensington Special Sales Manager: Kensington Publishing Corp., 900 Third Avenue, New York, NY, 10022. Attn. Special Sales Department. Phone: 1-800-221-2647.

Library of Congress Card Catalogue Number: 2024912205

The K with book logo Reg. U.S. Pat. & TM. Off.

ISBN: 978-1-4967-4400-5
First Kensington Hardcover Edition: December 2024

ISBN: 978-1-4967-4401-2 (ebook)

10 9 8 7 6 5 4 3 2 1

Printed in the United States of America

SUMMIT'S EDGE

Prologue

Off Route: A deviation from the planned climbing route (path to the top); such deviations can lead to dangerous positions, such as becoming cliffed out.

May 6, 10:28 AM
Above Hartsel, Colorado

The attack came out of nowhere.

One moment Nora Gleason was frantically reviewing the menu for a fancy dinner meeting. In the next her ears were ringing with the reverberating blast of a gunshot, and there was blood splattered against the wall of the luxury aircraft cabin.

The day had started like any other . . . minus being told to get on a plane and run the annual meeting for the Barron Pharmaceuticals Board of Directors.

She was a junior assistant; this was way above her pay grade. When she'd signed on for this job eight months ago, she thought she'd get a little experience to then take those skills and start moving up. Or out. Instead, she'd been thrown into the deep end, and, as a result, never felt like she could keep up.

That's certainly how Gloria made her feel. Gloria, Mr. Barron Senior's executive assistant, who was all "Yes, Mr. Barron" and "Of course, Mr. Barron" and "Right away, Mr. Barron," and who then shoveled at least half that work on Nora, while Gloria took all the credit so Mr. Barron Senior thought she could walk on water. Didn't he realize she had a stable of assistants to help her?

Gloria was supposed to be on this trip, until her obstetrician suddenly decided it was too risky for Gloria to fly at eight and a half months along. But just because Gloria was grounded didn't mean the show didn't go on. Oh no, now someone had to go in her place. And they'd picked Nora. Not because she was the best—that had been made clear—but because she was unattached, with no children, so it would be *easiest* for her to go.

It was like a pity assignment, except instead of kindness coming her way, it was days of sunup to sundown—and beyond—work. And while the boss was away, Gloria would no doubt be calling it in from home.

Nora sat seething at the rear of the plane. Normally, the chance to be on Mr. Barron Senior's luxury private jet would have been a supercool moment for her, but she was still peeved she had to go. Then was even more peeved when Mr. Barron Junior told her to sit at the back near the kitchen and the flight attendant. Like she was staff. Well, she was staff, but she was part of the team, not a support person like the flight attendant. Who, she admitted, seemed nice. The attendant had caught her eye and smiled as she'd settled the bigwigs in their seats and made sure they were comfortable, taking their drink orders so she could serve them as soon as takeoff was complete.

Nora sat in her big, comfortable, padded seat, which felt more like a lounge chair, with a table in front of her so she could get her notes organized while they flew to Napa. She'd never been to California. Hell, she'd never even left the Denver area before, but she knew she wouldn't be seeing California. She'd be seeing the inside of meeting and hotel rooms, and that would be it. Then she'd be back in a few days, probably without so much as a thank-you from the sainted Gloria.

Takeoff had been uneventful and beautifully smooth; it really was a glorious way to travel. It was too bad Mr. Barron Junior was so unpleasant, always focused on business and the bottom line, and was known to hold a grudge against anyone for *any* perceived wrong. Or else she might consider pursuing him. Only having his money and lifestyle might make up for actually having *him*.

Dream on, Nora. If you don't make sure these meetings go perfectly, you won't have him or a job.

She'd pulled out her slimline laptop, opened it on the table, and started to review the schedule of events, the food and drink required for each, what technology had been booked, and the related agenda.

Nora had been deep into double-checking dinner details when the world went to hell.

The gunshot was heart-stoppingly loud in the enclosed space, and the screams from forward in the cabin had her snapping her head upright to a sight she couldn't fathom.

Sid no longer sat across from Pat at the front of the cabin; instead, he was on his feet and the cabin wall beside Pat had become a Jackson Pollock painting of blood and brains. Then Sid had a second gun in his hand, and when he went to the cockpit, he kept the gun in his left hand fixed on the occupants in the main cabin, constantly glancing back to make sure no one moved.

No one did.

The sight of the pilot and copilot being herded into the main cabin was as terrifying as the guns. Who was flying this plane? And if no one was flying it, were they going to crash or fly into a mountain? No one lived in this area of the country without knowing how dangerous it was to fly here. How high were they at this point? Had they cleared the fourteeners?

Then Sid taunted Mr. Barron Senior, first by putting a gun to Mr. Barron Junior's head, then with his words. She was too far back to hear what he was saying, but she could hear the pleading in Mr. Barron Senior's voice, interrupted only by the captain begging to let him return to the cockpit—he could put down anywhere Sid wanted, he just had to name the place. But Sid wasn't budging.

Nora didn't recognize the man holding the gun. Physically, she did—this was the man who always offered her a cheerful "Good morning, Ms. Gleason" and asked about her weekend/holiday shopping/vacation plans—but that man wouldn't shoot a friendly colleague in the head. Except he had.

They were all going to die.

Her breath sawed as her heart punched against her breastbone and her vision began to swim. She was going to pass out, unless she got her head between her knees. But she was still belted in tight and the table was in the way—

Through the buzzing in her ears, she gradually realized she could hear a whisper from behind her and turned to peer into the kitchen, where the flight attendant hid. Nora couldn't actually see the attendant, so she turned back so as not to give anything away, but closed her eyes and strained to hear what she was saying. And picked up the word "hijacker." The attendant was telling someone outside the plane what was going on. Maybe there was hope after all.

The sharp *crack* of a gunshot sounded, followed by another in quick succession, and then it was chaos up front as Mr. Barron Junior and Mr. Varma jumped the man. While they rolled on the floor, the pilot and copilot scrambled over seats to get past them and ran to the cockpit.

Another gunshot followed by a cry of pain.

The plane suddenly angled sharply up as the pilot tried to climb out of the deadly mountain peaks, the acceleration pressing Nora deep into her seat as the plane pitched in the strong winds.

The plane lurched sharply downward as if thrown by a toddler's tantrum.

Agonizing pain.

Then it all went black.

CHAPTER 1

Approach: The walk or hike to the base of a climbing route.

May 6, 1:07 PM
J. Edgar Hoover Building
Washington, DC

"Meg! Brian! In my office, now!"

Meg Jennings looked up from the report she was finishing, her gaze shooting to Special-Agent-in-Charge Craig Beaumont's office across the bullpen. He was behind his desk, dressed in his usual dark suit and tie, his salt-and-pepper head bent, the phone pressed to his ear as he rapidly made notes.

She swiveled in her chair toward Brian Foster, her FBI Human Scent Evidence Team partner, who sat at the adjacent desk, dressed in his typical deployment-ready outfit of hiking pants, hiking boots, and a long-sleeved athletic T-shirt, his green eyes under the fringe of his dark hair narrowed on Craig's office.

"Sounds like duty calls." Meg dropped a hand down to rest on Hawk's warm fur, but her black Labrador already had his head up and his ears perked—years of experience had taught him to recognize the urgency in Craig's tone.

"Sure does." Brian looked down at the black-and-tan German shepherd lying at his feet, half under his desk. "Lacey, come."

"Hawk, come."

Together Meg and Brian rose to their feet, Hawk and Lacey instantly heeling at their handlers' left knees as they crossed the bullpen.

Meg stopped at the doorway, her hand on the jamb, waiting for Craig.

He waved them in. "Yes, I have two teams I can deploy immediately. I'll get them on a flight directly to Aspen inside of the next hour. Denver will take too long. We might have that time, but if we don't, we'd be delaying the search, or be sending the teams out in multiple waves." He scratched something incomprehensible on the yellow legal pad in front of him. Wondering what was going on in Colorado, Meg tried to read his notes upside down as she stepped closer to the desk to sink into one of the two facing chairs, but, as usual, couldn't decipher Craig's chicken-scratch handwriting.

Hieroglyphics, as Brian would say.

She wasn't concerned, since Craig would distill everything down to what they needed to know. And then would stay on top of the deployment, even from a distance. Her team was lucky to have such a competent supervising agent. She'd heard occasional horror stories from other units, and was thankful that wasn't the work life their group led.

"I'll let you know when they're in the air. Thanks." Craig hung up and put down his pen. "I need you guys to fly to Colorado immediately."

"So we gathered," Brian said. "What's going on?"

"Plane crash." Craig frowned down at his legal pad. "Somewhere in the mountains."

"Somewhere?" Meg exchanged a confused glance with Brian. "How are they going to deploy us if they don't know where we're going? And, I mean, we're good, but you said Aspen. Those mountain regions usually have great search-and-rescue teams, though mostly they don't use dogs because of the terrain. Dogs can't belay in a location where they have some of the tallest mountains in the country."

"In other words, why us?" Brian asked the question for her.

"We're still putting the incident together, but it looks like a hijacking."

"Federal case, then," Meg said.

"Correct."

"And they think there will be survivors? When they don't even know where the plane is?"

"Honestly, they don't know. But the bottom line is, if I don't deploy you now, you won't be on-site if there are survivors. Worst-case scenario is you fly there, turn around, and immediately come back." Craig held up a hand to stop Brian's next question. "Let me tell you quickly what I do know, then I want you two to go home and pack a bag."

Meg glanced at the backpack propped against her desk. "We have our go bags with us and can deploy from here."

"It'll be worth taking the time to pack correctly for this. The plane may have gone down on one of the thirteen- or fourteen-thousand-foot-high peaks—'thirteeners' or 'fourteeners,' as they call them out there. It may be late spring at lower altitudes, but there will still be snowpack and it could be seriously cold at night on the mountains. You need layers, and the right kind, at that."

"We'll need more for this deployment than we're currently carrying. Understood."

"I also don't know how long you'll be needed out there. It might be a day or two, it might be longer."

Meg froze in her chair. *Longer? Now? When they were less than two weeks away from—*

"I know," Craig interrupted her thoughts. "We're just under two weeks away from your wedding."

"I don't have any trouble with the deployment, but I can't be out there for two weeks. I booked off next week for this exact reason. To handle the last-minute stuff here and in Virginia, and to make sure I'm clear from any deployment."

"I know," Craig repeated. "I have my eye on the dates. I don't think this will go over a week; hell, you might not even be needed out there more than a day. But if it goes more than three or four days, I'll get Lauren and Scott to sub in. They'll be home from their water training in Louisiana by that time. And if they're not, I'll send them directly to Colorado." He held her gaze unflinchingly. "You'll be back in time."

"She better be back in time. Hell, *I* better be back in time. I didn't get ordained through the Universal Life Church so I could officiate this wedding for nothing," Brian grumbled.

Meg patted his arm. "We'll both be back in time. Or Todd is going to come looking for us." She winced. "And so is my mother."

"I believe it," Brian said. "Your mother can handle anything. I have no doubt she could handle a fourteen-thousand-foot mountain."

"Don't worry," Craig assured them, "I have this in hand. Everyone will be in Cold Spring Hollow on time, as planned, and we won't have to send out anyone to get you. Someone else will take over for us if it runs long. Okay?"

"Okay." Meg forced her shoulders to relax. "Tell us what you know at this point and we can be updated on the fly."

"That call was from the Denver field office. Special Agent Corey Newall. He and Special Agent Stacey Carlisle are assigned to this case and are on the way into the mountains now."

"How far is it from Denver to Aspen?"

"About a hundred miles as the crow flies, but three to four hours by car. It's a four-and-a-half-hour flight for you, so you may arrive within an hour of each other. Hopefully by then, they'll have found the plane, but weather is going to be an issue."

"Did the weather bring the plane down, or did the hijacker?"

"Unclear at this point. Here's what we know: It's a twin-engine Gulfstream G800, privately owned by Barron Pharmaceuticals. The plane can seat up to nineteen people, but the manifest says it carried thirteen passengers, plus a flight attendant and two pilots. The flight plan says it was headed for Napa County Airport under flight designation BA0649. It took off from a private airstrip just north of Colorado Springs, but there was a distress call seventeen minutes into the flight. The flight attendant made contact with a Denver air traffic controller, which is the only reason we know what was going on after he called the Denver field office. She reported a single male with a firearm taking control of the plane. At least one person was dead, but she could only stay on the line long enough to report the incident, so they don't have a good picture of what was happening. Denver tracked the plane west for about thirty miles when it disappeared from radar."

"They think it went down there?" Brian asked.

"The air traffic controller couldn't say. All he could say is he couldn't track it anymore. It might have crashed or the hijackers might have taken the ACARS offline."

Meg glanced at Brian, who shrugged. She turned back to Craig. " 'ACARS'?"

"They had to explain it to me too. It stands for . . . Aircraft Communications Addressing and Reporting System," Craig read from his notes. "It's the system that allows airplanes to communicate with air traffic controllers on the ground, and allows those same controllers to track the flight path. When that system goes offline, a plane is essentially invisible."

"Except by eye."

"Right. Except when you're in the mountains and line of sight is limited. They were already heading west, and the hypothesis at this point is they were trying to get lost in the"—he ran his index finger down the line of his notes—"Sawatch, Elk, or San Juan Mountain Ranges. Or the Flat Tops, just to the north."

"Picked a route so once there was no way to trace via radar, they also mostly stayed out of sight," Brian stated.

"Wait, isn't it an FAA regulation that private and commercial planes have to have some sort of emergency location transmitter that gets auto-activated when they land with enough impact?" Meg asked.

"Yes, but they're not picking anything up," said Craig. "There are a couple of theories on that. It might have been removed, or deactivated. Or, because it runs on battery power, if it wasn't maintained, it literally may be out of juice. Or the battery could have been removed ahead of time."

"It's accessible?"

"The whole system has to be accessible for maintenance. It's a privately owned, corporate plane—who knows who had access to it?"

"Now the plane is lost somewhere in a treacherous area with a series of thirteen- and fourteen-thousand-foot mountains and their associated lower ranges," Meg said. "Unless the hijacker was a pilot familiar with the area, or unless the pilots remained in control of the plane, their risk of flying into a mountain could be pretty high."

"That's the concern. Reports of the sound of a crash came in from the Elk Mountain area, and it seems too coincidental for it not to be from this plane." Craig scanned his legal pad again. "Primarily around the area of the double peaks of the Maroon Bells. Problem is, that whole area is socked in right now with rain and fog—and snow higher up—so there's no way to get air support into the area to search for a crash. Planes have gone down in the area before and there have been survivors. And if the hijacker survived . . ."

"It's highly doubtful he's going to sit around and wait for help to arrive to toss his ass in jail," said Brian. "Anyone else who survives will stick with the wreckage because it'll make them visible. But the hijacker will likely head out into the wilderness and try to get away."

"And that's where you come in," Craig said. "At that point it's not a rescue, it's a search. The kind of search you excel at."

Meg ignored the compliment, her mind focusing on what she knew of the geography. "I know a little about that area. Todd and his brothers are all outdoorsy types, but Luke, the youngest, likes to climb. He and a couple of his buddies have vacationed out in Aspen, and he's told us stories. It's a deadly area. One false move and you're falling at least a thousand feet to your death." A shudder rippled through Meg, and she fought hard to suppress her physical reaction. However, one quick glance at Brian told her he'd seen it. Luckily, Craig was studying his notes again.

This was going to be a nightmare of a deployment.

Brian was the only team member who knew Meg was deathly afraid of heights, though she had an inkling Lauren Wycliffe, border collie Rocco's handler, suspected. Scott Park, the last of the handlers, who paired with his bloodhound, Theo, the best nose in the group, seemed blessedly unaware.

More importantly, Craig was unaware. And Meg had no intention of ever telling him, because it would handicap Hawk. Hawk was an amazing search dog, with an excellent nose and the kind of drive Theo simply couldn't generate. He was an asset to every deployment. More than that, he *loved* the rescue life. He was in his element every time they went out on a search. Working a search lit him from the inside, and that joy was infectious. But if she told Craig about her fears, he'd only send her out on searches he deemed reasonable, which wouldn't do. The career of a working K-9 was often limited to only a handful of years. For some, depending on how physical the work, they might see seven or eight years after training. But for the physical exertion of search-and-rescue, a dog might only see five years of intense work. Hawk had been two when they joined the Human Scent Evidence Team three years before. Now, at five, he might only have two or three work years left, maybe four if they worked hard to keep him healthy and in shape. But in the type of job where any single injury, to either herself or Hawk, could sideline the entire team, she would not allow her weakness to shorten his career. She would not snuff out that light.

She'd handled heights before: the train trestle at Mono-cacy National Battlefield; the terrifying walk over an I-beam above a deadly drop at the Bowie Meatpacking Plant; walking the Ocoee Flume outside of Turtletown, Tennessee; the cliff where Rita Pratt died in the Boundary Waters Canoe Area; standing on the pile, the dead under her boots, after Talbot Terraces fell. She'd do it again now.

She met Brian's eyes and gave him a subtle nod.

We got this.

His return nod reinforced her confidence. *We do.*

I can do this.

I know. And if you need help, I'm there.

The smile she gave Brian was a combination of relief and gratitude. Together, with their dogs, they could work this deployment.

"There's more information coming," Craig said, oblivi-ous to the full conversation passing silently between his handlers. "But I'll have to get it to you en route. For now, I want you to go home and pack. Pack layers, pack water-proof shells; do your best to pack light because you'll be climbing with most of it. Assume you may be sleeping on the mountain. People there will have any emergency gear *you* might need, but only you can pack for your dog." His gaze dropped to where Hawk and Lacey sat, side by side, between Meg and Brian. "And they need to stay safe. We're nothing without them."

"You have no idea," Meg murmured, the quick flash of Brian's smile telling her he'd heard.

"Then get to Reagan Airport," Craig continued. "I'll have a plane ready for you, and you'll be in the air and on your way, ASAP. I'll leave it to the Denver agents to update you on the most current information they have when you land versus me updating you in the air each time I learn something. You won't be able to do anything with the information until you're down anyway, so I'll leave you to rest and prepare during the flight. Agents Newall and Carlisle will meet you at Aspen/Pitkin County Airport. Don't take your sidearms; they'll provide weapons for you, so you don't have to take them on the plane. I don't expect you'll be involved in any takedowns, but I don't want you unprotected, just in case. This is an incident where we already know weapons are involved, so let's play it safe."

"Got it." Meg stood, Hawk rising to his feet with her, Brian and Lacey following.

They were halfway to the door when Craig's voice stopped them.

"This one has the potential to be dangerous." Concern carved even deeper lines into Craig's normally craggy face. "We don't know who you're up against or what weapons they might have at their disposal. We don't know where the crash site is yet, and that in itself might be the most dangerous aspect of the deployment. Yes, I want the person or persons responsible caught, but not at the expense of either or both of you. Or the dogs. Be careful. Be safe. And stay in touch so I don't worry."

"We will. Regular reports, and we'll have our sat phones, so we'll never be out of touch. We'll keep you in the loop."

"Appreciate that."

Meg and Brian returned to the bullpen, shut down their computers, grabbed their go bags, and headed for the door.

Meg raised a hand to wave farewell at Craig, who returned the gesture. But the unease in his expression settled in her gut like a clenched fist.

This was going to be a seriously difficult deployment,

and her fear of heights was only going to complicate things.

She glanced down at Hawk, who seemed to sense her nerves and was already gazing up at her with eyes full of love, his tail wagging with enthusiasm.

She could do this. She had to.

Any other alternative could be deadly.

CHAPTER 2

High-altitude Illness: A potentially life-threatening illness caused by a sudden increase in altitude and the resulting lower oxygen pressure that can result in cerebral or pulmonary edema, coma, and, potentially, death.

May 6, 1:49 PM
Jennings/Webb Residence
Washington, DC

Meg unlocked the front door and let Hawk precede her into the front foyer. The Lab immediately trotted down the hallway toward the open concept kitchen and family room, disappearing from view as he angled toward the seating area clustered around the TV.

"Hawk, buddy. You're home early." Todd's voice floated down the hall.

She had multiple things to explain to Todd about this deployment, but he needed to come upstairs with her so they could talk while she packed. There was no time to waste. Lives might depend on it and she had a plane to catch.

She walked into the family room to find Todd, in jeans and a faded, short-sleeved T-shirt, comfortably ensconced in her ratty old recliner. It might look like hell, but it was the most comfortable chair they owned, and was especially loved by the men of the house.

By men of the house, she included Clay McCord, one of the *Washington Post*'s top investigative reporters, and her sister Cara's partner. Cara, McCord, and their three dogs lived in the other half of the Cookes Park duplex the four had purchased together nearly a year before. Both couples were in and out of each other's homes constantly, and Meg could count on McCord claiming her chair the moment he walked in the door if it was unoccupied.

"Hey." Todd Webb turned as she came in, his index finger marking his place in his book—a nonfiction account of the firefighters who lived through the London Blitz and kept the city from burning to the ground, a recent birthday gift from McCord—his other hand rhythmically stroking Hawk's back. Hawk leaned against the side of the chair in bliss. "You're home early. Everything okay?"

"Brian and I are being deployed and I need some things. Quiet day?"

"Yeah. Kind of feel like I needed it after yesterday's incident." A firefighter/paramedic with DC Fire and Emergency Medical Services Engine Company 2, Todd had been on duty last night when what would become a four-alarm fire broke out at a seniors' apartment building. It had been a grueling series of rescues, repeatedly running into the burning building to carry out trapped seniors. Some had mobility problems and couldn't manage the stairs to escape on their own with the electricity cut and the elevator locked out. Many more had gone to bed without their hearing aids, had woken late to the alarms, been disoriented, and unable to manage in the dark. Several had medical crises because of the shock of the alarm and the low oxygen in the smoky environment; so, for Todd, who wore two hats as both a firefighter and a paramedic, it had been a particularly busy night. But they got everyone out, and while some residents were rushed to the hospital, it didn't look like they were going to lose anyone. They'd also kept the fire from spreading to the adjacent buildings. Combined, it was a win in their books.

Todd had come home from his twenty-four-hour shift at nearly eight-thirty that morning, exhausted, sleep deprived, and ravenous. Meg had stayed long enough to throw together a high-protein breakfast for him, and to get his assurance he'd eat and go to bed for at least a few hours.

Meg ran a hand over Todd's dark hair, cut short to be comfortable under the helmet he wore so often. "You look much better after a couple of hours sleep than you did when you came home this morning. You were edging toward pale."

Brown eyes, flecked with gold, turned up to her. "I had more than enough energy to keep going through the incident, but by the end of shift, with no shut-eye, I was pretty wiped."

"You're not twenty-two anymore, old man." Meg softened the playful dig by pressing a kiss to the top of his head. "Come upstairs while I grab what I need and I'll explain. Time is tight."

"Sure. Hawk, shift it, bud." When Hawk was safely out of the way, Todd lowered the chair's footrest and stood, leaving his book behind in the chair.

Meg led the way upstairs, Todd trailing behind her as Hawk shot past them both to sprint up the stairs, past the study, around the corner, and down the hallway to the master bedroom.

As they went past, Meg's gaze dropped to the section of wall that had been repaired and repainted so the hole marking the vicious attack the previous summer was entirely erased. She didn't think of Giraldi's attack often anymore—she and Todd had cleansed their home of the evil that had invaded that night with the sole purpose of killing Meg and Hawk—but, every once in a while, the memory of the attack that had nearly killed her crept through. She would have died that night except for Hawk coming to her rescue at the very moment when things seemed bleakest, saving the day and helping to take down a killer.

Hawk was the best of dogs. That night, he'd given her life back to her—not for the first time—and, for that, she'd stand on a mountain beside him because it would make him happy, as well as save lives.

She walked past the spot in the hallway where she'd nearly been strangled, and toward the dog who waited for her at the foot of their bed, head held high, fringed tail waving proudly.

"Before I explain what's going on, I want to say first I know today's date. So does Craig. Our wedding is not in jeopardy."

Todd sat down on the cushioned cedar chest at the bottom of their bed, his gaze fixed on her, one eyebrow cocked suspiciously. "Why do I think I'm not going to like this deployment?"

"I can tell you, I already don't." She pulled a duffel bag out of the wardrobe and sorted through her athletic clothing.

Craig was correct—layers were going to be key. With it being late spring, grass would be growing around trees in full leaf as flowers bloomed at lower altitudes. But above, where the winds would be brutal and the air thinner, temperatures could be easily twenty degrees colder, even more as night fell.

On a search like this, you didn't stop when the sun went down. Any survivors of the plane crash—if they were lucky enough to survive a crash onto a mountain, in the first place—would likely be badly injured. Hours of hypothermia from being alone on a mountaintop at night could be deadly to an injured victim—especially one who was only barely hanging on. By the time they arrived in Colorado after their four-and-a-half-hour flight, they'd have only gained two hours of sunlight. And much of that sunlight, if not all of it, would be used up simply traveling to the site of the crash.

If they even knew where it was by that time.

She pulled clothes out of the wardrobe—three base layer, long-sleeved, wicking athletic shirts; an SPF 50 sun hoodie; two pairs of fleece-lined, water-resistant leggings; and a pair of waterproof hiking pants for over top.

She dropped the hiking pants on the growing pile on the bed. "Craig is sending us out to Colorado to the site of a plane crash."

Todd's eyebrows winged up. "Colorado? That's pretty far west for a deployment. You're going to lose hours just getting there. Why is he sending you? Wouldn't rescue crews do better with local search dogs?"

"Quite likely. But here's the wrinkle—it was a hijacking gone wrong. And there are hopes there will be survivors."

"Ah. One of which might be the hijacker. Hijacking makes it a federal case?"

"Yes. We're being met by two agents out of the Denver field office. There are concerns that if the man who hijacked the plane survived the crash, he's going to rabbit and try to get away over the mountain. Whichever mountain it is."

"They don't know?"

"At this point all they have is a plane that disappeared from radar because the communications system was somehow disabled, and reports of sounds of a crash in the Elk Mountains." She paused for a second, and then went all in on truth. "In the Maroon Bells area."

Todd froze in the act of running his hand down Hawk's

back, where he sat at Todd's knee. "Maroon Bells . . . that's where Luke went climbing last year with his buddies."

"Yes."

His eyes went unfocused for a minute, his brows drawing together. "Those are fourteen-thousand-foot peaks."

"Fourteeners, as the locals apparently say. So . . . yeah."

He met her gaze, held it. "How are you going to manage that?"

The laugh that broke free had a sharp edge to it. "It's not going to be fun, that's for sure."

"You know, someday you might have to 'fess up to Craig about your fear of heights. Brian won't be able to cover for you on this one."

"Not when he's right beside me, he won't." Meg pulled a brimmed khaki sun hat, with an adjustable chinstrap to keep it in place in high winds, off the top shelf and tossed it onto the bed. The Aspen area was socked in with bad weather today, but who knew what conditions tomorrow might bring? "You know how I feel about this."

"That you're shortchanging your partner if you limit where you can go. I get that, but what happens if you're fourteen thousand feet up and lose your nerve? Then they have to rescue you."

"Have I lost my nerve yet?" She grabbed her empty concealment shoulder holster from the top of her gun safe and tossed it onto the pile.

"No, but you've never tested it like this."

Temper flared, and she had to refrain from pushing back at him. "Are you concerned about the deployment, or the timing?"

"Craig says you'll be back in time?"

"He promised we'll both be back in time. Someone else will take over if it looks like it's going more than five or six days. But it's unlikely to. In that time, if we haven't found them, survivors will likely have died and the hijacker will either have died in the crash, died in the attempt to get away, or managed to escape."

"So then what worries me is the deployment. You're flying into Denver to meet with the field office agents?"

"No, they're already on their way to Aspen, which is hours away. They'll meet us at the Aspen airport." Meg stared at him, baffled, when he pulled out his phone and started Googling. "What are you looking for?"

He was silent for a minute, then refined his search before looking up at her, the concern in his dark eyes clear. "You're going from sea level directly to Aspen."

"Yes. Is that a problem?"

"It could be a major problem. It would be better to fly into Denver and stay there for a couple of days before going higher."

"You know that's not possible."

"Then you and Brian definitely have a problem. So do the dogs."

"With?"

"High-altitude illness."

The expression on his face made Meg pause stacking clothes to load into the duffel bag. "You're actually concerned."

"Yeah. You may be walking into something as dangerous as a fall from fourteen thousand feet."

Todd was as stable as they came—a logical, down-to-earth firefighter who called the shots as he saw them. He didn't fly off the handle or blow things out of proportion. If he was worried, there was significant cause.

Meg sank down onto the bench beside him, Hawk coming to stand between her knees. "I don't have a lot of time here. Break it down for me. What do I need to know?"

"High-altitude illness is serious stuff and covers a couple of more specific illnesses. It's not something we have to deal with in DC, but when Luke was going, I helped him research it so he and the guys from lower altitudes would be safe. This is nothing to mess with, and you're stacking the deck against you in a serious way."

"How?"

"Flying from sea level to any mountain airport is a risk, but it can be minimized, like Luke did by flying into Denver, which is only fifty-two hundred feet above sea level, and then staying there for two or three days. Then they drove to Aspen, which is seventy-nine hundred feet above sea level, stayed there for a day, and then moved up another five hundred feet to Snowmass, which they used as their base. From there they drove to the various trailheads, allowing them to acclimatize slowly. They also started taking acetazolamide a full twenty-four hours before they went."

"What's that?"

"A diuretic to help prevent and treat acute mountain sickness, the first domino to fall. Low oxygen pressure at that altitude leads to low blood oxygen concentration in the body, causing blood vessels to open more in an attempt to deliver more red blood cells carrying oxygen. That influx of blood causes the brain to swell. A headache is your first sign you're in trouble. Then you're looking at weakness, crushing fatigue, nausea, vomiting, and dizziness, a killer at high altitudes if you lose your balance. You won't sleep well and you won't want to eat. Then the spiral begins."

"It sounds like it's a good thing we're having this conversation."

"In spades, because you and Brian will be doing everything wrong. You're going too soon to take enough acetazolamide before you begin. You're flying straight to the higher altitude. You won't be drinking alcohol, which complicates things—"

"Definitely not."

"—but instead you're doing something worse. Instead of resting and acclimatizing when you arrive, you're immediately going out to do intense physical activity. You're not just going on a run; you'll be climbing a mountain. A highly strenuous workout that adds another layer—with every one thousand feet you gain, the risk grows. You're only supposed to go up in altitude about three thousand feet a day, but you'll be jumping approximately nine thousand feet in four hours, and then possibly another two or three thousand feet in the hours immediately after. On top of that, you'll likely be sleeping, if you get any sleep at all, at that same altitude, which is also bad because there's no break for your system. You could be looking at hypoxia, leading to a hyponatremia—low sodium in the blood that will screw up your blood pressure, causing the brain to swell more. Or, you could suffer a cerebral or pulmonary edema, where the capillaries leak fluid, filling the surrounding tissues, which can lead to a coma and death."

"Well . . . hell. Why didn't Craig say anything about this?"

"Sea level Craig, whose idea of the perfect vacation involves sun, sand, and as many rum drinks as he can down? His job is already stressful. He doesn't spend his vacations pushing his body to the limit; he spends it relaxing so he can come back to work to push himself to the limit there. It's doubtful he'd know about this stuff. In general, we don't tend to think about this kind of thing in this part of the country. I didn't learn about it in detail while training to be a paramedic; it's not relevant in this location. I learned all about it when I did a deep dive so I could make sure Luke would be safe."

"Can't take the older brother out of the firefighter/paramedic."

"Never. But whoever Craig was talking to out West should have filled him in. Someone screwed up, big-time. I know you have to do this, like I know risk is always a part of your job. Just like you know it's a part of mine, but this is an extra layer. It has nothing to do with bad guys or the risk around the geography of a chase. It's strictly about altitude and your physiological response to it. Some people handle altitude pretty well. Some people die. And we won't know where you and Brian fall on that scale until you're there and get into trouble you may not be able to get out of."

"What do we do?"

"First off, Craig needs to get you some acetazolamide. It should be taken twenty-four hours before your arrival at altitude, but four or five hours is better than nothing. Then you take it every twelve hours for the first two days at altitude." He opened the browser on his phone and did a quick search. "You're going to both need one hundred twenty-five milligrams twice a day. But he needs to get you the first dose before you go. If that's all he can get here, they'll have more there." He paused to do a second search. "And you need to take ibuprofen, each time you dose with acetazolamide. You need six hundred milligrams, which is a highish dose, but the point here is to use the anti-inflammatory effects to help minimize the swelling and inflammation in your brain caused by the high altitude. We have two hundred milligrams ibuprofen here. Take the bottle with you."

"I can do that."

"Then you and Brian need to be intently attuned to yourselves. But it's more than that." Todd ran a hand over Hawk's head, his fingers trailing off the dog's shoulder. "It's not just humans. Dogs can also get high-altitude illness."

A sharp stab of fear streaked through Meg. Putting herself at risk was one thing, but putting Hawk at risk was something else entirely. The thought of losing her heart dog—the canine equivalent of a soulmate—left her terrified.

Most dog owners were lucky if they found one heart dog, a dog who not only meshed, but bonded with them until they became an integral part of their identity. Meg had been blessed to have two heart dogs, but the loss of her first—Deuce, her German shepherd patrol partner when they were in the Richmond Police Department—after he had been shot while in the pursuit of a suspect, had left her emotionally wounded. After Deuce had bled out in Meg's arms, she'd quit the force and retreated to her parents' animal rescue, Cold Spring Haven, in the hills outside of Charlottesville, Virginia. It was there, only a week later, a black Lab puppy on the verge of death from a severe parvovirus infection was left on their doorstep. They named the scrappy little fighter Hawk, and by the time he was healed and well on his way to health and vitality, he and Meg were bonded.

Her fingers rose to touch the pendant she wore on a chain around her neck, whenever she wasn't out on active searches. A swirl of electric blue, black, and gray—a tiny bit of Deuce's ashes locked forever behind glass—the memory pendant was all she had left of him.

The thought of losing Hawk stopped the air in her lungs.

Todd grasped her hand, lowering it to his thigh and intertwining their fingers. "I know you—you're going to be more concerned about him than yourself. But I want you to be concerned for both of you. I need you both to come back to me. It's not just the wedding. We have our whole married lives in front of us."

She squeezed his hand and tipped her head sideways to rest against his shoulder. "I don't want to miss a second of that."

"Then let's set you up for success. We'd need a quick

word with a vet, but systemically, dogs aren't that different from us, so I wouldn't be surprised if acetazolamide
would work for them too. They'd have to tell us about
dosages, or they might recommend something else. Craig
can set that up. He has the power of the FBI behind him
to make things move. Once you're out West, watch for
the signs I've outlined. If you have a minor headache—
and I'd be shocked if you don't have at least that—monitor
it. It might not get worse. If it does, or if any other signs
arise, there are two things you can do. First, oxygen therapy. If the rescue teams are carrying oxygen, and they
might, you can artificially boost the oxygen in your blood.
That wasn't an option for Luke. What I told him was to
go no higher, and if there was no improvement, to go
down at least one thousand feet. That can also be an option for you."

"If that happened to either of us, as a team, we'd have
to drop out of the search."

"I know. And you're going to have to make that call on
the fly for both of you. You're also going to make sure
Brian knows all of this. He'll have to watch Lacey for any
signs of trouble."

"You know what a mother hen he is, especially since
the cougar attack last year. He won't let anything happen
to her."

"Neither of you will."

"Let's call Craig now." Meg pulled out her phone,
speed-dialed Craig, and put the call on speaker.

Craig answered almost immediately and skipped a salutation. "You're on your way to the airport?"

"In a few minutes. I need you to talk to Todd. He's
raised a medical issue and we're going to have to deal with
it, unless you want Brian and me seriously ill or possibly
dead. Or the dogs. Here's Todd. He can explain." She
handed Todd her cell phone.

"Hi, Craig. Sorry to be a wet blanket, but your guys out West neglected to loop you into some extremely crucial information." Todd quickly took Craig through the issue of high-altitude illness for the members of his teams.

As Todd explained the issue, Meg stripped out of the clothes she'd worn to work—her standard deployment outfit of yoga pants and an athletic top, and removed her memory necklace, laying it out neatly on the top of her dresser. Then she pulled on the base layer she'd need to decrease how much she packed in her bag so they'd be ready to hit the ground running. The backpack she normally wore on searches would be the only thing she'd carry onto the mountain, so the duffel with extra clothes would be left in whatever base camp they set up.

There were several seconds of silence before Craig finally responded. "Goddammit! What do I do? I need to send them."

"I know, and Meg knows how to manage as best she can and what to watch for, but you need to get acetazolamide in the doses I told you. Meg and Brian each need at least one dose before they're in the air. And you need to contact a vet and find out what a dog would need and make sure Hawk and Lacey take it before they're in the air. Then you have a chance of your teams coming back to you. Without it . . . well, I'm not sure how badly this could go." He looked up to meet Meg's eyes. "My gut says very badly."

"Thanks for bringing this to our attention. Heads will roll for no one in the Denver field office cluing me into this. Meg, when will you be on the road to Reagan?"

"In about five minutes. And I can be there in about twenty minutes, twenty-five tops."

"Someone will meet you there and you'll have the meds you need, at least for that first dose. Wait for them; you're not going up without them. I'll call you on the road with confirmation. You'll tell Brian?"

"I'll fill him in at the airport. But I know Brian—he'll take the meds on Todd's recommendation alone."

"Good. More soon." Then Craig was gone.

"Anything else you need?" Todd asked.

"A couple of things from the bathroom, then my water-resistant rain shell and my lightweight puffy jacket from the front hall coat closet." Both lightweight jackets could be rolled into compact tubes for easy carrying. "I need to pack food and treats for Hawk and energy bars for me. I'll fill the hydration bladder in my go bag once we land. Everything else we need is already there."

He grabbed her duffel bag. "Let's get you on the road then. Come on, Hawk."

Back downstairs, she quickly gathered the food and outerwear she'd need. She was packing the last of the food into her go bag as Todd ran through the list of rescue equipment he thought she'd need.

"Spare water bottle for electrolytes?"

"Yes."

"Climbing cord? Tactical knife?"

"Yes and yes." She zipped the backpack closed and turned to him, cupping his face in her hands. She went up on tiptoe to kiss him, stroking the slight scruff on his cheeks with her thumbs. "I have everything we need. And whatever specific mountain gear we'll need, they'll provide."

"You be sure to wear a helmet. Luke said the place is lousy with . . . What did he call it? Scree? Steeply angled slopes covered with loose rocks. Those rocks were constantly falling on his head." He gave her a stern look. "You *cannot* get another concussion. You risk being off the team permanently if that happens."

"I'll wear a helmet anytime there's a chance it's required. And I'll watch out for Hawk. I don't think there are helmets for dogs. But if there is, that's the area with them. They'll also have those full-body climbing harnesses for dogs, so if we need to belay, it will be an option. Though not one I'd look forward to."

"The rescuers out there are trained in high-angle roping because that's their bread and butter. If it comes to that, they'll equip you and talk you through what you need to do. Hopefully, you won't need to."

Meg shuddered at the thought as she shouldered the go bag. "We're ready. Hawk, come." She reached for her duffel, but Todd beat her to it.

"I'll walk you out."

Meg's SUV was parked up the street. The duplex was part of a historical neighborhood built just past the turn of the twentieth century, a good decade or so before cars were mass-produced, allowing ownership for the populace. Street parking was the name of the game for everyone in the neighborhood, but she'd lucked into a spot only about twenty feet from the duplex.

Meg unlocked the SUV and opened the back door. "Hawk, up." He leaped into his meshed K-9 compartment and immediately lay down, used to the routine of searches and the need to rest while he could, often during transport. Meg removed his leash and closed the door, took the duffel from Todd, then circled the SUV to open the hatch and toss the leash in. Her go bag and the duffel went next, then she slammed the hatch closed.

She stepped onto the curb to find Todd's gaze already fixed on her. His broad shoulders were stiff, his hands curled into unconscious fists, and worry lines carved deep grooves at the corners of his eyes and lips.

She sighed silently. She understood his worry—shared it

in reverse whenever he was called out to a fire, like last night's—but they'd agreed early on this was what they did and neither would ask the other to give it up. But they would both do what they could to make it easier on the other.

Stepping into him, she wrapped her arms around his neck, and was pulled closer when his arms locked around her torso. Her face pressed against the warmth of his throat, she said, "I promise to be careful. I'll watch for the signs you outlined. I won't take unnecessary chances with either of us."

"That's all I can ask."

"And I'll stay in touch as much as possible. I have my sat phone, and while satellite connections are infamous for delays, I should have a decent connection on top of a mountain. I'll never be out of touch. I'll update you as often as I can, even if it's just a quick text that all is well. Will that help?"

"Yes. Call when you have a moment, but I know you'll be busy, so I won't expect it often. I'll watch for your texts."

"I don't usually keep you in the loop so constantly, but I'll make a point of it this time, as there are a few extra complications. I'll suggest the same for Brian. He should let Ryan know what we'll be dealing with." Ryan Bennett, Brian's husband, was an archivist at the Smithsonian. Not part of the search-and-rescue world himself, he nonetheless kept tabs on Brian's deployments. "If Ryan has questions, can he call you for clarification?"

"Absolutely. Do I need to do anything for the wedding?"

"Not currently. If I'm only gone a few days, everything is fine. If I'm gone later than that, I may need to rope you, Mom, or Cara into a few tasks, but let's play it by ear. I know you're now off for three days; if I think of anything, I'll let you know. But I'm feeling pretty organized."

"You, Cara, and Eda are a force to be reckoned with. I kind of feel like all I have to do is show up."

"A bit more than that, but that's because you already have you and your brothers organized. We're collectively in good shape. You don't have to worry about wedding details."

"That's good. Then I can concentrate on worrying about you."

"That's not what I meant, and you know it." She pulled back so she could look into his eyes. "I need to go. This has already taken longer than I thought, but with good reason. We need to get there."

"I love you. Be careful, both of you."

"I love you too. And we will." She leaned in to kiss him goodbye, then gasped as he hauled her in closer and took the kiss deeper, not caring that they stood on a public street.

When he finally released her, she stepped away with a breathless laugh. "Wow. Trying to convince me to stay?"

"Will more of that do it?"

"Tempting. Very tempting. But duty calls." She stepped out of his arms before he could try again to change her mind and climbed into the SUV. Closing the door, she started the engine and rolled down the window. "Keep your phone on you at all times. Some of the texts may come at weird times. There's a two-hour time difference and we may be working all night."

"Rest on the plane if you can."

"I'll try. You know I don't sleep on planes well, but I'll rest my eyes at the very least. So will Brian."

"Safe travels. Know I'm with you all the way."

"You always are. I'll be back as soon as I can. And then we can really start our lives together."

A series of emotions flowed over his face—love, concern, restraint—then he leaned in and kissed her hard, one
more time. "I'm counting on that." He straightened, rap-
ping his fist lightly on the roof of the SUV, and then
stepped back.

Meg pulled away from the curb and drove down the
street.

A last look in the rearview mirror just before she turned
the corner showed Todd, standing alone, hands deep in his
pockets, watching as she disappeared from view.

CHAPTER 3

Belayer: A person who assists the climber by managing the belay rope, and who is responsible for counterbalancing the climber if he or she falls.

May 6, 5:10 pm
Over Wray, Colorado

Meg opened one eye as the facedown phone on her tray table chimed an incoming WhatsApp call. She pulled herself up straighter in the seat, where she'd been resting with her head tipped against the sidewall of the passenger compartment. Beside her, Brian also stirred, his eyes opening from where he sat, his head tipped back, a U-shaped travel pillow supporting his head.

The handlers were seated at the front of first class, their dogs lying quietly at their feet.

Meg massaged the back of her neck, and then tilted her head back and forth a few times.

"I'm telling you, you need one of these pillows. They look ridiculous, but I never come off a flight with a kink in my neck."

"I'll put it on my Christmas list." She flipped her phone over and was surprised to see McCord's smiling face on her screen, rather than Craig's serious expression. "Not who I expected." As Brian pulled off his neck pillow and leaned in to see who was calling, Meg accepted the call. She held up a finger to McCord as she dug in her pocket to pull out her Bluetooth earbuds so they could hear him clearly over the ambient plane noise, slipping one into her ear and giving the other to Brian.

McCord's face filled the screen, the backdrop of his kitchen behind him. From the angle of the camera shot, he was on his laptop. His blond hair was freshly cut, and with his wire-rimmed glasses shielding his blue eyes and sporting a pressed burgundy button-down shirt, he was looking distinctly professorial. "Hey, guys, wasn't sure I'd be able to get you."

Meg angled the phone so McCord could see them both as Brian sat back in his chair. "Wi-Fi calling works fine up here."

"You're still in the air?"

"Yes. Just entered Colorado's airspace, so we'll be down in the next half hour."

"Then things will get busy. So . . . Webb told me about your deployment."

"How's he doing?"

"Honestly, he's worried. He's going to stay worried until you're on the plane home. But he's handling it."

"He always does. But I'm sure you didn't call to give me an update on Todd."

"No. I wanted to pick your brain about what you know about the plane crash."

Brian chuckled, shaking his head, as he let the air out of his pillow, collapsing it down into a compact roll to be tossed into his duffel bag. "You're predictable, McCord."

"Of course I am. There's a story, I'm going after it."

"Literally?" Meg asked. "You're coming to Colorado?"

"Not at this point. I tried to sell Sykes on it, but he wasn't biting."

"Going to Minnesota last October emptied the coffers?" Brian asked.

"Nah. Craig paid my way there. I couldn't get him to take my money. He said I was part of the team, and the team flies on the government's dime. Sykes loves a good story, but I made the mistake of telling him the team had already been deployed. He knows you're my source of information, so he told me to get the deets from you. After I talked to Todd, it may be just as well. To be safe, I'd be stuck in Denver for days. Hopefully, it will be over by then."

"We can hope," Meg said. "I'm glad you're home and safe."

"So am I!" Cara's faint voice came from a distance, and McCord shifted his camera so Cara was visible standing at the counter.

Meg often thought looking at her sister was like looking in a mirror. Born eighteen months apart, they were frequently mistaken for twins, with their black Irish coloring—ice-blue eyes, pale skin, and long black hair—height nearing six feet, and confident mannerisms. But where Meg had gone into law enforcement, Cara had jumped into the world of dog training and rescue. "Hey, you. Sorry I didn't have time to say goodbye before we were in the air. There was no time on this one."

Cara leaned on the table beside McCord's laptop. "Todd filled us in. You be careful, you hear me? Don't make me come out there and get you. Same goes for you, Brian."

Brian saluted smartly with a wide grin. "Yes, ma'am!"

Cara patted McCord's shoulder. "I'll leave you to him. I know you'll be pressed for time, so just contact Todd; he can pass on updates for us. But keep in touch."

"I promise."

McCord moved in to fill the frame. "What can you tell

me? I may be able to dig up something helpful for you about the hijacker. It was a hijacking, correct?"

"Yes. We don't know much yet. The Denver field agents will update us with current info when we meet them after landing." She cocked an eyebrow at her camera.

"Uh . . . sorry." McCord looked seriously contrite. "Didn't think about that. You were resting?"

"We were." Brian's nod accompanied Meg's words. "We figure we're going to be on the go all night."

"Damn it. Want to go back to sleep?"

"I never got to sleep, was only resting. We're alert now. And, honestly, we're going to be landing soon, so it's not a problem. I'm just giving you a hard time because I can. Since we'll be on approach soon, let me tell you what we know before I have to put the electronics away."

"Shoot."

"The plane, a Gulfstream G800, left a private airstrip south of Denver. We haven't been updated as to who was onboard yet, but the manifest said a total of sixteen, including passengers and crew. The plane was owned by Barron Pharmaceuticals."

McCord whistled. "Barron Pharma?"

"Yeah. That means something to you?"

"It does. They've been on my radar for a while."

"Dirty financial dealings?"

"Sort of. Created a new opioid drug and then pushed it on the medical community, which then was given huge bonuses to prescribe it to their clients, often when something that strong wasn't needed. Problem was this drug— brand name Zelcone—is hugely addicting and people couldn't get off it."

"Kind of like what big tobacco did for decades," Brian stated. "Get people hooked, and then they can't stop."

"Precisely. They're permanently ruining lives and are hated by a lot of people. They've been sued many, *many* times, and have a slate of lawyers on retainer to keep bad press down. But word is leaking out. Especially since a generic analog of that compound is making it into street drugs."

"You mean they're selling Zelcone on the black market?" Meg asked.

"No, I mean they're cutting a generic version of it into common street drugs. With disastrous side effects. Someone buys meth from their dealer—which isn't pure to begin with, because these drugs are cut with other additives to increase the addiction or to stretch out the real supply—and then ODs from the Zelcone cut into the meth—"

"Wait," Brian interrupted. "Run that by me again. Why would someone mix Zelcone into the street supply if it's going to kill off the buyer? That doesn't make sense."

"That's not the goal. The goal is to make the addiction so strong, the buyer returns again and again for their fix. But the seller can't control how much of the drug the user will take. And sometimes that user dies, but there's always someone else to take their place. Now, this isn't directly Barron Pharma's fault; they aren't making the cheap generic version of their drug for the streets. Those drugs are often coming from out of country. But they're addicting a great many people, who then are so desperate to feed their addiction, they turn to dangerous street drugs for the fix that too often kills them."

"Right off the bat you can see a motive to hijack the plane," Meg stated.

"Absolutely."

"The flight attendant managed to make brief contact with an air traffic controller at the Denver airport seventeen minutes into the flight. She reported a single armed male onboard taking control of the flight, with one fatality. Then they lost contact. That air traffic controller contacted the FBI field office in Denver, which started the ball rolling."

"You have to wonder if the pilot's who they killed," McCord theorized. "But the gun is notable. Are we looking at an air marshal gone rogue or something like that? You can't just board a commercial aircraft armed."

"Remember, it came from a private airstrip. The kind where you stroll across the tarmac and climb the steps to a private plane. What kind of security is there at a place like that?"

"That's definitely something I'm going to find out." McCord's gaze shifted to one side of the screen as the tapping of keys sounded while he made notes. "I wonder who was onboard?"

"I'm sure they'll have that information by the time we land. Craig told us the plane's designation, but I can't remember what it was. BA . . . something."

"I can find that out. Where was it headed?"

"Napa County Airport."

"Going somewhere fancy in Napa. Or headed into San Francisco. If Barron Pharma owned the plane, you have to wonder if the CEO was onboard. Or his COO, who just happens to be his son."

"What are their names?" Meg asked. "They have to have the detailed manifest by now. But they clearly haven't released it, if you, of all people, don't know who's onboard."

"They're playing their cards close to their chest at this point. They haven't found the plane, and haven't released names. To answer your question, Barron's CEO is Kenneth Barron. The COO is Eli Barron."

"If they haven't found the plane yet, they don't know who survived and who didn't," Brian pointed out. "They're likely trying to protect the families. Especially if you're looking at a family that may have just had several members die."

Meg looked out the window, where a carpet of clouds flowed in peaks and valleys seemingly not far beneath them as they flew through the sunny sky. "There's almost complete cloud cover here. I wonder if we're looking at weather issues complicating the search. If you can't get anything up into the sky, you're depending on reports or searching on foot."

"That's where we come in." A chime sounded, and Brian's gaze shifted above their heads as the seat belt light came on. "We're about to find out. We're on approach."

Light in the cabin abruptly dimmed as they sank into the clouds, snuffing out almost all traces of sunlight.

This could be a bumpy landing. Meg gave her seat belt a tug to make sure it was well secured. "McCord, we have to go. Did this help?"

"A ton. I may not be able to join you in person, but our standard deal still stands," McCord said. "You'll keep me in the loop?"

"Absolutely. We're going to be up against a wall from the beginning, so I probably won't have time to call you. But I'll text you information, or ask Craig to feed it to you if our hands are full. Which they very likely will be."

"Works for me." McCord's gaze rose from where he would have been watching Meg and Brian on the screen to stare into the camera. It was like he was making eye contact with them. "I know the challenges you're up against because of where you're going, and I know the extra challenges the geography is going to give you. Be careful. Take care of each other and the dogs. And let the hijacker go if tracking him means your lives. Someone else can try to pick up the trail later if needed. We want you both back here in one piece."

"We hear you. Todd has given us our best shot at a safe deployment considering the circumstances. We took our first dose of acetazolamide before we took off. Craig even found a vet to tell him what dosage the dogs needed based on their weight, so they've also had their first dose. The local agents will provide the rest of the doses we'll need."

"Ladies and gentlemen, this is your captain." The voice came over the loudspeaker. "We're preparing to land in Aspen, where the temperature is fifty-three degrees Fahrenheit and the local time is 5:24 PM. We expect some turbulence as we make our approach. Please remain in your seats and keep your seat belt buckled at all times until we get to the gate."

"That's our cue, McCord. We're about to land. Do me a favor and let Todd know we've arrived and I'll text updates as I can, but remind him they may be few and far between."

"I can do that. I'll let Ryan know, too." McCord had Ryan's number in his contacts lists from their urban exploration case a year and a half before, something that had come in handy when Lacey had nearly died protecting Brian from a cougar attack shortly thereafter. Unbeknownst to anyone on the teams, McCord had reached out to Ryan on his own, arranged for his flight from DC to Chattanooga, Tennessee, and then for a rental car to get him to Chatsworth, Georgia. Ryan had walked into the vet's office just before Lacey's prognosis—a good one, thank God—had been delivered by the vet.

"Thanks, McCord," Brian said. "Ryan and I both appreciate it."

"No problem."

"More when there's more," Meg said.

"You got it." McCord gave a single wave of farewell, and then was gone.

The plane lurched suddenly and Meg felt as if her stomach might ricochet into her throat. She grabbed both arm-rests, her right hand bumping Brian's where he'd grasped the extra-wide armrest between them.

Hawk raised his head and whined quietly. Meg released one armrest to stroke down his back. "It's okay, bud. Just stay down. Stay, Hawk."

He put his head down on his paws.

"Hang on," Brian said, and the plane lurched again and then wobbled slightly, side to side. "It looks like it's going to be a bumpy ride."

Meg had to wonder if Brian meant the landing, or the search that loomed so large before them.

CHAPTER 4

Backcountry: An undeveloped and isolated wilderness accessed only by trails; a remote area, without easily accessible basic technology or medical care.

May 6, 5:34 pm
Aspen/Pitkin County Airport
Aspen, Colorado

"Glad we're finally down," Brian murmured as he and Meg led their dogs toward the aircraft exit.

"I'm with you there," Meg agreed. "I've had bumpy small aircraft landings in remote areas for searches, but this one came amazingly close in a much bigger plane."

"Those are some high winds. And we're not even out on the peaks yet."

"Well, as Todd looked up, we're seventy-nine hundred feet above sea level and in a valley with steep walls, so we're essentially in a wind tunnel. But yeah, I suspect it may only get worse from here." She shrugged her shoulders, seating her go bag more securely on her back as she maneuvered her duffel in front of her in the narrow space.

Just after they finally landed, as they were taxiing toward the terminal, one of the flight attendants had informed them they'd be the first to exit the aircraft, and the

Denver field agents were waiting for them on the tarmac. As soon as the plane braked to a stop and the engines wound down, the door was opened and boarding stairs were rolled into place. Meg and Brian had grabbed their bags and headed for the exit with the dogs.

They stepped out onto the landing of the boarding stairs and the wind slammed them full in the face, catching Meg's breath and whipping her loose hair into a cloud around her head. But the landscape around them equally stole her breath.

She'd been out West a few times, but never in Colorado, and never at this altitude, as it was something she happily avoided. Now she was torn as the beauty of the landscape filled her with equal parts awe and terror.

The airport was cradled in a low-lying valley surrounded on both sides by towering peaks, many rising two or three thousand feet above Aspen's already-considerable altitude. Dark clouds scudded across the low sky, pushed by ferocious winds, hiding the tops of the surrounding peaks. The deep green of trees marched up the hills around them, but the upper reaches were dotted with patches of snow. The air felt fresh, and while it bore a sharp snap of spring chill, it also carried the scent of seasonal blooms, earthy soil, and recent rain.

"This is something else," Brian murmured. "Gorgeous."

"See if you think that when you're balanced on top of one of those mountains and you can't see twenty feet in front of you because you're standing inside a cloud. From the look I had of the map, these aren't the tallest mountains in the area. We haven't seen anything yet." Meg forced her shoulders to relax. If she was this tense already, she wasn't going to be able to move a few thousand feet up in the air. *Get it together. You can do this.* "Hawk, come."

She led the way down the narrow boarding steps, loosening the leash to let Hawk precede her down the steps, with Lacey, then Brian, following. They stepped onto the rain-drenched tarmac and scanned the airport. A long, single-story building, embellished with stone pillars and wood accents—to resemble a ski lodge, Meg assumed— the airport had a single entrance off the tarmac under a wide portico. Lines of boarding stairs, baggage conveyor belts, luggage carts, and trucks were neatly parked at the edge of the tarmac, ready to be put into action with each incoming flight.

Meg's gaze panned left and she found the Denver field agents standing under an overhang beside a pillar. The man and woman were dressed in hiking boots and athletic clothes, but even out of the standard Bureau uniform of dark suits, Meg pegged them as agents simply from her stance and his haircut. "I have them. This way."

As Meg and Brian started across the tarmac, the two agents came out to meet them partway.

The man, tall and whipcord-lean, with perfectly trimmed chestnut hair, which rippled in the wind, blue eyes, and a welcoming smile, held out his hand. "Corey Newall, Denver field office. You must be Meg and Brian." He grinned down at the dogs. "And this must be Hawk and Lacey."

"Yes." Meg shook his hand and then indicated her dog. "This is Hawk. Lacey is the shepherd."

As Brian shook hands with Newall, the woman said, "I'm Stacey Carlisle." Petite in stature, but moving with athletic grace, Carlisle's blond hair, wisely pulled into a ponytail, was liberally shot through with silver, which, for her years—Meg placed her in her late thirties—looked more like brilliant highlights than early graying. She shook hands with Brian and then looked between the two handlers. "Can I meet your dogs? I mean, they're here to work, but I'm a sucker for dogs."

"They're not working yet." Meg looked down at her dog, standing patiently at her knee. "Hawk, sit. Say hi."

Hawk sat and politely extended a paw to Carlisle. Her smile went wide as she shook his paw and then held that same hand out for him to sniff before she skimmed it over his head and down his back. "Smart boy, Hawk. Handsome boy."

Meg laughed as Hawk sat up straighter, his tail thumping the tarmac. "He knows it too."

"And this is Lacey." Brian had Lacey greet the agents in the same way.

Carlisle straightened and stepped back, waiting until Newall had greeted both dogs. "We need to get on the road. Did you check bags?"

"No, this is it." Meg picked up her duffel. "We travel light."

"You'll travel lighter on the peaks. Come on, we'll update you in the SUV."

Newall and Carlisle led the way across the asphalt to a black SUV that shouted *Feds!* parked at one end of the terminal, just off the main tarmac. They tossed their duffels and go bags in the rear compartment beside two loaded backpacks—one with a rifle strapped to it—and then Carlisle climbed in behind the wheel, while Newall took shotgun. Meg and Brian let the dogs jump in first, then had them lie down so they could get in as well. Floor space was tight with two large dogs, but Hawk and Lacey were companionably curled together, their leashes dropped on the mat beside them, while Meg and Brian kept their boots pressed against the doors.

Carlisle twisted around to look. "Sorry, you're kind of squeezed. We don't have the typical vehicle you'd normally use. The dogs are okay?"

Hawk's head was down on his front paws, his cheek pressed to Lacey's. "Hawk *loves* Lacey," Meg said. "He's probably thanking you right now. We're good."

"It's nice they're so friendly." Carlisle started the engine and drove away from the airport, toward a small employee parking lot that led out of the complex.

"First of all," Newall said, "we messed up and owe you an apology. We had a miscommunication on our end. We thought our SSA, who talked to your SSA, filled him in on the issue of high-altitude illness. He thought we did. So, in the end, no one did."

"That's a big ball to drop," Carlisle added. "But someone on your side caught it?"

"My fiancé," Meg said. "He's a firefighter/paramedic with DCFEMS. Normally, this isn't something he'd be an expert in, but his younger brother came out to the Maroon Bells last year and he studied up so he could tell him how to do the altitude change safely."

"She says 'fiancé,' " Brian interjected, "but he's practically her husband. She's getting married in twelve days."

"Oh no." Horror filled Carlisle's voice as she made a right onto Airport Road. "I remember the last two weeks before my wedding. I was run off my feet. And we just pulled you out here?"

"Her fiancé is at home. He can fill the gap," Newall said.

"Spoken like a true man." Carlisle's eye roll was in full view in the rearview mirror. "You guys have no clue. When you got married, who did ninety-five percent of the organizing?"

"Well . . . Trudy did . . ."

"I rest my case. Meg, I'm sorry. We'll try to wrap this for you as fast as possible for everyone's sake, especially yours. But we needed help. You guys are the best, and it saved a ton of time not having to make deals to use another law enforcement body's teams. That can make things . . . complicated."

Meg waved away the concern. "We totally understand. Luckily, I'm super organized and I have my mom and sister standing by if I need help. We're getting married at my mom and dad's place, and they have a lot of the heavy lifting already in order."

"From someone who's been-there-done-that, that's a relief. Okay, back to the task at hand. Corey has the meds you need. You've already had one dose of acetazolamide?"

"Us and the dogs, yes. And Todd also advised us to take ibuprofen at the same time to counter any inflammation, so we've done that too."

"Even better. You know what to look for, as far as symptoms go?"

"Yes."

"We'll also keep an eye on you. We'll keep you safe. We may pester you every twenty minutes with questions about how you're feeling, but we'll do everything we can to keep you safe and healthy."

"Appreciate that. We want to be part of the search, not part of the rescue."

"That's the number one rule of rescue—don't make additional victims. Look after yourself, your teammates, and the victim, in that order. Speaking of which . . ." Carlisle rolled her window down and pointed to a building on their left. "See that building across Highway 82?"

On the other side of the road stood a building that looked like the architect had grafted a two-story log ski chalet onto a fire station. Over the pitched front entrance, C.B. CAMERON RESCUE CENTER was spelled out in large, block letters against horizontal wood cladding. A series of four transparent garage doors stretched across the southern end of the building under MOUNTAIN RESCUE ASPEN. A four-story rescue tower loomed at the southernmost end of the building. As they shot past, Meg noted that while the garage was flooded with light, it was deserted, every emergency vehicle missing from its designated spot. *Already deployed.* "That's the local rescue group?"

"Yes. They're amazing. We're lucky they're local, as they're one of the best, if not *the* best, in the country. They're a team of volunteers who all have day jobs and who will drop everything at a moment's notice when they're needed. They'll go through absolute hell to get to you, and they *will* get to you. You just need to hang on until they do. Everyone on that plane needs to hang on." Carlisle merged the SUV onto CO-82 and hit the accelerator. "Looks like they're already in the field."

"We're hours behind the crash," Brian stated. "We expected to be behind the first wave of rescuers."

"For sure we're behind the hasty team," Carlisle said, referring to the first search teams deployed to start scouting before the search proper was set up, "but it takes longer than you might think to organize a rescue of this size—all those people, all that equipment. Especially if it could be a long and dangerous search, needing extra equipment. Right now, there's still snowpack in the higher ranges, which means we might need crampons and ice picks. Someone needs to organize food, and get the vehicles where they need to be. At least they now have a common launching site for the trucks and gear in that station, which speeds the response."

"They didn't before?"

"Mountain Rescue Aspen has always been a volunteer organization, and for years it ran out of a cabin on Main Street. But there was hardly anywhere to park, let alone store all the equipment, so a lot of it was kept at people's houses. There wasn't even a room big enough in the cabin to house the approximately fifty members for a meeting. A memorial donation decades after the 1977 plane crash that killed C.B. Cameron jump-started hopes of a new facility. Fund-raising did the rest and that facility has been open for a few years now. They keep everything under one roof—all the trucks, ATVs, and snowmobiles, as well as all the climbing and medical gear—and it gives them a place to meet, to organize, and to do community training in climbing, planning and navigation, and avalanche safety." Carlisle met Meg's eyes briefly in the rearview mirror. "The backcountry can be incredibly dangerous. People go out for a day trip and die. They fall when a rock gives way underneath them, they walk off a cliff in the dark because they lost their route, or they get lost and die of hypothermia overnight because they packed for a day trip, or only for a few hours and are unprepared for the situation they now find themselves in. We'll have comms while we're out there, but the same risks hold for us as well, though we'll be better prepared."

"It sounds like you know a lot about this," Brian commented.

"Definitely more than me," said Newall. "Stacey's going to be our mountaineering lead through this incident."

"Not just me, but we'll get to that," Carlisle said. "But I do know this area and its dangers. I was born and raised in Aspen. Grew up on these mountains, so I know the whole area very well. Volunteered with Mountain Rescue Aspen on and off through college when I was home for summer or Christmas vacation. And have worked the odd case or two with them since then—a child kidnapped from his family while camping, rumors of some guy in the mountains with a grenade launcher . . . which turned out to be a telescope. They're a solid group who knows their stuff and their mountains. And they've done plane crashes before."

"Many times?"

"We get about three or four crashes a year from Sardy Field." Carlisle must have seen Meg and Brian's confusion because she clarified. "That's the local name for Aspen's airport."

"That's a lot of crashes," Brian stated.

"It's a tricky airport. As you can see, it's an extremely narrow valley, surrounded on all sides by tall peaks with multiple points of entry and egress. If the pilot isn't familiar with the area, they can fly up the wrong valley. If they don't gain enough altitude for the valley they're in, while thinking they're somewhere else, they can hit a peak taller than the one they expected. The air is thinner here, so there's not as much lift as you'd get at sea level, so they can't climb as fast. When you need enough lift to clear a fourteener, you simply might not have it if you're in the wrong place. Then . . . *bam*."

"Sounds like we're going to be in good hands. What do we know about this particular plane crash? Do you have better info on the plane and who was on it? Last we heard, there were sixteen onboard a plane owned by Barron Pharmaceuticals, flying out of a private airstrip."

"And one person was dead by GSW," Meg added. "So at least one weapon is involved."

"We've been able to update a lot of information since then," said Carlisle as they sped up CO-82, the four lanes divided by a narrow green space. "Including where we believe the plane went down."

"That's still not nailed down?"

"That can be hard to do," Newall said, "especially under current conditions. We're heading up West Maroon Road to a viewpoint we're using as a staging area, though we'll use the Maroon Bells Trailhead about a mile and a half farther on as base camp because there's more room. Reports of the crash point to a location around Pyramid Peak. Considering where it was coming from, it's likely on the east face of the mountain, but it's also a possibility it cleared Pyramid and hit North Maroon."

"Either is a nightmare," Carlisle muttered.

"Why?" Brian asked.

"They're both fourteeners, but it's the kind of rock

that's really the problem. These aren't solid peaks. They're composed of sedimentary mudstone. You think of stone as something that's strong and solid, but this particular type of stone fractures easily. So what's up there, all the way to the peak, looks more like piled, shattered fragments. The slopes leading to the peaks are steep and almost entirely covered in scree—small, fragmented, loose rock. Above the tree line, which is at about eleven and a half thousand to twelve thousand feet, it's all rock, and way too much of it is scree. The only way up is to scramble and you're always at risk of slipping. Fall with any kind of speed on scree and they'll act like rollers; you'll pick up velocity with nothing to hold on to." Carlisle glanced at the dogs on the floor behind her. "I'm not sure how they'll manage."

"You'd be surprised." Brian stroked a hand over Lacey's head. "These dogs are parkour experts. They'll likely do better than us. They're lower to the ground and on four smaller feet, so a partial footing for us is a whole footing for them." He quickly glanced sideways at Meg. "Do you think the crash site could be fourteen thousand feet up?"

"It could be, but if so, the site will be spread over the face of the mountain. There's nowhere up there to hold a crashed plane. It would shatter and fragment, with pieces possibly scattering down thousands of feet."

"With almost no chance of survivors," Newall added. "The be-all and end-all is we don't know. We're not getting much in the way of local reports of the crash. Any nearby campsites aren't open to summer bookings until the end of the month. Considering the weather today"— Newall peered out the window at the ominous overcast skies—"pretty much no one is out on the hills. Furthermore, these are federal, protected wilderness areas, maintained by the US Forest Service. No one lives in much of the area. There were a number of reports of sounds of a crash in the peaks, and they're trying to triangulate the location. Even if it's narrowed down to the Maroon Bells—that's Maroon Peak and North Maroon Peak collectively—and Pyramid Peak, it's still an immense search area. Mountain Rescue Aspen has called in its members and is working on a plan. If the dog teams need to split up, we're"—Newall waved an index finger between Carlisle and himself—"going to split with you, adding one Mountain Rescue Aspen trail expert to each group. We'll travel together, unless there's no option but to split into two groups. In which case we want to make sure we have one dog-and-handler team, one agent, and one trail guide to keep things as safe as possible while still tracking a potential perp and making the arrest."

"That makes sense," Meg said.

"We have the full manifest at this point," Newall continued. "The plane, a twin-engine Gulfstream G800, could have carried up to nineteen, but this manifest logs sixteen. There were three crew members—two pilots and one flight attendant. On the passenger list, we have thirteen, all employees of Barron Pharmaceuticals, starting with the CEO, Kenneth Barron. Also present, his son, the COO, Eli Barron, and the CFO, Eliza Sheard."

Meg and Brian exchanged glances—they were not at all surprised to hear McCord had correctly predicted who was on the plane when it went down.

"Seven members of the board of directors were also on the plane," Carlisle continued. "Corey?"

"Got it here." Newall pulled out his phone, opened an email message, and read the names aloud. " 'Andrew Blenn, Henry Corum, Jin Dai, Hannah Jewitt, Carolyn Miles, James Worland, and Ajay Varma.' Then, to round out the group, there's one assistant, Nora Gleason, and their two security guards, Patrick Connolly and Sid Drubek."

"The assistant and security guards notwithstanding, that's a pretty substantial list of the top people at the company. If someone wanted to cut the head off Barron Pharma, this is a good way to do it," Brian said.

"It sure is. Are you aware of the current accusations around Barron Pharma?"

"Yes. If the plan was to take the plane out entirely, whoever took control clearly thought it was worth his own life to cut that head off."

"There's been a lot of loss associated with Barron Pharma's products, especially Zelcone," said Newall as they entered a roundabout and Carlisle took the first exit onto Maroon Creek Road, a winding stretch of asphalt flanked by low hills, with rail fencing, bushes, and trees bursting with spring growth. "But motive is secondary to actually finding the plane itself and seeing if anyone survived."

Meg's eyes were fixed on the towering hills all around, which encroached ever closer the farther south they drove. The heavy, charcoal-gray clouds mirrored her foreboding, even while they hid the worst of the threat from her eyes as they settled around the peaks, sinking ever lower. "What's the theory on what happened?"

"It's sketchy at this point, but we're starting to form a picture." Newall slipped his phone back into his pocket. "They took off from Peyton Airfield, outside of Franktown, south of Denver, at ten ten this morning, local time. Here's the thing with private airstrips—there's no security at a lot of them. It's a private plane, owned by a Denver-area business. The security in a situation like this is who they're letting onto their own planes. We'd assume they wouldn't let anyone on they didn't trust. It's how private flight differs from public flights, where there's no way to know everyone getting onboard, so security screening is the way around any threats. But in a case like this, they should have known every passenger."

"Clearly, the weak point in this scenario," said Brian. "Does that plane have a locked cockpit door?"

"It's not a requirement for any plane with a capacity of less than twenty. A lot of these small planes don't have a cockpit door, period. This one did, but not one that locked, and certainly not one reinforced like a commercial jet. Getting through it would be simple, especially if there was a weapon onboard."

"No airport security would make that child's play," Meg stated. "In fact, there were two security guards, so you'd expect two weapons in play. There was a death reported; it makes you wonder if that was one of the security guards being taken out."

"It also makes you wonder who the hijacker is," Brian said. "You're looking at a limited group. The Barron Pharma execs would have been familiar with each other, at least at the top. Are any of those people new? Not Barron or his son, but the CFO or anyone on the board?"

Newall shook his head. "We're in contact with Gloria Seghers, Kenneth Barron's executive assistant. She organized this annual board of directors meeting, but she's eight months pregnant and her doctor wasn't comfortable with her flying. A junior assistant went on the trip in her place, at the last minute. However, Ms. Seghers is a font of knowledge. The newest member on the board of directors joined five years ago. The junior assistant has been there eight months. The security guards come from an outside contractor, but one has been assigned to Barron Pharmaceuticals for three years, the other, six months. No one is truly short term and there were zero red flags for anyone. Whoever the hijacker is, they put in a considerable amount of time preparing for this. Keeping in mind the flight attendant reported the hijacker was male; that narrows our list. But as part of the crew, she wouldn't know one suited business type from another. That gives us a pool of nine individuals."

"Seeing as the flight attendant didn't identify the hijacker as one of the known crew, we can assume they weren't involved."

"The pilots have been a regular part of Barron's crew since he bought the plane four years ago. The flight attendant is the newest, having flown with them for only about three months."

"But the plane would have stayed under everyone's radar for a lot longer if the flight attendant hadn't raised awareness. The plane had a comms system in the back. If one of the pilots was the hijacker, they'd have known about it and made sure she couldn't use it."

"Agreed," said Carlisle. "Because we're out in the field, we're getting additional assistance from other agents in the office. They're trying to find out more."

Meg met Brian's eyes. He gave her a head cock toward the front seat and a nod.

"We actually have another tool at our disposal," Meg said. "Clay McCord from the *Washington Post.*"

Both agents in the front went silent.

"I hear what you're not saying," Meg said as the road arced to the left around a football field surrounded by bleachers. "You should have seen me the first time we worked with McCord. It was during the spree bombings on the East Coast two years ago. For a while there, we even thought he might be the bomber."

Brian let out a self-deprecating laugh. "From our current perspective, years later, we really missed the boat on him early on. He could have been so much more useful."

"He still managed to get useful fast. In our next case, he

helped save my sister's life. Here's the deal SSA Beaumont and EAD Peters have worked out with McCord. He gets full access to our information—all of it, no holding anything back, or else we hobble him. In exchange he gives us everything he's found out, which is always useful and plentiful. He then sits on the story as it builds. And then continues to sit on it until the case is closed. He only goes to press with it once he's been given a green light by the Bureau. His editor understands the agreement and is okay with it, so there's no pressure from within the *Post* to blow us off. They get a superior scoop in the end, so it's worth the investment of time and information to them."

"It's also worth the investment to us," Brian finished. "And you won't find a better researcher. The stuff he can find out . . . it's impressive. The man can dig."

"Your superiors are fine with him?" Newall's tone was heavy with suspicion.

"They are. They've learned he's trustworthy and gets results. He also has contacts no one in law enforcement does, because he's *not* law enforcement. We've all seen it before, doors closing in our faces because we show we're law enforcement or we simply smell like it. He doesn't have any of that. He's so good, where we used to negotiate this agreement on a case-by-case basis, it's now auto-approved."

"You're going to forward the names on the manifest to him?"

"Does SSA Beaumont have the list?"

"Yes."

"McCord may already have it, then, but I'll make sure he does. He can't help us if we keep him in the dark. Bring him into the light so he can work with us."

"If you say so." Carlisle flexed her fingers on the steering wheel a few times as if trying to release stress at the thought of bringing a journalist into the case. "It sounds like you've had a kind of experience with the media we've never had."

"We hadn't either up to the time we met him, which is why it took him a long time to win us over," said Brian. "You won't regret this partnership."

They drove past a high school and district theater as, ahead of them, a taller mountain materialized out of the clouds, slowly morphing from mist into a solid form that seemed to rise forever. Meg's gaze was drawn up the thick green of forest rolling darkly over steep slopes, but its rocky heights remained hidden from view.

They'd be lucky to have forest to protect them from the winds and from a fall. To hold the scent of a target on the run. But where they were going, thick forests couldn't flourish in the cold, wind, and low oxygen.

Then it would be just the teams, the rocky peak, the winds, the sky. The void below.

And a deadly drop in every direction.

CHAPTER 5

Climbing Area: A geographic area with multiple climbing routes.

May 6, 5:59 pm
Maroon Creek Road
Aspen, Colorado

Emergency vehicles overflowed the tiny viewpoint parking lot, pulling onto the grassy verge until even that was full, then they simply filled the road around it. Cars, SUVs, and pickups streamed down the road past the staging area, pulled off to the side as their occupants jogged in from beyond.

As they slowly drove by the parking lot, Meg got a quick view of a crowd of people clustered in groups. Each emergency vehicle had every compartment door open and she caught glimpses of piles of ropes, webbing, tarps, a steel litter, snowshoes, climbing hardware, and the wooden handles of what she supposed were ice picks. Then they were past, squeezing slowly down a road where vehicles lined both sides.

Carlisle pulled off to the right in the first available grassy spot and cut the engine. She slung one arm over Newall's seat as she looked into the back. "Assume we're leaving immediately following the briefing. Grab the gear you need from your duffels. We made it into the midfifties today, but it's going to be colder above. Then it's going to be colder still overnight." She shot a look past Brian's shoulder and out the window. The sky, already dark with heavy clouds, was deepening into the gloom of dusk. "Those clouds say there's a good chance of either rain or snow tonight, depending on whether we stay above freezing or not. And chances are likely better than fifty-fifty we won't."

Brian shuddered.

Carlisle gave him a pointed look. "You're not in DC with the cherry blossoms. This is the backcountry, where winter never truly leaves. Dress for it. The last of the daylight will be gone soon; I promise you won't get overheated."

"Understood," said Brian. His gaze slid to Meg. "We better bring the dogs' coats."

"We better bring anything we might possibly need because once we're up there, there's no coming back for it."

"We can help you carry too. We're each only packing for one, you're packing for two," Newall said, opening his door. "But we're going to be paired with you for the whole time. To help us build the best teams, who's stronger? Has better endurance? Same for the dogs."

Meg and Brian stared at each other for a minute before Meg answered. "Honestly, we're matched as teams. And that might be because we always work out together, run several times a week, do parkour a few more. We can manage the same challenges, and the dogs are also equally matched."

"That's good," Carlisle said. "Okay, Meg you're with me; Brian, you're with Corey. The goal is for all of us to stay together until we find the survivors. Two teams give us flexibility if the hijacker has disappeared and the trail splits or becomes indistinct. Or . . ." She trailed off, suddenly unsure.

Meg immediately realized the real reason for two teams instead of one—redundancy. "Or if one of us or one of the dogs gets hurt. Or killed. Then you still have a second team already up there."

Carlisle looked vaguely uncomfortable, as if caught with her hand in the cookie jar.

"It's okay." Brian patted Carlisle's arm. "We're not only professionals, we're practical. It's a whole different playing field at altitude. And stuff happens. We understood that when we accepted the deployment."

"Could you have said no?"

"To Craig, yes." Brian's tone held no doubt. "It would have left him in the lurch, having to figure something else out. But we didn't."

Gratitude shone bright in her eyes. "We're glad to have you with us. And we'll do everything in our power to make sure no 'stuff' happens. Beaumont said you both preferred a Glock 19, so Corey has those for you, and a couple of different styles of holsters, so you can pick your preference."

"We brought our own holsters," Meg said. "Craig told us you'd be supplying firearms for us, once we got here, so we came prepared. We both use concealment shoulder holsters on a search like this. Keeps the weapon strapped close when we're active, and we're going to be active today."

"Good thought," said Newall. "We should do the same. Let's move."

Meg and Brian spent a few minutes reorganizing their bags, while the dogs waited patiently in the second seat. They added layers for warmth, as well as resisting water, be it rain or snow. Meg pulled on her hooded long-sleeved sun shirt over her athletic base layer, then a fleece layer.

She slipped her arms into her shoulder holster, cinching it under her breasts, and secured the Glock that Newall handed her into the holster hugging her left side. She seated it under an elastic strap, so with the flick of one thumb, she could pull the weapon with her right hand and be ready to fire in just over a second. She layered her thermal waterproof puffy jacket over the holster and waterproof pants over her leggings. Her hiking boots were waterproof, unless she stepped in a puddle deeper than the top of the boot, but she had spare socks just in case.

As was de rigueur for cold-weather rescue scenarios, the handlers had taken care to not bring anything made of cotton. Meg loved natural fibers, but they were verboten in the great outdoors on a search, especially one in extreme wet and cold, as cotton was easily saturated, didn't dry quickly, and sucked every ounce of heat from the wearer once wet.

She braided her hair, letting the braid dangle over her shoulder, then added a thermal cap. She wasn't cold yet, but she knew she'd need it. She tucked her gloves into her jacket pocket.

After making sure everything she needed for Hawk was packed, and double-checking their lifesaving meds were securely tucked into place, she zipped the pack closed and slid her arms into the straps, shifting it slightly to seat it comfortably. She did one last check to make sure the go bag straps didn't interfere with her access to her weapon, then zipped her jacket closed again.

Ready.

Brian, already wearing his pack, gave her a nod. After commanding the dogs to jump down and giving them a minute to take care of business, Meg and Brian buckled them into their navy work vests—with FBI in large yellow block letters, so there was no mistaking their affiliation—and leashed them. Right now, in the midst of so many law enforcement and rescue teams, their affiliation was key. Later they'd swap out the work vests for the warmer coats they'd surely need.

They turned to find Carlisle and Newall watching them. Both wore backpacks, clearly prepared to tackle this incident according to their own strengths.

Carlisle's backpack had a short, squared shovel blade strapped under a swatch of matching nylon to the back of the pack, its short handle rising toward the base of her skull. A bright blue helmet was snapped onto one of the straps holding the shovel in place.

But it was Newall's pack that caught Meg's attention, and she partially circled him for a better look at the pack she'd only glimpsed previously. The rifle was strapped to the side of the tactical backpack he wore, one with pockets for extra magazines, a side pocket to seat a rifle buttstock, and webbing straps up the side to snap-buckle the receiver and barrel securely to the pack. The long rifle barrel towered a good six inches above Newall's head. "A Remington 700. With a Leupold Mark 6 scope?" Meg asked.

Newall's eyebrows shot skyward. "You know your firearms. And accessories."

"I do. I was Richmond PD before I joined the FBI. When I was at the academy, it was a toss-up for me whether to aim for SWAT, because I had a real knack for sharpshooting the 700—to the great displeasure of Sergeant Collins, my fossil of a firearms instructor, who thought women didn't belong in law enforcement—or to follow my real passion for the dogs. The dogs won." Meg opted to leave out the tragedy of the loss of Deuce and to stay in the present. "When I got Hawk, I moved to search-and-rescue, and we found our place in the FBI. Like you guys, we're required to do our time at the range to keep our proficiency sharp. In our capacity we try not to ever use firearms—with our dogs, we're a tool, not a weapon—

though we never know when we might need to protect ourselves and our dogs. The Glock 19 is my standard weapon now, but I trained on a 700 using .308 rounds at the academy."

"What was your longest shot back then?"

"Consistently? Six hundred yards. I kept trying for seven hundred, but never nailed it on the regular. And then I took that left turn into K-9 patrol and didn't need to keep up that kind of distance."

"I can regularly hit eight hundred and have gone higher, but it's not a sure thing in the field. Too many complicating factors. But this is why you have Stacey and me assigned to this case. She's a climber and knows this kind of terrain and the rescue aspect. We know from the flight attendant's call that we have guns in play and the possibility of an armed suspect, so we wanted a longer-range sharpshooter on the team."

"Smart."

"You're both ready?" Carlisle asked.

"Yes."

"This way then. We need to find the on-site rescue leader. The coordinator will be back at the station, but we'll have someone on-site as well. He or she will liaise with the groups."

With no vehicle coming, they walked down the middle of Maroon Creek Road, back toward the tiny, overflowing parking lot. "There's us and Mountain Rescue Aspen. What other groups are involved?"

"The Pitkin County Sheriff's Office. The US Forest Service. Quite possibly volunteer firefighters from Snowmass. Maybe even a team from the Bureau of Land Management. When there's a crisis up here, it's all hands on deck. But the sheriff's office runs the rescue. If not Sheriff Cox, then one of his deputies. They're intimately involved with Mountain Rescue Aspen and are part of the

Incident Command System. Have you ever worked a search needing ICS?"

Images flashed in Meg's memory like a slideshow—tumbled concrete, twisted metal bars, a forest of tiny red flags. The anguished wails of those left behind. A tiny infant, dressed in a fuzzy shell-pink sleeper, so cold and motionless, still cradled in her dead mother's arms.

Meg cleared her throat before trusting her voice. "Yeah, we've done ICS. In spades." She met Carlisle's gaze, which suddenly looked cautious as she studied Meg. "Brian and I and two other handler teams were the first on the pile when Talbot Terraces fell in DC in December." Meg didn't ask if the field agents were familiar with the catastrophe. For a three-week period moving into the turn of the year, all of America had watched. Waited. Hoped.

In vain. Todd's rescue of Kevin Vaughn had been the last live rescue from the rubble. After that, no one else had survived.

"Oh Christ," Newall murmured. "You worked that?"

"For weeks." Brian's tone was flat. "Even after they told us to go home. By that point we felt we owed it to the victims. We didn't leave until we were finally deployed to new incidents."

"Then you know ICS. This will be a big scene from our perspective, but I suspect not so big from yours."

"Let's hope it has a better outcome."

They walked quietly for another minute until they came to the edge of the parking lot.

Meg recognized the organized chaos of the beginning of an operation. From the scrambling to organize gear, to determining teams, to figuring out locations, it was all familiar. From chaos came order, and, really, couldn't come without it.

"There's Sheriff Cox." Carlisle pointed to a tall, rake-thin man in his fifties. He stood between Mountain Rescue

Aspen vehicles—a king cab Suburban, the tailgate on its cap wide open as rescuers hauled gear out onto the grass, and a larger emergency truck. His cool steel-gray eyes were laser-focused on the surrounding buzz of activity while another man talked to him. The sheriff looked like he was ready to join one of the teams himself, dressed in a khaki department parka with the star of his office high on the left breast, a matching khaki cap, waterproof pants, and heavy hiking boots.

His gaze shifted to their group as they got closer and Meg noticed the cool gaze warming slightly as it landed on Carlisle. But it went calculating when it dropped to take in the dogs.

"Sheriff!" Carlisle hailed as they approached. "Our teams are here and ready to go. This is Meg Jennings, with Hawk, and Brian Foster, with Lacey, out of DC."

Cox nodded at Meg first, then Brian. "Appreciate you coming out here to give us a hand." Cox's voice was smoky whiskey poured over rough gravel. "This is going to be a hard search. You're up to the task?"

"Yes, sir," Brian answered. "Us and the dogs. This is the kind of thing we train for. We'll have the endurance to stay on the hijacker's trail . . . if he survived."

"You've come a long way if he hasn't." His gaze slid to the FBI agents. "But the Bureau didn't want to chance it, so I hear."

"We don't," said Carlisle. "When are we sending teams up?"

"Just about to. You arrived just in time for the briefing."

"Hasty team is away?"

"Two teams, one for the Bells, one for Pyramid. But without a firm location yet, they're not truly functioning as hasty teams."

"More like a couple of teams who got away a little early."

"Yeah. We're in radio communication, so they'll let us know if they find signs of the crash and we can redirect. But I'll get into this shortly. Make sure you sign in with Deputy Snyder." Cox turned away as a deputy called his name from where he bent over a map spread out on the hood of a Pitkin County Sheriff's Office Tahoe. Another man, dressed in a hunter green parka and pants, with heavy boots and a knit cap bearing the stitched emblem of the US Forest Service, was sketching out areas on the map with his index finger.

"Do you know who this Deputy Snyder is?" Newall asked.

"Yes. Snyder's been around for years. I've worked with him before." Carlisle scanned the crowd, her gaze finally stopping on a deputy near the rear of a US Forest Service truck. Dressed in the same parka as Cox, he held a clipboard and was surrounded by rescuers. In head-to-toe winter gear, all distinguishing characteristics, even gender, were erased, but everyone looked ready to hit the trails as soon as they were released. "There. Come on, let's sign in."

After making their way to the front of the line as the previous group dispersed, they had their names added to the growing list on the clipboard, then pulled back to wait for the briefing.

Meg tugged the zipper of her jacket a little higher as the wind, blowing in explosive gusts, kept trying to slither inside. She studied Hawk, sitting patiently at her knee, watching for signs of a chill. They'd be fine once they got going and were active, but the waiting period could cool and stiffen his muscles if they waited too long, which would slow down the beginning of the search.

"We're really running on limited info here if we're basically just doing exploratory teams," Newall murmured.

"I kind of expected that might be how this starts."

Carlisle cast her eyes skyward and frowned. "That ceiling is so damned low. We may lose lives if anyone survived, simply because we won't be able to find them soon enough." A shout to their left drew her attention to where another deputy had stepped on top of a raised, flat boulder about thirty feet from the parking lot, and was waving both arms over his head and bellowing for rescuers to come closer. "Looks like the briefing is starting. Come on. Let's find out exactly what kind of fresh hell we're in for."

CHAPTER 6

Start Zone: The location where an avalanche starts; this area will include characteristics of slope incline and direction, sun and wind aspects, forest cover, as well as snow depth and type favorable to the formation of an avalanche.

May 6, 6:24 pm
Maroon Creek Road
Aspen, Colorado

"Hawk, heel." Meg instinctively tightened her grip on the leash to keep her dog close while they were surrounded by so many heavily booted rescuers—most already laden with backpacks and equipment—not willing to risk an injury before they even began. But the move was unnecessary, as Hawk instinctively stayed at her knee. A quick check showed Lacey in a similar position to Brian.

They followed Carlisle and Newall toward the gathering group, crossing bright green spring grasses and weeds, stepping over rocky patches or clusters of small boulders, and avoiding low-lying boggy areas, still cradling the results of recent rains. The ground sloped down at an angle, continuing on another 150 yards to where a twisty creek broke from the shelter of flanking pine trees. Even from this distance Meg could see how high the water level was and how fast it was moving. *Spring runoff.* Her gaze rose to the rising peak on the other side of the creek, the top lost in heavy, dark clouds. *Bet there's still snow up there. If so, that water is going to be* cold. *We need to do our best to stay out of it, or hypothermia could be a real problem.*

Keeping the dogs close, they joined the men and women clustering around the deputy. Their professional affiliations mostly lost in heavy waterproof outerwear, to Meg's eye, they looked competent and prepared. This wasn't their first rescue; this wasn't even likely their first plane crash if what Carlisle said about the annual number of plane crashes was accurate.

They tried to keep to the edge of the group as much as they could, but needed to be close enough to hear. People crowded in, making a full circle around the deputy because there was simply that many of them, and Meg pulled Hawk closer, then stepped over him, straddling his body, sheltering him from inadvertent encroachment. No one here would want to hurt one of the search dogs, but many of them weren't looking down and were focusing on the deputy motioning them closer.

"Good idea." Brian copied her move, having to adjust his stance around his larger dog. Lacey looked up at him in confusion, but didn't object.

"Let me through." Cox pushed his way through the crowd to join his deputy, who stepped off the rock, allowing his sheriff to step up. Gloved hands on hips, Cox took in everyone around him. "Thanks for coming out. This is a great response. Now, we want to get this search started right away. The feds are still gathering specific information about the flight and its passengers, but we know what's important to us already. We're looking for a twin-engine G800, owned by Barron Pharmaceuticals. There was one fatality at the time of the report, so we're looking at a max of fifteen survivors. The plane went off the radar over Hartsel, no reported line of sight after that. About twenty minutes after it went black, we started receiving reports from folks who heard the crash.

"The weather and time of year are working against us. Winter's over, so the skiing and snowmobiling seasons are done, and summer climbing's not going yet because it's cold and muddy in the hills. And the few brave hikers we might have had all wisely stayed home because of the clear risk of rain, sleet, or snow—take your pick with this temperature range—and the extremely low ceiling. We'd have been luckier if this had happened in February or July; you guys know what an offseason May is. They don't call it 'mud season' for nothing. Anyway, those few remote reports narrowed down the search area to an extent, but it's not a small range and it's definitely not easy terrain. Without a specific location, finding any trace of the plane or its trajectory is job one. Two hasty teams are already deployed, but there's no word back from them, so we're flying blind. And we're going to stay that way, because there won't be any air support. Winds are over fifty miles per hour with gusts even higher, and the ceiling is way too low. No chopper pilot is going to risk himself or his bird in these conditions. It would be a suicide mission, and then we'd have one more rescue to do."

"What about the drone?" someone called from the crowd.

"Burt tried it from a location where there was no risk of collision. Here at nine thousand feet, he had pretty good control. But the ceiling is sitting around ninety-five hundred feet and the winds are brutal. He guessed he couldn't see farther than about ten or fifteen feet above that altitude and wasn't confident about control in those winds. We send it up, we'd have to be right on top of the crash to see it and will likely lose the drone before that happens.

We can't risk a piece of equipment crucial for future searches on this particular search when the elements are working against us." Cox scanned the group, and Meg felt the intensity of his gaze as it passed over them. "We have no choice but to proceed on foot," he continued. "District Ranger Wekerman knows this area like the back of his hand and has spent a long time combing the maps. Running on the assumption the plane came from the east, based on last-known location and direction, the east faces of Pyramid and the Bells are likely our best bet when we account for reports of the crash. But that doesn't count out a strike on any of the three peaks and the plane fragmenting down the west side. Likely no chance of survivors if that's what happened.

"Deputy Snyder says we have seventy-eight rescuers on-site currently. We're going to break into multiple groups to increase our chances of finding the crash site. Once a site has been identified, we can then reroute the greater group to that location." Cox's gaze rose to the valley between the two wide mountain bases. "Two-thirds of you will follow Maroon Creek Road to the Maroon Lake Trailhead. From there, you'll pass Maroon Lake, follow West Maroon Creek, and then split, one group to cover the western face of Pyramid Peak, one to cover the eastern face of the Bells. Of those groups some of you will take the standard trails up both peaks, but most will not. The hazard of this search is going to be intensified for those of you going off trail. I know you're experienced, but I don't want anyone cliffing out. Hang on a second." Cox turned as a deputy approached and bent down for an update.

" 'Cliffing out'?" Brian murmured to Carlisle. "What's that?"

"That's when you get yourself into a position where you can't proceed farther up the peak, but can't go back down either. Now, unlike most hikers, this group should have the technical equipment to get themselves out of that position, but sometimes you can be so cliffed out, you need a chopper rescue."

"And that we can't do."

"Not right now anyway."

"Sorry about that," continued Cox as his deputy disappeared into the crowd. "The remaining group will follow East Maroon Creek to the east face of Pyramid Peak. There is no standard route on this side of the peak because it's simply too hazardous, so you'll have to take great care. Nonetheless, this remains what many feel is the most likely location of the crash."

"What about the west side of the Bells?" someone called. "That's everyone deployed, with no one covering that side."

"For now. Rocky Mountain Rescue has offered their services. I know we don't usually go out of county because we have what we need here, but because we're forced to do this search entirely on foot, I think we need the extra manpower. They're going to cover the west side of the Bells. They'll ATV the five or six miles from the Maroon-Snowmass Trailhead on the west side of Willoughby Mountain until they have to go on foot. They'll be in place to start within the hour. But we won't wait for them."

Cox surveyed the group, his face somber. "The odds are against us. Chances are good no one survived. If they did, and we don't reach them tonight, it's likely they'll die of hypothermia. The clock is ticking. But safety is priority one. Adverse conditions for them will affect you as well." He tipped his head back, squinting at the leaden sky, its thick clouds surging and boiling, with streaks of virga—rain or snow streaming from clouds, but evaporating before reaching the ground—in the distance. "My left knee says it's going to come down, and it's never wrong. Stay safe, stay in communication. Base camp is being set up at the Maroon Lake Trailhead and we'll be in constant contact with Dirk Slocum at Mountain Rescue Aspen headquarters. You need people, you need resources, you need help, we'll find a way to get it to you. Now Deputy Snyder is going to give you the team breakdown."

Fifteen minutes later, as the group began to break apart, with a large number of rescuers heading at a brisk pace along Maroon Creek Road toward the lake, two men in Mountain Rescue Aspen red parkas and carrying heavy packs approached the group. The man in the lead was tall and broad, with a face like weathered granite, but his brown eyes were warm. He grinned at Carlisle and slapped her shoulder hard enough to nearly knock her off balance. "Stacey! Good to see you."

"You too, Ben." Carlisle regained her footing and turned to the handlers. "Meg, Brian, this is Ben Hensley; he'll be our Team Four leader. Ben's an old-timer in the rescue group and knew me in my college days. Ben, this is Meg and Brian from the FBI Human Scent Evidence Team. And these are their dogs, Hawk and Lacey."

"And this is Rob Fifer."

Fifer was considerably younger than Hensley, easily twenty-five pounds lighter and still two inches taller. Even with a pack that had to weigh at least forty pounds, he walked with a spring in his step that telegraphed barely contained energy, and had laughing green eyes and tufts of carrot-red hair sneaking out from under his knit cap. "Just call me 'Fife.' Everyone does."

"Nice to meet you, Ben, Fife." Meg shook hands with both men, then stepped back so Brian could do the same.

"I was told we'd need to gear you guys up." Fife peeked at the glimpse of shovel and helmet showing behind Carlisle's pack. "You look prepared."

"I have everything I need to overnight on the peak,"

said Carlisle. "I used to do summers and Christmas vacation with MRA, so I've lived the routine."

Fife brightened. "Cool." He side-eyed Hensley. "You didn't tell me that."

"I told you'd they'd do fine. That's how I knew they'd do fine. Whatever Stacey hasn't prepared, we'll take care of." He looked down at Hawk and Lacey. "How about your dogs? Any concerns about going up there with them?"

Brian shook his head. "There may be some areas the dogs can't scale, but if we're on the run after the hijacker, I doubt he'll be able to either. The trick may be getting to the crash location. But the dogs are parkour experts. They won't let you down. Like us, they've already had a dose of acetazolamide. And we'll keep dosing on schedule."

"And we'll keep an eye out for signs of high-altitude illness." Fife bent down toward Lacey, then hesitated. "Can I meet them?"

"Yes. It would be better if you do. We're going to be spending a lot of time together. Better for them to be familiar with you."

Fife held out a hand to Lacey, who sniffed it and then held still as he ran a hand over her head and down her back. "Pretty girl." He looked up. "I love shepherds. Grew up with them."

"They're great dogs."

Fife looked sideways to where Hawk stood by Meg and his pale complexion flooded with ruddy color. "Not that Labs aren't great."

Meg's easy laugh let Fife off the hook. "It's okay to have a particular species favorite. The thing that matters in the end is both dogs will get the job done for you."

"Agreed."

"So . . . we're ready to roll?"

"We're going to take you to the equipment stores and

make sure everyone has what they need." Fife eyed the handlers' go bags. "What's in there?"

"All the food and clothing we need for this search," Meg said, "as well as medical supplies, because when we're out on a search, we can't pop back to civilization in a flash in case of emergency. Not so different from your job, I imagine."

"Not so much. You're going to need to carry more. Any objections to swapping out to a bigger pack?"

"As long as we can climb in it, no. And as long as someone holds on to our own packs until we get back."

"We can do that. Stacey, do you need any equipment?"

"I don't have the climbing equipment I know you guys are packing, but I have my bivouac sack, sleeping bag and pad, goggles, extra socks, water purification tablets, a whistle, binoculars, foldable trekking poles, headlamp, and my avalanche transceiver. I had enough time to borrow equipment from a friend to outfit Corey with the same. He's not a climber, but he's a long-distance runner, so he'll do fine."

"You're carrying an avalanche transceiver?" Brian asked. "Is that a risk at this time of year?"

"It's always a risk up here," Hensley said. "Just the degree of risk changes depending on the season. Winter is worst obviously, but in late spring like this, you can still get wet slab or loose wet avalanches on certain faces of the mountain. We're assigned to the east face of Pyramid and a wet slab could be a real problem down some of the larger couloirs—one of those steep, narrow gullies you see often high on a peak. They're like a chute for the snowpack that piles up in them. If the top goes, it all goes, and God help anyone standing at the bottom." Hensley turned back to Carlisle. "If you have room in there, we'll pack in some more rope and a harness for you. If we need to build a rope system, you'll be useful."

"No problem. We can squeeze more into both packs. Let's get everyone else equipped."

Hensley caught Carlisle's arm in a light hold when she started to step after Fife. "Hey, what's your opinion on this?"

"On what?"

"Don't bullshit a bullshitter. What do you and the Feds think happened? Barron Pharma isn't exactly one of the good guys."

Carlisle tossed Meg and Brian a pointed look. "Ben's a bit of a straight shooter."

Hensley's laugh was a sharp bark. " 'A bit'?"

"Understatement. It's nice to see you haven't changed, even after all these years. There's something comforting in that." Carlisle exhaled, her shoulders falling. "Needless to say, we don't have anything concrete so far. And while this hasn't been released yet, it will likely come out while we're on the mountain. The plane was not only owned by Barron Pharmaceuticals, but it carried the CEO, COO, CFO, and the entire board of directors on it."

"Whoa." Hensley pulled back slightly. "If everyone dies, they've wiped out the brains of the company."

"Pretty much. As you said, Barron Pharma isn't one of the good guys, if we're to believe the many accusations. The theory we're running on is that someone had a grudge. If we can find survivors, though, that will tell us the real story." Carlisle's gaze rose to the dark sky as a gust of wind whipped around them. "On that note, let's grab the equipment and helmets you guys will need and head out."

"Hawk, come. Heel." Meg purposely fell into step with Brian. "How are you feeling? Any effects so far?"

"I wasn't sure how hard or fast it would hit us, but nothing so far."

"Me either, but Todd said activity will make it worse, so we'll see how that goes. The next hour may tell us how the night will play out." Meg studied the mountain's massive footing that disappeared into the clouds. If the base was that large, how high could it go?

Too high.

Brian elbowed her. "Your brain is so loud, I can hear what you're thinking. We got this, you know. We'll get through it. *You'll* get through it."

"You don't think it's going to be a challenge?"

Brian's gaze followed hers to scan the landscape. "I admit this could be tricky. We've never covered a site like this. The dogs have never managed this kind of terrain. Forget the altitude; I'm more worried we're going into terrain they won't be able to manage. But we need to trust the team we're with. They know what they're doing. They'll make sure we do too."

Meg wanted to take Brian's words to heart, some of which she knew were to boost his spirits, as well as hers, but they were walking into a treacherous situation. An armed man, who might be loose on the mountain, the treacherous landscape and the wildlife it might contain, and the added risk of encroaching bad weather.

They wouldn't let the risk stop them, but trepidation would accompany them both onto the mountain.

CHAPTER 7

Route Finding: Planning a route/climbing path in unfamiliar terrain using available topographical maps, climbing apps, GPS, and a compass.

May 6, 7:11 pm
East Maroon Creek
Aspen, Colorado

They followed East Maroon Creek into the valley between Hunter and Pyramid Peaks, clinging to a narrow path on the east side of the creek as it rushed back toward the staging area. Hensley led the group, followed by Carlisle, Meg and Hawk, Brian and Lacey, Newall, and finally Fife bringing up the rear.

Meg and Brian wore their newly borrowed, considerably larger packs. When out on search, they always packed a lot of gear, but their goal on most searches was to cover as much ground as possible, as quickly as possible. Speed necessitated a more compact and lighter pack. In this situation speed took a definite backseat to straight-up survival, so the packs were considerably larger, heavier, and contained everything Hensley and Fife considered necessary to make it through a brutal winter-like night on the peaks.

Hensley and Fife also each carried extra equipment in case survivors were found alive. Depending on the crash site's location, even if someone was on the brink of death, it might be too dangerous to attempt a descent in the dark. As rescuers they had to be prepared for anything, but the main goal was to return from the search alive, intact, and with as many survivors as possible.

Meg shrugged her shoulders, resetting the heavy pack, and checked once again that the path to her firearm wasn't impeded by the straps. She hoped she wouldn't need to use it, but she'd be ready to take action, as would Brian, if the hijacker had survived and acted against them first.

If anyone had survived.

The first goal was finding the crash site. They had their directions, as did the four other teams preceding them. They were to follow the creek to a specific set of coordinates, then veer west. This would spread the five teams out over the eastern face of Pyramid Peak. Even with that many teams, given the size of the mountain, the rescuers would still be spread thin across the terrain. There was strength in numbers, but no one searched alone; that was simply too dangerous. There was a minimum group size of four rescuers, though they were the largest group with six, plus two dogs. They would stay together until the plane was found; only if there was a trail to search might the dog teams split up. In the meantime, if a modified ascent route had to be found for one dog because it couldn't traverse a vertical wall, it made sense for both dogs to be on that modified route; the dogs were evenly matched and what one could manage, the other would as well. There was no point in handicapping two teams, instead of one, when time was of the essence.

It was up to Hensley and Fife to find the safest route up the peak from their maps and knowledge of the area. Some mountains had multiple established routes to reach the summit; this one had only one and it was on the west side, so the FBI agents and handlers put their faith in Mountain Rescue Aspen—in their personnel, their training, and their equipment. Meg took her cue from Carlisle, who confidently strode along behind Hensley. Carlisle knew what she was doing, even if she might be a little out of practice. As long as she was satisfied with their progress, Meg would assume they were on the best and safest track.

It had been a brisk walk, but even so, covering the nearly two and three-quarter miles that carried them just over six hundred feet higher had taken them nearly ninety minutes. Their pace had been better before they lost the light, but once dusk crept in, they had stopped to pull out their headlamps—small but brilliant LED lights on an elastic strap to be worn over the head or climbing helmet—so their path remained lit.

So far, so good. Meg's breathing was definitely faster than it would normally be for an equivalent hike back home, but she didn't feel like she was straining yet. Hawk looked good as well. How long that would last, she didn't know.

She wished it weren't so overcast; this far away from big-city lights, the skyscape would be glorious and evocative of what she'd seen in the Boundary Waters Canoe Area. A view of the night sky might have given her a needed boost, knowing Todd could be standing in DC, looking at the same stars. He felt a long way away tonight.

Instead, as the last of the sun's rays leached away, they were left in darkness, with only the beams from their headlamps to light their way. Though once or twice, Meg was sure she caught a brief flash of light hundreds of feet above to their right, where she imagined one of the teams would be as they made their way up the steep slope, scanning the area around them as they went.

That would be them soon enough.

With the day's light gone, the temperature started to drop, exacerbated by the chill wind whistling through the valley, funneled by the surrounding peaks. It made Meg glad they were moving at a brisk pace to keep everyone warm.

Hensley slowed and then stepped off the path into long grass studded with tumbled rocks of various sizes, his face lit below the headlamp by the light of the topological map open on his GPS unit. "This is where we go off the established trail. I've sketched out a route that will keep us in the trees for a while. A lot of the slope is scree, but on that kind of angle, it's treacherous. If lives weren't on the line, we'd never attempt it in the dark like this. And we won't be able to avoid it all the way, but we can for some of it."

"If we're in the forest, are we avoiding the scree?" Brian asked. "That's why you set our path like that?"

"By and large, yes. When we hit those areas, there aren't any trees, because there's no soil for them to grow in. So we'll stick to the trees for as long as we can. Though once we're above eleven thousand feet or so, we'll clear the tree line. From then on, it's nothing but rock." He glanced down at the dogs. "This could be really hard going for them. And hard on their feet."

"We have Velcro strap boots with thick rubber soles for them, if needed," Meg said. "Dogs actually do well for traction without the boots because they can feel the surface under their pads, but yes, it may get to a point where sharp rocks are a bigger disadvantage to them. We'll constantly evaluate and can put them on and take them off as needed."

"Good. Let's head up."

"The dogs should run unleashed from here on in." Brian bent and unclipped the leash from the loop on the back of Lacey's work vest. "We're about to get to the point where they'll need to climb solo from us, for our safety and for theirs."

"Agreed." Meg unclipped Hawk's leash, and coiled and tucked it into one of the side pockets of the large pack, knowing it was unlikely they'd need it again until they were back down at nine thousand feet.

The path Hensley set away from the creek dipped down briefly before angling slightly upward as they wove through a thick cluster of pine trees. After they entered the copse, the wind dropped from sharp-bitten gusts to wisps of breeze weaving through the dense, wide trunks. The ground under their boots was hard-packed soil, studded with rock, but even here, grasses and ground cover broke through, reaching for any minimal sun making its way through the heavy canopy.

Crossing a flat span of dirt that allowed her a moment to take her eyes off her feet, Meg swung her gaze up the massive trunks to find the lowest branches easily twenty-five feet overhead, with the rest of the tree disappearing into the dark beyond, probably at a total height of at least two to three times the lower branches.

"Ponderosa pines." Fife's voice came from behind them, audible now that they were out of the worst of the wind. "You find a lot of them at this elevation. Higher up, we'll be getting into hemlock, white pine, red fir, and aspens."

"Thus, the name," said Brian.

"You know it. Bet this is pretty different than DC, with its cherry trees, oaks, and maples."

"Sounds like you know a lot about trees," Newall said.

"Most of us at Mountain Rescue Aspen have day jobs. Helps when your day job has some flexibility so you can drop what you're doing and run. I own a landscaping company, so trees are my business. I know what we have here, and what will and won't survive in this climate. But running my own business allows me to set my own hours.

And my clients understand that sometimes I have to leave their job to save lives. Rescue is a way of life around here."

"You know it," Brian echoed with a grin.

"Yeah, you guys get it."

"Get it," Carlisle said, looking over her shoulder. "Hell, Meg is getting married in less than two weeks, and here she is climbing a mountain."

"Seriously?"

Meg's eyes were fixed on the path, but she could hear the smile in Fife's voice. "Seriously. Make sure you get me up there and back down again or my fiancé will kill me."

"That's always the goal. Getting up and down again, I mean. Not keeping your fiancé out of jail, though that would be good too."

The forest continued for a few hundred feet more, and Meg could see in the light of her headlamp the space beyond the trunks opening out again. But she wasn't prepared for the landscape beyond.

"Watch your step here." Hensley left the forest first and stepped to the side, allowing Carlisle and then Meg to follow him.

At first Meg wasn't sure what she was looking at as she scanned the area with the beam of her headlamp. The light was bright, but only illuminated a limited area as she tried to piece the landscape together from those brief snatches.

It looked like a giant had carelessly tossed several fistfuls of massive matches onto the slope in front of them. But some of those matchsticks still had a few dead pine branches attached near the top. The rest had been wiped clean away by an unimaginable force—the same force that had tossed the towering ponderosa pines to the ground as if they were weightless.

"What the . . . ?" Brian murmured behind her, then

sharply inhaled as he put the picture of the landscape to-gether.

Meg ran her beam of light straight upslope and, as an icy shiver snaked down her back, fully understood what she was looking at: the hundreds of toppled pine trees, studded with massive boulders, and the slope that angled down in front of them before it rose steeply up the side of the mountain, its surface scoured clean as far as the light could reach.

Avalanche.

CHAPTER 8

Scrambling: A type of ascent categorized between hiking and rock climbing requiring the use of hands, but not climbing equipment.

May 6, 8:56 pm
Pyramid Peak
Aspen, Colorado

The force of the avalanche must have been unimaginable as it roared down the side of the mountain, ripping away anything—living or mineral—in its path. It might have slowed when it hit the bottom of the mountain's skirt and angled upward again, but clearly still had a head of steam from the way it mowed down heavily rooted eighty- or one-hundred-foot trees as if they had no substance to speak of.

Meg's light wasn't strong enough to see long distances, but she had the feeling it could have been as much as the length of a football field before the wall of snow finally stopped. And half this forest was leveled by then.

It made her think of the mountain—even the modest amount visible below the low clouds—and how much of it had long, pale tracks rolling down the hillside, interspersed with swaths of dark forest. Those tracks may well have been the slide paths of a series of avalanches.

"Crap." Fife broke the silence. "I haven't been up here since that rescue in February. This is March's persistent slab avalanche?"

"Yeah." Hensley's expression was grim. "Lost four skiers. They never had a chance."

"But that's a winter avalanche, right?" Meg asked. "The whole hillside was covered in snow, so there was a lot of mass?"

"Yes."

"We don't have to worry about that kind of massive slide?"

"Right, but it doesn't mean there's no risk. You don't have the volume of snow, but up high, there are still significant snowfields. It's about being in the wrong place at the wrong time. We're all wearing avalanche transceivers in case we get caught in one, but having one is no guarantee of survival. It improves it, but it's no guarantee."

"It will help us find you when you're buried," Fife added, "but it doesn't do anything to prevent the trauma you can suffer being pummeled by rocks, or hitting a tree, or going off a cliff. And while it helps us find you probably four times faster, thirty minutes is all you have. Really, your best chance of survival is in the first ten minutes."

Hensley nodded in agreement. "Fife raises a good point. You guys need to be prepared in case you end up in that kind of scenario. You've got your transceivers set to transmit and not search, correct?"

Meg pictured the compact, handheld device Carlisle had given her before they'd started, and had shown her how to set and lock the dial to transmit, and how to change it to search mode, if needed. She'd said the transceiver had fresh batteries, so it would last on transmit for a week, but there was an extra set of batteries, just in case. Most importantly, she'd shown Meg how to keep her electronics from interfering with the beacon's signal, placing the transceiver in Meg's left hip pocket and having her move her satellite phone to her right breast pocket. Maintaining twelve inches between the two units would ensure her safety.

"I made sure they're set up correctly," Carlisle said. "And their sat phones are spaced far enough away there's no interference."

"Good. Those beacons can be picked up by our transceivers, once we put them into search mode. If anything happens to any of us, the rest of the team will be able to find you. The question, really, is, how fast we can find you? God forbid you're caught in an avalanche, you can improve your chances of being found by doing a few things.

"First, if you see an avalanche form, try to get out of the way. It sounds obvious, but lots of people stand and gawk at it in terror. If that happens, *move.* Even if you can't get out of the way, getting to the outer boundaries versus the center of the path can make the difference between life and death. If you're caught by the snow, the number one thing to do is shut your mouth and clamp your teeth tight. If you get a mouthful of snow, it could suffocate you if you can't dislodge it. You're going to be swept along, and chances are good you'll lose track of which direction is up, but do your best. Try to stay at the top of the slide by kicking and doing a backstroke motion with your arms." He demonstrated, windmilling his arms backward. "It will be exhausting, but you have to keep at it. The lower you are in the snow when it stops, the harder it will be to save you." Hensley looked from Meg to Brian to Newall. "With me so far?"

"Yes," chorused all three.

"Once the slide starts to slow, assuming you haven't hit a tree or been knocked out when your head slams against a boulder," Hensley continued, making their chances brutally clear, "this is when you can make the biggest difference to your own rescue. Wave one hand vigorously and repeatedly in front of your nose and mouth to clear an airspace, because once the snow stops moving, it will be like being encased in cement. Punch out with your other hand in the direction you think is up. Depending on how deep you are, you might even break the surface. Many people have been rescued because of a hand reaching for the sky out of the snow. After that, all you can do is wait for us to find you." Hensley paused to meet everyone's eyes in turn. "And we will find you. You have to hang on until we do. Fife, Stacey, and I have done this before. Any of us could do it alone; together we can do it faster. You just hang on."

Hensley pointed at the field of fallen trees. "Everyone be careful crossing these. The avalanche will have dragged a lot of rocks down with it and they'll be wedged in here too. We may have some climbing to do." He turned to Carlisle. "It would have taken more time to detour around this than cross it."

"Time is of the essence." Carlisle studied the shadow beside Meg, where Hawk stood. "The dogs will be okay? From what I can see, the trunks are eight to twelve inches in diameter, but some of them are piled on each other."

"This is the kind of parkour we train for," Brian said. "The hardest part will be the lack of light, but we'll help them."

They stepped into the felled forest, working as a team. Anyone who found an easier way through redirected the team to follow. Meg and Brian led the dogs, finding a path, lighting each next step—up onto a trunk tipped on an angle over another, off it from the other side, around it completely if the way was clear, or straight down the length like walking a balance beam—and the dogs enthusiastically made their way across.

"Lacey, up," Brian called from the far side of a snarl of large boulders and thick tree trunks, snapped like thin sheets of balsa wood. He slapped his palm on the top of a boulder, and the shepherd lightly sprang onto it and then hopped down on the other side, on his command.

Meg followed with Hawk. "We must be nearly through at this point." She paused and directed her headlamp toward the upward slope that had crept ever closer with each step. "Yeah, maybe another thirty or forty feet and we're through."

"Good. Let's get out of this godforsaken maze and make some real progress."

After a few minutes they were at the bottom of the hill that held the forest—both the living and the remains of the dead—staring up the eastern face of the mountain.

As her heart thumped, Meg wondered what they couldn't see. Then she considered if perhaps it wasn't better to ascend in the dark so as to lose all sense of altitude. Maybe it would be less terrifying if she couldn't see more than twenty feet down.

"This is where the going gets hard," said Hensley. "Make sure the dogs are watered, drink some yourself. Once we start up, there may not be a good place to stop for a rest. And while you're doing that, I'm going to give you a crash course on scrambling, because ten minutes spent here could save your life. Or save us a rescue that could take hours." He turned to Newall. "You ever done this? Any kind of climbing?"

Newall's light flashed back and forth as he shook his head. "No, I'm a runner, and while I've run hiking trails, never anything like this."

"Running's good. You'll have solid leg strength. You'll need it. More so than arm strength. Okay, you three are essentially newbies, but you're all in good shape, which will help a lot. This is a class-four mountain, but the worst of it is toward the summit and a lot of this lower section is class three."

"I don't know what that means," Newall interjected.

"It's the classification system most people use in the US. All you need to know in this case is the system goes up to class five, which is the serious rock-climbing level. Class three is what we'll mostly be looking at here—hopefully— and that means scrambling, which is essentially an easier method of rock climbing. We won't be using ropes unless we have to, and those will be in the class-four sections. It all depends on where the plane went down. For class-three scrambling we'll mostly be looking for solid footholds and, less often, handholds."

As Hensley talked, Meg unbuckled the chest and waist straps of her pack and lowered it to the ground. She quickly found and pulled out Hawk's collapsible bowl, opened the valve on the tube for her hydration bladder, and emptied a portion of water into it. She set down the water dish and Hawk moved in immediately to lap; the dogs knew on a search when food and water were offered to take advantage, as it might be hours more before their handlers were able to do so again. Meg took a few long pulls from the tube herself and then dug out Hawk's high-energy food—only a little, as she wanted Hawk to get the nutrients and energy, but couldn't afford to be weighed down with a full meal—and an energy bar for herself.

"Situational awareness is going to be key," Hensley continued. "That means knowing exactly where you are in each moment in relation to where you've been and where you're going. And that's going to be hard, because we're doing this in the dark. Normally, in daylight, you'd take the time to pause and look three hundred sixty degrees around you. Even if you're following a set route, it can be easy to lose your way. There are multiple couloirs up a mountain; it's easy to mix up which one you safely came up when it's time to go back down." He met Fife's eyes. "You and me, that's our job. We know this mountain, but we're not taking the standard route. It's on us to get us all up there safely. And back down."

"We got this." Fife's tone was sure, which abated some of Meg's constant unease.

"The most important thing with scrambling over the kind of terrain we have here is not to rush. Yes, we're on the clock, but we're no good to potential survivors if we're dead, so we're going for a slow and controlled pace, especially because we may not be able to see the drop-off just beyond us. That kind of pace will help you keep your balance and conserve energy. It will also help the dogs stay with us, because they aren't going to be able to haul themselves up with a handhold or two. This is where the dogs will be at a disadvantage—for us the rule is three points of contact. You won't always need it, especially at the beginning in the trees where the slope won't be so extreme. But farther up, it's going to be tricky."

Hensley turned to the two handlers. "You each saw the harness at the bottom of your packs when you were repacking?"

"Yes," Brian said.

"We knew you were coming, and while Mountain Rescue Aspen doesn't usually use dogs and doesn't have harnesses for them, I have some buddies who climb with their dogs. I borrowed two full-body dog harnesses to fit your dogs. They're what we'll need if we have to lift or lower the dogs in exposed areas, or if we need to give them a hand with ropes in a tricky spot on the route. We may not need them, but we have to have them with us up there or we don't have the option."

"Options are good."

"In our world we live by options because we never know how a rescue will go sideways. And most of them do in some way. So, while we hope we won't get to the class-four areas and need the ropes, we can't be sure at this point, so we're prepared for it. If we're going to need the ropes, we'll prep you at the time. We're going to be scrambling right off the bat, so that's where we'll start. As I said, three points of contact is paramount on steeper slopes. You don't move a hand unless you already have two footholds and a handhold. You don't move a foot until you have a foothold and two handholds. And you test every surface. Just because a handhold looks solid doesn't mean it is, and you want to test it before you remove any other points of contact. If you still have three points of contact and the new one gives way, you're still supported." Hensley's face turned toward the side of the mountain, his headlamp illuminating very little. "We're not going to be able to see the exposure up there, but assume any fall will be fatal. It might not be, but the odds are it will be, because even if you don't fall all the way, by the time someone gets to you, you may be gone." He read Meg's grimace correctly. "Not pleasant, but not bullshit. You need to know what you're getting into before we begin."

"We get it." Meg dropped a hand to Hawk's head to show she was speaking for both of them. "It's risky, but we're up for it. Any more tips?"

"A couple of things. Make sure your packs are cinched tight to bring your center of gravity in. You also don't want any weight shifting up there, because that could be enough force for you to lose your balance and fall. Look for solid footholds, so you're letting your lower body carry your weight, instead of your upper body, or your arms will tire early. You may only get the toe of your boot on a rock, but if it's secure, it will be enough to step through."

"Don't forget about rockfall risk," Fife interjected.

"Right. Often, if we're out for a climb on a nice day, our biggest threat is not the mountain, but what can come off it, especially from climbers above us. In this kind of terrain, with fields of loose stone, dislodging a rock is a real threat, not necessarily to you, but to whoever is below you, be it person or dog. It happens to the best of us, even when we do our upmost to watch out for it. Be alert to rockfall from anyone who is above you, and if you realize you've loosened a rock, yell 'Rock!' so whoever is below you can prepare. Assume this is going to be the issue from the beginning, so helmet up now." Hensley checked the time. "Let's get started. Stay in the same order, unless it's not working for us. We'll stick together as a group—this will minimize the risk of severe rockfall, as nothing will have a chance to pick up extreme speed before it hits. Strikes from a distance are much more damaging. Helmets on!" Reaching his hands behind his head, he unsnapped his white helmet from where it was hooked around the top loop of his backpack.

"Should we use the trekking poles?" Brian asked as he snapped his helmet strap under his chin and gave it a tug to make sure it was snug.

"I like them," Fife answered. "At least where the slope isn't too steep. Kind of puts you on four legs, like the dogs, and they're handy when the scree is small. But once the slope gets steep, crawling with your hands works better for me than the poles. Everyone is different, see what you think. But I'd suggest trying them. When they're not working for you, fold them up and ask the nearest climber to tuck them into your pack for you."

Meg and Brian helped each other by digging through each other's pack and pulling out a long cloth bag. Inside lay what looked like a bundle of fourteen-inch metal tubes connected by a sturdy cable, but which seated into each other to form robust poles with the ability to adjust the height and then lock solidly in place.

Brian slipped his hands through the wrist straps and leaned his whole weight on the poles. "These things are solid. Not budging at all."

"That's good." Meg tested her own poles. "One of them collapses up there, it could be a fatal fall." She studied the two dogs, who stood with their faces turned up to their handlers. "I think we need to make sure that while this is going to be like parkour to the dogs, they can't attack the slope with their usual playground or stone-wall enthusiasm."

"Agreed. No leaping and jumping. No landing can be guaranteed safe, so they'll need to essentially walk the whole route, unless they can't step the distance. Then we need to be ahead of them to make sure their landing spot is solid. If it supports us, it will support them."

"We're on the same page. Good."

Moving onward, Hensley led the way, taking them a little south to hug a line of trees running up the slope—mature trees, so this must have been the outer edge of the avalanche track—and then to the west, up the slope, which stayed at a gentle rise for only the first few minutes, and then angled to about thirty degrees. There was no established route to follow, and they wove around trees just inside the tree line, pushing through low ground cover, carefully picking their way over and around the jagged, protruding rocks that pierced the hard ground, waiting to trip or unbalance the unwary.

Meg and Brian were careful to keep their heads down at an angle, making sure they could look up to avoid stepping into a tree, but keeping the light low to not only light their own way, but the dogs' as well. Both dogs trotted easily beside their handlers, their noses down, not to scent the path—that command hadn't been given, since there was no trail to follow yet—but as part of their own route finding. The forest was alive with scent for the dogs; once or twice early on, Meg had heard scurrying in the undergrowth around them. But the dogs stayed on task—they were wearing their work vests and had been told to heel; they were on the job and they knew it. Hensley kept the team to as brisk a walk as he dared in a dark minefield of rocks and vegetation. Newall had been the only one so far to trip over an unseen hazard, but had quickly caught himself on one of his trekking poles.

A long, tremulous scream rent the air, rising for several seconds, then dropping quickly. It was followed by another, then another.

Brian jerked to a stop. "What the hell is that?"

"We're pissing off a northern saw-whet owl," Fife's voice came from behind. "He's probably newly returned to the area for the season and we're in his territory. He's telling us to get lost. They're called that because that whine sounds like the sharpening of a saw blade."

"Apt description." Digging one of his poles in between two rocks, Brian climbed after Meg. "Hang on, buddy; we're leaving your turf."

They were now in full dark, and the temperature had dropped a good fifteen degrees from before dusk, but physical activity kept the team warm. Luckily, the rain or snow Carlisle had predicted stayed away; yet Meg had a bad feeling they were on borrowed time.

They'd been hiking steadily uphill for about twenty minutes when Meg slowed her steps, turning her left ear toward a new sound. "Am I hearing water?"

"At this time of year, probably," Carlisle said, only slightly breathless. "Lots of runoff from above. We'll want to avoid that if possible, since wet rocks are slippery, and some of those runoff streams can move pretty quickly depending on how fast the snowpack is melting."

Another few minutes drew them closer to the sound as the trees started to thin. Winding around the thick trunk of a pine, Meg turned her head briefly toward the sound. Water sparkled in the beam of light, where it splashed over a series of larger boulders, all smaller debris long washed away. "Hawk, come this way." Meg stepped away from the water; it was wild and beautiful, a series of cascading waterfalls winding through the flanking greenery, but she couldn't risk her dog getting wet and chilled.

Shortly thereafter, Hensley led them in a slightly more southerly route, out of the trees and over rougher terrain, covered only by shallow grasses, short stubby ground cover, and the odd clump of hardy ferns growing against a rock.

He stopped when another clump of trees rose out of the dark before them. "We're going to head up this couloir. It has the advantage of still having tree cover on either side, but according to my map app, the slope is going to increase quite a bit. And while we've been in the trees so far, we're getting to the point where it's safer to depend on the rocks than the trees for holds. I'd also recommend stowing the trekking poles at this point so you have both hands free. There are gloves in your packs, but try not to use them for as long as you can." He nodded down at Hawk and Lacey. "Like the way the dogs use their pads to feel the surface beneath them, you need to be able to feel the rock with your fingertips and to have a really solid hold on it. At a certain point your hands will get so cold, you'll get clumsy and can't feel the rock. You need to switch to gloves before that, so watch for chilly fingers." Hensley unlocked one of his poles and folded it into sections. "We're going to lose most of the trees soon and then it's going to be real scrambling. There's no sign or sound of the crash so far, so we'll keep going up."

They took a minute to collapse their poles and pack them into their bags, and then they were off again.

Meg took in the terrain above them. The slope was easily forty-five degrees now, and her lamp showed about twenty feet of narrow, rocky gully, full of loose rocks ranging from fist-sized to small boulders. But which were loose and which were solid enough for climbing? And how was she going to be able to guide Hawk's path?

She turned to look down the hill, past Brian, Newall, and Fife, but her headlamp beam dissolved into the gloom. It was on the tip of her tongue to ask how far they'd climbed, but she bit back the question.

Better not to know.

"Hawk, stay. Let me test this out." Remembering what Hensley said about three points of contact, Meg planted her boot on a boulder, tested it, and then transferred her weight to it. Pushing up, she grasped two rocks, one solid in the hillside, the other rolling under her grip, so she chose another. Only then did she step up to test a new foothold. Now with four points of contact, she released one hand, reached out, and tested a new hold. It was solid, so she moved one foot. She was slow to begin, being meticulous in her choice of hand- and footholds, but as she climbed up a few feet, she could feel a rhythm already settling in.

She could do this.

Calling her dog to follow her, showing him the first holds to support his weight, she climbed into the unknown.

CHAPTER 9

Edging: Only being able to use the edge of a boot on a foothold, rather than the full width of the foot.

May 6, 9:50 pm
Pyramid Peak
Aspen, Colorado

"*Rock!*"

Her headlamp fixed on the area directly in front of her, Meg jolted when Hensley's bellow came out of the darkness above. Her head snapped up to see Carlisle swinging off to the side ten feet uphill, and the blur of a spinning, bouncing object careening downhill another ten feet above her.

It was headed straight for Hawk, who was more centered in the path slightly behind her after she'd angled to the right for her next set of holds. Hawk, who hadn't been taught the *Rock!* command, as it was brand-new, wouldn't be able to get out of the way quickly with his current precarious balance, his legs spread wide to find the solid holds Meg had pointed out for him.

At this angle a hard rock strike could knock him off his feet and then there'd be no stopping his fall down what could be over a thousand feet by now.

Doing a lightning-fast switch between her left hand and her right, and holding onto that one handhold for dear life, Meg lunged for a jagged boulder, getting her left foot onto it, and extending her body out, twisting sideways to block her dog.

The rock struck the center of her back with a force that wrung a cry from her and pushed her facedown into cold, rough stone before she dimly registered it ricocheting into the trees to the south. Her cheek pressed against chilly mudstone, Meg sucked in air through gritted teeth, her heart hammering, and a cold sweat blooming as she waited for the earth to fall away beneath her, for the battering fall that would steal her breath just before it took her life. But the hand clamped onto the rock, and the left knee she'd managed to get up as she dove, held her braced. She stayed frozen, terrified any movement would send her spinning away.

"Meg!" Brian's shout of alarm cut sharply through the quiet night.

"I'm okay." She forced herself to do no more than raise her head, turning it to find Hawk, looking ready to bound to her side. It was what he'd normally do in this situation, but she didn't want him falling in his hurry. "Hawk, I'm okay. Slow. Come, but slow."

Rather than rushing, Hawk picked his way carefully toward her, at one point getting a supporting hand on his rump from Brian, who closely followed, until he was beside her, as she cautiously pulled herself into a crouch. He pushed his nose against her, leaving a streak of dampness followed by the sleek softness of his fur.

"I'm okay, buddy. Good boy."

A hand landed on her shoulder, and Meg looked up to find Carlisle crouched down above her. "You okay?"

"Compared to past injuries, this is nothing."

Hensley climbed down to stop just above Carlisle. "God, Meg, I'm sorry. A foothold gave out on me."

"Not your fault. If anyone is experienced enough to try to avoid that happening, it's you."

"I tried to give everyone a warning."

"You did. I had time to move. Actually, I wasn't even in the way."

"But you got hit?"

"Because Hawk *was* in the way. I put myself between him and the falling rock." She met Brian's eyes. "Even if we could teach them a command for 'rock,' we'd have to build in a direction because they couldn't make that call on their own."

"It could be done, but I don't know they'd ever be able to react in time, because I don't know *we'd* be able to react in time. Not that we could teach them fast enough for it to be useful on this search, even if we could make it all come together." Brian rubbed a hand over her back. "You're really okay?"

Meg could still feel the sting of the rock's impact—staying close together may have decreased the potential damage, but it still hurt like crazy—though it wasn't bad enough to slow her down. Of greater concern to her was the headache she'd been conscious of for the last half hour that had moved from a faint pang to a low-level aching buzz. She promised herself she'd continue to monitor and would bring it up if needed. For now, she'd keep to the current injury. "I'd be lying if I said I didn't feel it, but it's not that bad. At least it didn't hit me in the head. Todd warned me about not being able to afford another head injury."

"You'll be able to continue?"

"Absolutely."

As Brian planted himself and then let Meg use his shoulder to push herself to her feet, Meg couldn't help but think of the wedding dress hanging in Cara's spare bedroom closet—a halter style that showed off her toned back. Unless that back was marred with an ugly black-and-purple contusion.

You're still twelve days away. Don't borrow trouble.

She straightened and found her balance again. "I'm up." She rolled her shoulders, feeling a twinge in her trapezius muscle just to the left of her spinal column. On the bright side, though, the rock had hit muscle and not bone, so there was no damage to her spine. "Let's keep going."

"What do you think is the best plan for the dogs?" Brian asked.

"I think we're doing it. Hensley is route finding, I'm following and modifying only if necessary for Hawk and Lacey, then pointing out the route for them, and you're there to stabilize Hawk and give him a boost if needed."

"And Corey is doing the same for Lacey." Brian turned to look at Newall a few feet downhill. "Thanks for that."

"No problem. They're at a definite disadvantage here." Newall's headlamp beam flowed over rock as he scanned the terrain around them. "Up is one thing. I'm honestly not sure how we'll get them down."

"Don't assume we'll be coming down this way," Fife interjected from below. "Once we find the crash site, we'll reevaluate. If there's any way to make it around to the standard route on the west side without having to summit the peak, that's the way we'll go. And if we're too high, we may have to wait until the weather clears tomorrow, like they're calling for, to get a chopper in the air to pick them up from wherever we are. As you said, options are good. And we'll have more of them in eight to twelve hours."

"But we can't wait that long to find the crash site or we may not have survivors anymore." Hensley straightened from his half crouch. "Let's take this as a reminder about taking care not only for yourself, but for anyone who follows you. Onward and upward."

They pushed on. They were well inside the low-lying clouds at this point, and the mere twenty feet their headlamps had shown them previously was now only half that. Meg could see Carlisle, but Hensley was lost visually. She could still hear him ahead of her, but the path she followed was now Carlisle's, who she trusted kept Hensley in view. As a group they were aware of the worsening conditions and purposely stayed closer together.

Hensley called a halt on a narrow, flat plateau of patchy ground cover and rocks big enough for six humans and two dogs, with a little space to spare. "We're going to stop here and have a water and snack break." He studied Meg and Brian, who were breathing hard.

"This is definitely harder than I thought it would be," Brian half wheezed. "I told you we're in good shape and here we are getting our asses kicked. We look like we're new to this."

"You're new to the altitude is all. It's going to exhaust you faster than the same hike at two thousand feet."

"That pretty much sums it up."

Meg unbuckled her pack and lowered it to the ground. "I'm never this tired hiking. And I can feel Hawk dragging too. Must be the lack of oxygen."

"Not the lack of oxygen, but oxygen pressure," Carlisle clarified. "You're pulling in the same amount, but there's not enough atmospheric pressure to push it into your lung tissue, so you just breathe it right out again."

"So near and yet so far," muttered Brian.

Meg checked the time on her fitness tracker, calculated. "We're short of the twelve hours since our last dose, but it's close enough I don't mind front-loading a bit."

"Agreed. Dogs too."

"How are you two feeling?" Carlisle asked as she dug through her pack. "Any effects so far? Headache? Fatigue?"

Meg looked at Brian, who suddenly seemed intently interested in his dog. *Todd won't forgive you if you hide this and something goes sideways. And it may force Brian to admit if he's feeling it.* "I have a headache."

Carlisle's head snapped sideways. "How bad?"

"Not terrible. I've been monitoring it for a little while. Todd said he'd be surprised if we didn't get at least that. The question is, how much worse might it get?" Meg turned to Brian. "How are you?"

His lips pursed briefly, confirming to Meg he'd also been hiding symptoms. "About the same. It's there in the background." He ran a hand down Lacey's heaving back as she panted. "My Lacey-girl is all in, but I suspect she's not feeling top-notch either."

"We're definitely taking ten," Hensley said as he scanned the area. "There." He pointed to the northernmost section of the plateau, just before it sloped steeply up again. "That looks like the flattest area. Take the dogs over there. They can lie down and rest for a bit."

"Appreciate that, thanks. Hawk, come." Meg led Hawk to the spot Hensley indicated and was pleased to find a big enough area for both dogs. "Down, boy. Down. Take a load off."

"Lacey, you too. Down."

Both dogs lay down, arranging their bodies around any protruding rocks. Hawk lay his head on his paws and loosed a gusty sigh.

"They're tired." Meg pulled out Hawk's water bowl, filled it, and set it in front of him. He greedily lapped beside Lacey, who had her own bowl, both still in a prone position as if too tired to rise. "I'm not sure they're going to be able to do this." She kept her voice low so only Brian could hear her as Hensley, Carlisle, Newall, and Fife discussed their ongoing route. "We've been climbing for hours and it feels like we're getting nowhere."

"You know that's not true. You're getting discouraged because we're struggling." Brian dug his satellite phone out of his zipped jacket breast pocket and opened the GPS app, giving it a moment to triangulate not only their latitude and longitude, but their altitude. "I have us at just over ten thousand seven hundred feet. That nowhere we're getting is over eleven hundred feet up from where we started."

"I guess that also explains the headache." Meg pulled out the bottle of meds and tapped out a dose of acetazolamide and ibuprofen for Brian and then another for herself. "It's not just the exertion, it's the altitude. We're a long way from the top of this fourteener, if we have to go that far." She downed the meds with a few swallows of water.

"We're not going to make the summit. The dogs can't do it and there's no place for us without them."

Meg tucked Hawk's dose into one of the pill wraps she'd brought for the meds, and added it to a bowl of high-energy food, where it disappeared in seconds. "Good boy. Lacey's had hers?"

"Yes. We're good. Though I'm going to swap her vest for her coat. The temp is dropping too quickly and while we're moving and warm, she's okay, but I don't want her getting chilled while she's resting."

"Good idea. I'll do the same for Hawk."

"Then sit down and breathe for a few minutes. You need some recovery time, too."

"Yes, Dad." When she finished with Hawk and had him resettled, she sat down in a small clear patch of grass, folding her legs into her best attempt at a lotus position given the outer wear and hiking boots, closed her eyes, and centered herself, slowing her breathing.

"Cara would be so proud of you." Laughter filled Brian's tone. "Look at you, doing yoga on a mountaintop in a helmet and hiking boots."

Meg didn't open her eyes, but one corner of her mouth twitched. "Be sure to tell her, so she can be."

Quiet fell over the group as they took ten minutes to rest and recharge.

After taking two minutes with her hands tucked into the lowered zipper of her jacket and under her armpits to warm them to the extent she had full feeling again, Meg pulled out her satellite phone and sent a couple of texts.

The first was to Todd. **Hello from 10,700 feet. Taking a rest while climbing. All well so far but still no crash site.**

Her second went to Craig. **Been climbing for hours. Keeping up. Dogs managing. No crash site yet. Will update as able.**

Craig responded almost immediately with a thumb-up emoji. It was well after midnight DC time, but Craig must have been sleeping with his phone.

Todd was only about ten seconds behind. Someone else was sleeping with his phone, or hadn't gone to bed while waiting for news. **Rest is good. Don't push it if you can help it. How are you feeling?**

She knew he'd be worrying, but would want nothing less than pure truth. **Mild headache and the fatigue is kicking my ass. Hawk's too. But it's manageable for both of us. And before you ask, we've had more acetazolamide and ibuprofen and the dogs had more acetazolamide.**

Todd sent a heart emoji.

Please let Cara and McCord know how we're doing. Going to rest for a few minutes before we start again. Love you.

Will do. Love you back. Be safe.

She tucked her phone away to see Brian doing the same thing with his. "Talked to Ryan?"

"Yeah. He left his phone on his pillow with the volume

cranked so he wouldn't miss me if I had time to touch base. He was glad to hear from me and said to text any time."

"Same basic message from Todd, along with questions about symptoms and medication doses."

"I would expect nothing less. Ryan is worried about us stepping off a mountaintop; Todd is worried about that and us ballooning our brains this high up."

"Sometimes it really sucks to be our partners, doesn't it?"

"It sure does. How's the back?"

Meg rolled her shoulders, wincing slightly. "Definitely aches. Can't wait to see the bruise. Definitely can't wait to see if there's still any trace of it in twelve days."

"Keep your glass half full. Surely, it will be gone by then."

They settled in for a few more minutes of rest, and Meg closed her eyes and tried to relax the way yoga taught her, slowing her breathing, steadying her heart rate.

All too soon, Hensley called for them to get moving again. Meg and Brian both grabbed energy bars as they repacked the dog bowls, and when they stood, they both felt better suited to carry on. Meg thought her headache had backed off a bit with the short rest. She was sure it wouldn't last, but she'd take it.

They climbed for nearly another thirty minutes, finally coming to the end of the couloir, cresting a rise, and following the downhill slope that angled both up into the next couloir and down toward East Maroon Creek, fifteen hundred feet below. Everyone was constantly conscious of the ramifications of a fall, but never more so than when they were purposely moving downhill. Faced with a field of scree bordered on one side by a ragged scattering of pine trees, Meg opted to move downhill on her ass with her feet braced in front of her, Hawk beside her upslope, the light of her headlamp lighting both their ways. Brian, seeing how well this worked for her, followed her lead, rather than climbing down backward like the more experienced climbers. Neither cared if they looked like idiots, as long as they and their canine partners made it down safely. It was only about two hundred feet down the hill, but it took them a full ten minutes to cover the route carefully, meeting the other climbers at the base of the next couloir.

"Where to from here?" Brian asked, straightening and brushing grit off the seat of his pants.

"Straight up." Hensley's beam of light illuminated a short span of the terrain above them. "It's going to be steep, but all routes are at this point. This route is the best I could find, while still keeping us in our section for searching. It will be a range of more and less steep areas, but we're less than a quarter mile from the ridge of the saddle."

" 'The saddle'?"

"There are a couple of lower-lying areas on Pyramid Peak that have high sides at each end and a lower section in the middle—essentially the same shape as a saddle. The largest is called the 'amphitheater,' and it's south of us on the far side of the peak." Hensley pointed up and diagonally to their left, in a southwesterly direction. "On the northeast section of the mountain is another saddle, and the ridge of that saddle is what we're aiming for. From up there, we'll be on level ground. Narrow ground—in some places only a foot or two wide—but level. And from there we can cover over a mile of the mountain north to south, but nearly two thousand feet up from where we started and almost twelve thousand feet high in total. We'll have a much larger range to be able to cover, carefully mind you, because a misstep in either direction would almost certainly be fatal."

"Level sounds good to me," said Brian. "We can go slow."

"I haven't seen or heard anything that hints at the crash site. No lights, no voices, no debris. I've recovered a few plane crashes in my time, and the debris field can spread wide. But nothing so far."

"It's a big mountain." Standing, hands on hips, Newall was breathing hard.

Meg realized it wasn't just the dawn runs that kept herself and Brian fit, but all the parkour they did with the dogs—over and around playgrounds, on hiking trails, up and down the "*Exorcist* steps" in Georgetown or, one of their favorites, the Spanish Steps on 22nd Street NW. They didn't send their dogs off to do the challenges on their own—they joined them, and it made them ready to face this challenge head-on. Sure, they were a little breathless, but much of that was due to the altitude, not the exertion. Newall had the advantage of being acclimatized to the altitude and had the fitness of a runner on his side. She couldn't imagine how the canine teams would be managing if they were unused to both the altitude and the extreme exertion.

"It is. But that's why we have as many teams going as we do. It's nearly midnight and we've been out here for five hours, hard climbing for three, but we might not be able to find it for more than a day. Hopefully, the weather will clear when the sun rises in about six hours."

Six hours? Meg checked her fitness tracker, shocked to find it was almost 2:00 AM by her body clock. No wonder she felt exhausted. The effect of the brief rest McCord had interrupted on the plane had dissipated long ago, and adrenaline would only get her so far.

"Let's take ten here before the big push upward. That's going to take care and energy, so prep for that."

As always, Meg and Brian cared for the dogs first, then themselves. Sitting on a large rock, Meg called Hawk in close. She ran her hands over him, looking for signs of pain, and then checked his paws for cuts or abrasions from the rough rock, finding none. She didn't need to rest her hands on his rib cage to know he was breathing hard; they all were. She slid her fingers along the inside of his right rear leg, coming to rest at midthigh. His femoral artery pulsed under her fingertips. She pushed back her cuff to reveal her fitness tracker, waiting until it hit a ten-second mark, and started to count, stopping when it hit fifteen seconds later, then multiplying that value in her head.

Which gave her 116 beats per minute. His heart rate was accelerated, but she knew since they'd been resting for a few minutes, it was coming down from something higher, probably something over 130.

"What's wrong?" Brian's eyes were fixed on her face, lit by his headlamp.

"Hawk's heart rate is pretty fast."

"Too fast?"

"Not dangerously fast now, but it's dropped since we stopped. It's one-sixteen."

Brian made a grunt in the back of his throat and then pulled Lacey in closer, his hand searching for the same spot. "Time me."

"Ready?" Meg paused as the seconds ticked up. "Go." She waited the fifteen seconds. "Stop."

"Thirty. So one-twenty. Faster than Hawk, but females are often a little higher than males. I'd guess it was maybe around the one-thirty-two or one-thirty-five mark before we stopped. They're working hard in a low-oxygen environment. I'm sure our own heart rates are high." He checked his fitness tracker for a current read on it. "Yeah, higher than normal. You too?"

Meg checked her own tracker. "Yeah. You're probably right. Still, we need to watch for this too. If they cross the one-forty boundary, that starts to get into danger territory.

We need to take a quick break to check midclimb if we can do it safely."

"And watch them like . . . uh . . . hawks." Brian gave her a sheepish grin.

Five minutes later they were climbing again as the pitch rose. Any patch of green was now few and far between. Even the trees were thinning out drastically to just the odd single tree here or there, which indicated to Meg they had to be getting close to the eleven-and-a-half- to twelve-thousand-foot mark—the tree line. The walls of the couloir rose steeply around them, but Hensley's path kept them at a reasonable slope—if about forty degrees was reasonable—as they climbed ever higher.

"Watch your holds, and be careful with the dogs," Hensley instructed. "The moisture in the air is getting heavier and I'm feeling it on the rocks. They're starting to get a little slick. So not only test them for stability, but test them for friction."

"Great," Brian muttered. "Like we don't have enough challenges."

Meg looked down at Hawk, where he stared up at her. She could see the exhaustion in his every movement, could see the toll the night's exertions and the lack of oxygen were taking on him. But when he looked at her, his big brown eyes were full of trust, and his tail, previously low and still, wagged several times. If Meg needed anything of him, he would give his all until he was pushed to collapse. "Brian, I'm beginning to worry."

"You and me both. I'll freely admit this is exhausting. Even with breaks and snacks, it has to be draining them. Not sure how they're going to manage this steeper section."

"Me neither." Carlisle moved farther away, and Meg knew she needed to speak up. "Ben, Stacey! Can we hold for a second?"

Carlisle dropped into view. "You guys okay?"

"The dogs have been doing well so far, better than I anticipated, and are sometimes finding their own way to manage the slope better suited to their body conformation and weight than what's working for us. But they're starting to struggle and it's pretty steep here. Can we change the order a bit? Can I have Hawk follow you and then I'll follow him? I want to be there if he slips."

"Of course."

"It means you'll have to choose your route so it's also appropriate for Hawk."

"I can do that." Carlisle tested a lower handhold and then dropped to a crouch, both boots planted with one hand extended down toward Hawk. "Will he go past you?"

"He will when I tell him to." Meg craned a look over her shoulder. "Brian, does that work for you? Have Lacey follow me, so you're behind her if she slips?"

"At this point I think that will work best," Brian agreed. "After a few hours they know what we're doing and that we're a group. And Lacey would follow you anywhere."

"Good. Let's rearrange then." She tested a foothold to the right, then called Hawk to climb to her. He stood puffing for a moment, then Meg directed him higher. "Hawk, follow Stacey. Stacey, call Hawk."

"Hawk, come." Carlisle kept her hand extended in welcome and to convey what was becoming a familiar scent. "Hawk, up."

The Lab looked unsure momentarily, then he picked his way carefully uphill as Meg stepped in behind him in case he slipped. "Lacey, come." A quick glance behind showed her the shepherd was already following, with Brian bringing up the rear.

The climb was definitely more challenging in this area. Meg's already-cold, bare hands were starting to feel stiff and slightly clumsy, and the rocks were definitely slick. Even so, she didn't want to put her gloves on yet, fearing they wouldn't have the grip of her bare skin.

At least it hasn't started to rain or snow yet. That would probably doom us.

Checking that Hawk successfully made the next step, Meg reached up and tested one hold, then another, before reaching up with her left boot. The foothold was a little higher than she'd like, though her yoga pants and own flexibility allowed for it; still, it made for an awkward angle. Going up on the toes of her right boot, she planted her left boot, testing the hold. A little more weight, a little more—

Her boot slipped off the moist surface, pushing her into the rock face, and her heart punched into overdrive as the image of sliding past Brian, Newall, and Fife to tumble helplessly down the slope filled her mind. But lightning-fast reflexes, hours of training to maintain peak physical fitness, and sheer stubbornness kicked in and she gripped the handholds hard and hauled herself up.

"You okay?" Brian called.

"Yeah." She paused to take two deep breaths to slow her speeding heart, but didn't dare take more as her dog was moving ahead of her. "Watch this spot. It's getting slick."

"It's all getting slick, but thanks. Have Lacey follow you to avoid that spot."

Moving off to the right, Meg called Lacey to follow her path as they moved ever upward.

Ten minutes later the ground pitched down a little, and Meg called Hawk to hold for a fifteen-second count of his pulse—132 beats per minute—before she released him and the climb continued.

The terrain pitched steeply upward. They'd known it was going to happen at some stage, and, at a certain point, it didn't matter if they were five hundred feet above East Maroon Creek, or two thousand feet—a fall from either height was guaranteed to be fatal.

That thought dampened the palms of her hands, even though they were too cold to sweat. *Stop that. Don't become a self-fulfilling prophecy.*

"Guys, it's going to be steep for a bit, then it will improve." Hensley's voice floated to them from above.

Looking up, Meg could just see his outline in the light of Carlisle's headlamp, all details of him disappearing into clouds that seemed to thicken with every ten feet of height gained.

Suddenly there was a buzz of static and then a sharp voice burst from the radio Hensley wore in a chest harness, strategically positioned to be more than a foot from the transceiver in his hip pocket. "Command to all teams. Team Six has identified part of the crash site." In the quiet night air, disturbed only by the sound of boot or canine nails on rock, heavy breathing, and the odd curse as a hand- or foothold didn't play out, the words carried clearly.

Everyone found at least three solid points of contact, Brian coming to a halt only a few feet below Lacey, and Meg closing the distance between herself and Hawk as each dog balanced on the uneven slope just above them.

Meg didn't like the extreme angle they were on. She wasn't sure the dogs would be able to manage if it went any steeper, and then they might be . . . *What was the term Cox used? "Cliffed out"?* Or they'd need to use those harnesses in their bags to rope the dogs either up or down.

Every headlamp swung forward to spotlight Hensley, who had dropped down a bit toward them and leaned into a half kneel, with one knee on the slope and his other leg braced. Stabilized, it allowed him to take both hands off the slope to dig out his radio.

Meg, following his example, lowered one knee to the unforgiving, uneven surface, but refused to release her handhold. If anything happened, she'd need that hold to keep Hawk from tumbling down the slope.

No longer half covered, the radio's message came through loud and clear. "The tail section of the plane has been discovered on the east face of Pyramid Peak."

Meg's head snapped sideways to meet Brian's eyes in the glow of their headlamps. That's where they were, but the mountain was miles long. Were they close or on the wrong end altogether? And just the tail? The plane breaking up on impact wasn't a surprise, but Meg had hoped they'd find the plane in one piece, indicating a softer landing.

Really, how could anything land softly here? Deep in the clouds, among the tumbled rocks, with every surface at a terrifying angle?

She couldn't shake the feeling there was no one to find alive.

That didn't matter at Talbot Terraces. We kept at it until we brought everyone home. We can do that here as well.

More radio static, then, "All teams to divert. Prepare to receive coordinates."

Hensley muttered something under his breath, jammed the radio into its harness, and pulled out his GPS. Twenty-five feet down the slope, Fife did the same.

"Command to all teams. Here are the reported coordinates." A slow stream of longitude and latitude numbers followed, then a pause, then the same numbers again at the same slow pace, allowing everyone listening to enter and then double-check their directions. Then, "Sellinger reports they're at eleven thousand four hundred seventy-five feet. All teams check in with their current coordinates. Team One, go ahead."

As Hensley waited for Team Four's turn, Brian, similarly balanced on one knee, unzipped his jacket pocket and pulled out his phone. The illumination coming from the screen lit his face under his headlamp with a ghostly glow. "I have us at about the same altitude," he murmured. "But I don't know where those coordinates are. We may be a half a mountain away from that location."

Up ahead, they could see Hensley bent over his GPS, more as a combination of bright headlamp and dimmer screen; but from how close they were together, it was clear he was working on their location and its relative position to the crash site.

"Team Four," the radio squawked.

"Team Four reporting," Hensley said, and then read out their coordinates. "I have us at eleven thousand five hundred sixty feet. We're less than a quarter mile from the crash site, but it would take us less time to get there if we go up the last hundred yards to the northeast ridgeline and then travel north along it to descend at that latitude. It's about one hundred twenty-five yards at that point. We could possibly be there in about thirty– to forty-five minutes."

"Team Four, you're the closest to Team Six. Proceed."

"Are there any reported survivors?"

"Team Six is exploring the site. Stand by." The radio operator then moved on to Team Five, and the reports continued.

Hensley dialed down the volume and turned to look down the hillside to where everyone stared at him. "Fife? Did you catch all that?"

"Got it!" Fife yelled. "Good plan. We'll hit the ridgeline and take it north."

Relief pulsed through Meg. Her headache was getting a little worse, and she could only imagine what Hawk must be feeling. It sounded like they might be close to topping out altitude-wise and wouldn't need to push closer to fourteen thousand feet.

"Move on out!" Hensley shouted.

Above her, Carlisle found her next handhold and pulled herself up, then called Hawk to follow.

"Lacey, come." Meg tested a foothold and stepped up, looking back to see the shepherd following.

The end of the climb was in sight.

But was there anyone alive to find? And where was the rest of the plane?

CHAPTER 10

Technical Route: A route requiring the use of climbing equipment (ropes, harnesses, or ice tools, etc.) to navigate safely.

May 7, 12:12 am
Pyramid Peak
Aspen, Colorado

It was a relief to finally reach the top of the ridge. There was no stopping to recharge now, not when the crash site was so close, but simply moving across the ridge of the mountain was so much easier, it felt like a rest.

Meg and Brian walked with their dogs in front of them, their headlamps lighting the way. While it wasn't a flat path of solid rock, and care still had to be taken over loose scree, some sections were more than thirty feet wide. The narrowest, so far, had been five feet. The wind whipped around them viciously, but the extra width gave them some security against its intensity.

Meg felt like she could take a breath for the first time in hours. She was sure her blood pressure was appreciating the break, at the very least. So were her hands, which were now gloved, as no handholds were required to navigate their current route. Staying warm was important, as the brutal wind gusts felt like they pushed the temperature below freezing. Meg pulled her cap down and her collar up to best protect her face from the cold.

It wasn't the time for anyone to let their guard down—a fall from the ridgeline would be as catastrophic as a fall while climbing—but at least there was the space to stay in the middle of the nearly flat terrain, providing some relief from the exposure on both sides leading to certain death.

They covered the ridgeline at a steady pace, keeping close together as a group. In front, Hensley would occasionally pause to check his GPS, then continue.

Meg was surprised to find a scattering of sturdy pines here at the upper reaches of the tree line. For some reason, the rare greenery among the desolation of the brutal rock raised her spirits. Somehow life always found a way, even under these harsh conditions.

It was also as if the elements finally realized they'd made the rescue attempt hard enough for the exhausted teams as the thick fog dissipated slightly and headlamps cut considerably farther into the night. It wouldn't be enough to get a chopper in the air, but it would help the rescuers on foot and make their climb significantly safer.

They were about five hundred feet along, by Meg's estimation, crossing one of the narrower sections of the ridgeline, her eyes on the ground in front of her dog, when a flash of light to her left caught her peripheral vision.

She jerked to a halt, turning to face the west side of the ridge, but after thirty or forty feet, all she could see was cloud behind the beam of her headlamp.

Had she imagined it?

"What's wrong?" Brian had stopped behind her.

"Wait. Ben, Stacey, hang on! I may be losing my mind, but I thought I saw a light in the saddle."

Hensley peered down into the dark, the beam of his

headlamp lighting a steep slope running downhill before it disappeared into the mist. "I don't see anything."

"Maybe we're doing this wrong," Fife said. "Meg, were you looking that way?"

"No, I had my eyes on the path. I thought I saw it out of the corner of my eye."

"Exactly." Fife flipped off his headlamp and stared into the dark. "You saw the light in the dark. When we're shining our lights down, all we're getting is our own light bouncing back at us. It has to be a strong light to get through this. Plant your feet, get the dogs to stay, and everyone turn off their headlamps."

The thought of standing twelve thousand feet up on the edge of the ridge in the dark and gusting wind made Meg's skin crawl, but she commanded her dog to sit and stay, braced her feet in a wide stance, and switched off her headlamp.

When the last headlamp went out, it was exactly as dark as she imagined it would be, and Meg dropped one hand down on Hawk's head to comfort them both.

Then she saw it again—that brief flash of light.

"I saw it!" Brian's enthusiasm pushed his words to a near shout.

"So did I!" Excitement rang through the exhaustion in Newall's voice.

"Me too," Hensley said. "Lamps on. Then watch out, it's about to get loud." He cupped his gloved hands around his mouth as if to propel the sound in only one direction, and bellowed, *"HELLO!"*

Everyone stayed stock-still, some with eyes closed to concentrate, some staring in the direction of the cloud-swathed saddle. But if there was a return call, it was lost in the whistle of the wind.

Hensley repeated the call, and they waited in vain.

"Nothing. But we may not be able to hear them. In no wind a shout will carry four, five hundred feet. But in these conditions—"

The wind, whistling around the group, carried a new scent to Meg. "Wait." She cut Hensley off, then closed her eyes again, drew in a large breath through her nose, concentrated. Her eyes flew open. "Do you smell that?"

"What?" Brian asked.

"Fire. And not just fire. Burned electrical components and plastics. It's faint. In a wind this strong, it's hard to catch."

"You can identify those smells?" Newall asked, then closed his eyes and inhaled through his nose. "I think I smell something? Or I may just be projecting because you mentioned it. It's not strong if it's there."

"My fiancé is a firefighter. I've been to scenes. I've been to the fire station when they're back from a blaze and the smell is absorbed into their gear. Into them." She looked down into the blackness of the saddle. "It's down there. And when it crashed, it burned. The wind is mostly blowing the scent from the fire away from us."

"But we all saw a light, so either we're looking at emergency lighting or at least one person survived." Hensley pulled out his radio. "Team Four to command."

The response came back almost immediately. "Go ahead, Team Four."

"We're currently at the top of the northeast ridge. We've spotted a light down below in the saddle to the west. It's faint because of the cloud cover, but they should have emergency LED flashlights on the plane, and we may be seeing a signal from a survivor. Has the rest of the plane been identified at this time?"

"Negative."

"We need to check this out. Do you have sufficient personnel coverage for the existing section to the east of us?"

"Affirmative." A crackle of radio static, then: "Two deceased found in the tail section. No survivors."

Meg and Brian exchanged a look under crossed lamp beams. Two dead left fourteen still as potential survivors. Unless the initial fatality wasn't one of the two already found; then they had a pool of thirteen potentials.

"We're going down into the saddle to check this out." Hensley's lamp beam slid sideways to shine over the two dogs. "The terrain from the ridgeline into the saddle is too steep. We're going to have to rope down, using the canine harnesses."

"Confirm current coordinates."

Hensley read out their coordinates and altitude.

"Confirm crash site as soon as you find it. Other teams are already en route, and we'll divert them to you at that time."

"Affirmative. Team Four out." Hensley put the radio away and pulled out his GPS, then spent a moment considering the map before he put it away.

"We're going to need to rope down?" Meg tried to sound casually interested, as if her blood pressure and heart rate weren't spiking at the idea.

"Yeah. According to my topo app, the top part of the slope is anywhere from sixty-five to eighty degrees. The dogs wouldn't be able to manage it; truthfully, it would be safer for us to rope down as well. We'll help you; you won't need to belay. Just carry the weight of the dogs on your harness."

"*On* the harness?"

"Yeah, we'll explain once we have it set up. It will be easier if we go this way. Satellite photos say there are trees farther ahead. We passed a few, but I'd like a better selection for an anchor. Come on."

Meg and Brian didn't question Hensley's strategy. They'd both been present when Todd and Luke had used two trees as anchors near the cliff leading down the beach at the Boundary Waters Canoe Area. The brothers had body-rappeled down the cliff to find one of the victims of a night of murder. But they'd only needed two things to accomplish their goal—an anchor and the rope.

Right now, they had one, and needed the other. And they'd need harnesses, which the Mountain Rescue Aspen team already had handled.

They'd only covered about another one hundred feet when Hensley slowed, then stopped.

Carlisle stepped up behind him and froze. Then she turned around and looked back at the rest of the team. "This is definitely it."

She and Hensley moved sideways so the others could move in, directing their headlamps down to the ridge and then into the saddle.

Meg's breath hitched at the sight of the damage.

There was no mistaking what had happened here; the destruction to the ridge said it all. Though, really, the tail section had been the first clue. Lights coming from the far side was the second. This part had been inevitable.

A massive object had struck the ridgeline, obliterating several vertical feet of solid rock. Perhaps whoever was at the controls had been trying to get the plane up and over the ridge, but the angle and force at which they hit was sufficient to cleave the plane in two, the tail section sliding back down to come to rest several hundred feet downslope, and the remainder of the plane skidding down the side of the saddle and into the low-lying area hundreds of feet below them.

A trough of destruction ran down the inner edge of the ridge as far as their beams could light. To Meg's inexperienced eye, it carried roughly the correct dimensions for the passenger compartment of a small jet.

"Assuming we're not imagining that light, I'm amazed

anyone survived this," Brian said quietly. "The impact alone could have been enough to kill everyone. And yet someone survived."

"Possibly several someones," Meg said. "Maybe the hit slowed them down enough that the plane's angle changed, tipped them forward, so what was left of the plane skidded downhill instead of soaring to the next peak." Meg turned to Carlisle on her right. "If that really is someone shining a light down there, we need to be prepared that it's the hijacker."

Carlisle laid a hand over the lump of her service weapon that lay against the left side of her rib cage under her jacket. "You and I are on the same page. We need to be prepared for anything as soon as we get there. We know there's at least one firearm in play. For the sake of anyone caught in the cross fire here and just trying to survive, I feel bad about an aggressive initial stance, but it's the way it has to be. If the hijacker didn't make it, then we can relax. Otherwise, he needs to be contained before we do anything else. Now is not the time for him to threaten anyone. They didn't survive the hell of a plane crash to die as the hijacker escapes."

"He's not escaping," Brian said. "Lacey and Hawk can track him, even if he tried to run hours ago. If he survived, he's had time. It was daylight when they crashed."

"But now? That would be suicide," Newall said. "Up here, in the dark, in the cold? Maybe he had daylight initially, but there's no way he's not injured in at least some way, so he's not going to move like an experienced hiker. He won't have climbing gear or a headlamp. Not to mention, he doesn't know where he is and would get lost. If he's out there, he's straight-up lucky it isn't snowing yet."

"Death from hypothermia wouldn't be unlikely, snow or no snow," Carlisle stated.

"Let's keep moving." Fife pointed to where Hensley was

carefully picking a route over the newly cut ridgeline. "We can't afford to let anyone else die of hypothermia before we get there."

They kept to the inside rim of the saddle, to shorten the distance of any potential fall. All six humans and two dogs made it across the rough-hewn trough safely, and within four minutes were standing at the edge of a scattering of pine trees that ran up the slope on the creek side, over the edge, and then down toward the base of the saddle.

Hensley laid his hand on the thick, sturdy trunk of a pine so tall it disappeared into the surrounding cloud. Bracing his foot against it, he gave it a solid shove. "This should do nicely. It's big and solid."

"Looks good to me." Fife stepped past the handlers and dogs, unclipping his backpack and swinging it to the ground.

Standing at the edge of the downward slope, her head-lamp pointed into an abyss that disappeared into the blackness, Meg forgot how to breathe for several seconds. The thought of moving down the slope in the dark, even with the rope and harness, made her slightly lightheaded. "How far down is it into the saddle?"

"About three hundred feet." Hensley's voice came from behind her. "But we'll only need to rope you through the vertical section. That's only about two hundred feet straight down. It's an easy class two scramble down the rest."

Meg shuddered.

"Better a two-hundred-foot controlled descent than a fall," Brian murmured beside her.

"My head knows that. My gut thinks they're the same thing." She pulled in a big breath, then pushed it out, hoping to blow out some of her stress with it. "Let's do it. Maybe, if we're lucky, some of the booze bottles I'm sure were on that plane are still intact. I'm going to need a drink."

"You and me both, sister. Too bad we're not supposed to drink on the job."

"To my everlasting sorrow. Especially right now."

They turned around to find Hensley and Fife on their knees, bent over their open packs, rapidly unpacking gear. Fife tossed a coiled rope onto a loose pile of rocks.

"Time to put on those harnesses we brought you," Hensley said as he pulled out a palm-sized burgundy metal device that Meg recognized from Todd's work at the fire-house as a brake system and emergency belay device. She eyed the device. "That will hold both of us?"

Hensley followed her gaze. "The MPD? As long as the two of you don't weigh more than six hundred pounds, we're good."

"MPD?" Brian asked.

"Multipurpose device. Because it can help with both raising and lowering loads, belaying, and just as a general pulley system. In this case it will give us the friction we need to lower you down safely. Don't worry about the equipment. We'll make sure it will take your weight. Fife, you got the quad length sling?"

"Right here." Fife handed over a coil of flat, woven blue webbing about an inch wide.

Hensley shook out the sling, grabbing both ends, the closed circle of the sling long enough to hang loose even with his arms extended wide. He swung one end of it around the tree, caught it with his other hand, and then ran the sling back and forth to flatten the width against the bark at about thigh height. Bringing the two ends together, he tied them in a tight square knot, leaving the two equal loose ends free. Fife handed him an open carabiner, which he hooked through the twin loops and closed off. He gave the system a hard yank and nodded in satisfaction.

"Let's get the dogs harnessed." Meg pulled back a few

feet, Brian following, and they removed their packs and sorted through the contents.

While they had their packs open, they watered the dogs again, took a few gulps for themselves, and then dug out the harnesses.

The harness was similar to what Meg had seen Hawk wear when a West Virginia aviation trooper had rescued him off a cliff face after he nearly plunged to his death with Daniel Mannew at the end of their pursuit of him up Great North Mountain. It had a padded belly and back, with thick webbing straps running up the chest to the shoulders, behind the front legs and around the stomach, all secured by sturdy double-back buckles to ensure no slippage. Two additional leg loops with similar fastenings ensured there was no chance of the dog slipping out of the harness. A large attachment point in the middle of the back and another in front of the tail clipped the dog into the climbing system.

"Is it safe to strap them in over their coats?" Brian called.

"Yes. Just like you'd wear a harness over your climbing gear," said Hensley. "Just make sure the buckles are tight. To be certain, we'll check it before you go down. Stacey, can you give them a hand while we build the brake system?"

"Sure." Carlisle knelt down next to Meg, who had pulled the webbing straps loose and was slipping the harness over Hawk's head. "That's good. Now slip the webbing back through the buckle . . . right . . . now double it back and snug it up." She tested the fit around Hawk's rib cage. "Perfect. Now do the same around his belly. Right, like that." She turned to Brian. "Looks good there too. Now undo the leg straps and wind them around their thighs, then buckle them again. Great."

Within a few minutes the dogs were ready.

"We're going to need harnesses, too, I assume?" Meg asked.

"Yes." Carlisle gave Meg a clinical appraisal, then Brian. "Let me see what the guys have." She walked to where Hensley and Fife had a long length of climbing rope attached to the MPD. About fifteen feet of rope lay on the ground toward the edge of the drop; the larger coil lay on the ground just to the left of the brake system.

Brian pushed to his feet, grasped the attachment points on the back of Lacey's harness, and lifted. Lacey didn't make a sound as her feet left the ground—just hung, fully trusting Brian in whatever he needed of her. "Good girl." He set her down. "She's not sliding out of this."

"They're secure," said Meg. "Now let's hope we will be, too."

"It'll be okay. They're not going to toss us over the edge."

Carlisle returned with two climbing harnesses. "Large for you, Brian. Small for you, Meg." She laid a harness in front of each handler, seating the leg loops inside the oval of the waist belt. "Step into each leg loop and then pull up the waist belt and shimmy it into place."

Meg stepped into each loop, one at a time, making sure the loop rested on top of her foot, and then pulled up the waist belt, the leg loops falling into place on their webbing straps.

"That's good." Carlisle knelt down in front of Meg and slid the leg loops a little higher. "Now pull the waist belt tight over your hips. Not that it should happen in this scenario, but you want to make sure if you somehow flip upside down, you won't slide out of the harness." She waited as Meg tightened the webbing in the double-back buckle. "That fits well. Brace yourself. I'm going to test it." Grasping the two metal rings on each side of the harness, she gave it a hard downward tug, but the harness stayed firmly in place. "Perfect." She turned to Brian. "How are you doing?"

"I think this is right."

"Looks good. Can I check it?"

"Go for it." Brian held firm as Carlisle yanked on his harness. "Didn't budge."

"Good. Come on, they're ready for you."

Meg and Brian called their dogs and followed Carlisle to the tree.

"So, how does this work?" Meg could hear the nerves in her own voice, suspected Brian could as well, but hoped anyone unfamiliar with her couldn't.

"It's pretty straightforward," Hensley said from where he straddled the anchor and MPD. "We're going to use a couple of webbing slings to attach your dog to the carabiner we'll attach to your belay loop—that loop on the front of your harness. Then you'll be attached to the rope coming out of the brake system by that same carabiner." He patted the MPD. "Back here, I'll be letting out the rope slowly, allowing you to essentially walk down the side of the ridge with your dog hanging behind you." He picked up the rope that fed into the MPD. "I can control the speed." He pulled the rope parallel to the ground. "When it's flat out like this, there's very little friction and the rope moves more quickly." He pulled the rope almost to a ninety-degree angle. "When it's in this position, there's lots of friction, which slows it right down."

"What if you need to stop it?" Meg asked. "Say the dog is unbalanced or we're spinning and we need to pause?"

"We can do that using this handle here." He drew an *S* over the front of the device. "This is how the rope is wound through. The progress of the rope is controlled by the metal swing brake inside." Hensley tapped on the T-bar handle protruding from the front of the MPD. "This release handle controls the swing break. When it's released, the friction increases so much the rope stops moving. Then there's the parking brake. If I engage the parking brake, it locks out the system and I could walk away and you'd stay hanging partway down."

Cold fear sluiced through Meg at the thought of hanging there, with her dog, in the pitch blackness of night, hundreds of feet over a bone-breaking field of rocks, while being tossed by brutal gusts of wind. Her mouth went so dry she couldn't articulate the fear.

Hensley must have realized from Meg's wide-eyed expression of horror she thought it might be a real possibility. He held up both palms, his fingers splayed wide. "Not that I would. I'm just saying there's a backup fail-safe. There's no way the rope is going to whiz through and you're going to crash to the bottom."

Another fear layered on in Meg's mind. Hensley's demonstration to reassure them this was a safe operation was actually having the opposite effect.

"To let the rope out," Hensley continued, "all I have to do is slide my hand under the release handle, engage the gears, and we're in motion." He demonstrated, grabbing the rope with his left hand, and then sliding his palm-up fingers under the T-bar, which he then lifted and rotated 180 degrees. "If there was load on the rope, it would play out. If anything goes wrong, all I have to do is this"—he pulled his hand away and the T-bar snapped back into place—"and the system stops. Does that make sense?"

Meg merely nodded, but Brian said, "Yes."

"Good. Because you're not belaying on your own, you'll have both hands free for handholds, or to keep your dog from swinging. We'll send one of you down first, then the other." He turned to Fife. "I want you to go down before them; that way you can monitor from below and let me know via radio how things are going. Then the handlers and dogs, then Corey and Stacey."

"What about you?" Newall asked.

"I'm the most experienced climber, so I'll rappel down after quickly breaking down the brake system, in case we need it again. I have the equipment I need, and we'll leave the rope in place in case we stay socked in and need to come back up this way. But we shouldn't need to, because going down the saddle to the north face of the mountain will be a much easier and less technical route. We'll make sure the equipment gets recovered later. But it's worth leaving it in place so we have an additional route at our disposal, if needed."

Fife was already stepping into his climbing harness and cinching it tight, doing a self-check, and then repacking his backpack.

"I can get the dogs ready while you lower Fife," Carlisle offered. "What are you thinking for the connection?"

Hensley pointed toward a pile of white webbing. "Use two double slings per dog. Loop the sling over the back attachment; use a carabiner on the tail attachment so the ass stays below the head. It will also help keep the dog from spinning. Use one of the large, pear-shaped, locking carabiners on the belay loop. Put the dog behind the handler, one sling attached on one side, the other on the other side. The third tie-in is the descent cord, locked into the loop below the double figure-eight knot. Make sure they know how to open the carabiner at the bottom to get off the rope, but if they have trouble, Fife will help them."

Hensley turned to Fife, who had already tied himself into the rope, looping a carabiner through his belay loop and then to the descent cord. "Ready? This isn't going to be a real belay, more like a supported downward scramble. You can control your angle to the rope by shortening your footholds."

"Got it. This gives us a test of the system. Let's pick a spare radio channel."

After agreeing on a channel and setting both radios to it, Fife walked backward to the edge as Hensley slowly let out the rope, then, using the rope for tension, found a foothold and started to walk his way down the steep slope, using his hands to push off the rock face.

Hensley let the rope play out, holding it at about a forty-five-degree angle, maintaining a constant speed. After about a minute, he keyed his radio. "How's that for speed?"

"Perfect for the dogs. Give me a little more."

"Affirmative."

Carlisle went over to the equipment and brought back everything she'd need for the two teams. "Let's get you and Hawk set up and nearly ready to go."

Brian opened his mouth, but Meg subtly shook her head to dissuade him from his offer. The wait was making her heart pound with the thought of being out there with nothing to support her but a rope. Logically, she knew it was safe, but she was having trouble getting that message from her head to her heart, which was pounding as if the end was near.

She was going to force herself to do this sooner or later. The sooner she began, the sooner it was done. Brian meant well, but he could wait.

Following Hensley's instructions, Carlisle showed Meg the twist and push needed to open the gate on the autolock carabiner, then attached it to Meg's belay loop. Then she took two webbing loops—only about half as long as the one Hensley had used to anchor the system on the tree—and threaded one through the attachment point on the canine harness over Hawk's back and then through itself, pulling it tight, and then attached another autolock carabiner to the tail attachment point and slipped a second sling onto it before locking it. "This should be a quick descent for Fife. As soon as the rope is back, we'll get you attached."

It felt like the longest eight minutes of Meg's life, waiting for her turn to step out into thin air and walk down a rock wall. She'd seen Todd do essentially the same thing—and he'd been without a harness and had used a specific method of winding the rope around his own body—and even that had made her nervous, despite knowing he'd trained for that kind of climbing in his role as a firefighter.

Finally the rope was unwound from the MPD, then pulled back up and neatly recoiled. Hensley double-checked the equipment, and they were ready to go.

Carlisle positioned Meg with Hawk behind her, then clipped the tail sling from the dog harness into the carabiner from Meg's right side, and the back sling into the carabiner from Meg's left side, locking them together with only a little slack. She took the descent rope and clipped it in, letting the carabiner's autolock gate close, adjusting the pear-shaped carabiner so the narrow end pointed up to hold the rope and the two slings flanked the rounded bottom.

Meg stared down at the knot, following the doubled cord in a figure eight. "So that's it? We're holding on with one knot?"

"That's an extremely strong knot. Weight on it only pulls it tighter. It's not going to unravel on you partway down. And the climbing cord is rated for considerably more weight than the two of you combined." Carlisle met Meg's eyes in the glow of their headlamps. "Don't be nervous. You're going to be fine."

Meg stripped off her gloves and stuffed them in her jacket pocket. "Easy for you to say. You do this for fun."

"And I remember being nervous the first few times too. Don't worry. You're in good hands."

"Just get us down there in one piece. What do I do next?"

"Back toward the edge, taking Hawk with you. Ben will keep the rope taut. When you're at the edge, lift Hawk up so he's suspended and then step out backward."

"Okay." Meg took one moment, closed her eyes, filled her mind with the image of Todd walking over the edge of the cliff, how he'd managed the change in angle. She opened her eyes and stepped back. One step, two. She lifted Hawk enough off his feet so she could step back once more and he was dangling.

You can do this.

She stepped off the edge.

CHAPTER 11

Belay Descent: A descent where the climber descends down a slope with the aid of a moving rope.

May 7, 1:04 am
Pyramid Peak
Aspen, Colorado

The trip down wasn't as hard as Meg imagined.

The first few steps had been terrifying, trying to keep from slamming into the rock face, trying to move to minimize her hips swinging, which would start Hawk swaying from side to side. She'd anticipated she'd feel Hawk dragging on her harness, but the climbing cord essentially took all his weight, allowing her to move with relative freedom within the safety of her own harness. She'd had to wipe her palms off on her pants several times, but as they progressed, the cold sweat dissipated, her heart rate slowed slightly, and she was able to hear the wind in her ears again rather than nothing but her own pulse.

She checked on Hawk as often as she could, and each time her gaze locked on his, she saw the same emotion—love, trust, determination. His steadiness bolstered her.

It's what partners did for each other. Their partnership

wasn't all about her caring for him. Most would never understand, but so much of what they did was because of Hawk. Not just because of his amazing nose and ability to follow commands, but because of his spirit, drive, and strength that held Meg up when she might have otherwise stumbled.

Hensley kept the speed constant and manageable, and Meg used her legs to keep herself and Hawk away from the wall. Only rarely did she need to reach around to steady him, though she talked to him all the way down, telling him what a good boy he was. He remained limp and calm, hanging just behind her knees, and his lack of struggle helped Meg settle into the downward climb.

One thing was very clear: They'd never have made it down this slope—cliff, really—with no assistance. They would have both ended up in a bloody tangle at the bottom of the drop. Between the nearly right angle and the damp slickness of the rock, it would have been insane to try without climbing gear.

Within eight or nine minutes, just as Meg felt she was getting into the rhythm of the climb, the pitch of the slope changed and she had to push off more with her legs, changing their angle from her torso so Hawk would continue to dangle unimpeded.

"I can see her, nearly there," Fife's voice came from below her. "Slow it down. That's it. Keep it coming. Meg, you have about fifteen feet to go. I'm going to steady you when you get there. A little more, a little more." Hands clasped her harness on either side, the bulk of a radio pressed into her left hip. "Ben, cut it!"

The rope stopped moving.

"Doing great, Meg. You too, Hawk. Now get your feet under you. I'm going to lift Hawk." Some of the weight that had settled around her hips as they stopped lifted. "Did Stacey show you how to open the carabiner? Twist and pull?"

"Yes." Meg rubbed her hands together to brush off grit from the handholds of her descent and then found and opened the carabiner. But her hands were clumsy with the cold, and it immediately snapped shut on her. "Sorry, hold on. I need to try again."

"You need to hold that gate. They're built to stay closed as a safety precaution, which can sometimes make it a challenge to open until you get used to them. " His voice sounded slightly strained as he suspended the seventy-pound dog with one hand. "Give it another shot."

Meg got it on the second attempt, and stepped slightly up the slope to slip the rope down and off the carabiner. Twisting a bit to the right, she slipped off first the one sling, then to the left for the second. "He's free. You can put him down."

Fife's relieved exhalation brought a smile to Meg's lips. "He's down." He brought his radio to his mouth, keyed it. "Rope is free. Bring it up and let me know when Brian and Lacey are on their way down."

"Affirmative," Hensley responded. "Good work, Meg. Any comments before we repeat with Brian?"

Meg took the radio Fife extended to her. "Not for you. The speed was perfect. Can Brian hear me?"

There was a pause, then Brian's voice, loud and clear. "I'm here. You okay?"

"I'm down." Meg left out the fact that her hands were still shaking and her knees wanted to buckle. "The ride is actually pretty smooth—just keep pushing off with your hands and feet so you don't wind up kissing the rock wall. When you get to the bottom, you'll find Lacey is bumping the backs of your knees, so you'll have to go from a more vertical position to an *L* shape."

"Did Hawk spin? Is that something I need to guard against?"

"Some swaying, but the way they arranged the slings coming around us, it's stabilizing. Good luck."

"See you in about ten."

Meg handed the radio to Fife. "Am I going to need my harness for this next part?"

"No, should be a fairly easy descent into the saddle from here. You can take Hawk out of his harness, too, then set up your trekking poles. That will help you manage the angle down."

"Thanks." Meg moved off about ten feet, finding a flattish rocky outcropping large enough for her to sit on and Hawk to climb on beside her. "Up, boy." He landed lightly beside her and pushed his cold nose against her cheek. She ran her hands across his head and neck. "What a good boy you are. So brave and calm." She gave him a kiss on the top of his head. "My hero."

Hawk's tail rapped a dull tattoo against the rock.

"Let's get you out of this harness and get you some food and water." Cupping her hands, she blew on them to infuse some warmth into her nerveless fingers. As soon as Hawk was comfortable, she was going to dig out her gloves and let her hands defrost. She wasn't sure how cold it was, but it felt like as low as the midthirties. And now they'd stopped moving, and her body wasn't circulating activity-warmed blood, the chill was setting in with a vengeance on any exposed skin.

Her hands were clumsy releasing the webbing straps pulled tight from Hawk's weight during the descent, but she finally got them unbuckled and slipped the harness off over his head. She folded it up and then opened her pack. "Hawk, I have an idea. Down, boy." He hopped down, balancing on some uneven rocks a level below, but it gave Meg room to find and pull out the sleeping pad she'd been given. The pad was meant to be inflated and used under her sleeping bag if they stayed for the night, but could also be quickly packed away when they needed to move on. In this case it would be a flat double layer of protection between her dog and the cold rock. She shook it out and spread it across the rock—it was big enough to cover the whole space, giving enough room for both of them—and then had him jump up. She flipped back one corner and set his water bowl on the rock, protecting the pad from splashing while he drank, and then poured out another small meal of high-energy food.

If they were about to find what remained of the plane, it could be a while before their next break. Definitely a "smoke 'em if you got 'em" moment.

Meg shucked off her own harness and tucked it into her pack. Sitting beside her dog, she downed some water, then opened and quickly consumed an energy bar. She tucked the wrapper away, tugged the collar of her jacket up to her nose so it bumped the bottom of her helmet at her neck, and slid on her gloves. As soon as Hawk finished, she had him lie down beside her, pressed against her leg so he could rest, but also get some of her warmth. He was clearly feeling the cold, because instead of his usual elongated position with his head on his paws, he curled into a ball like a cat, his paws contained within the ball to warm them.

Part of the problem was the wind. Their current position felt like standing on a big-city street surrounded by skyscrapers funneling the wind between them. The sides of the saddle essentially did the same job and the wind whipped ferociously. She angled her body to do her best to block Hawk while he rested.

Meg studied Fife as she waited. He stood in the same spot, radio in his gloved hand, his head tipped up and his headlamp beam disappearing into the mist above. She scanned higher, but didn't see any hint of Brian's headlamp above.

It looked like the clouds weren't shifting at all. They'd been beyond lucky there'd been no precipitation so far—climbing was hard enough, but climbing in ice and snow would have been damned near impossible for the handlers and the dogs—but she had a bad feeling it wasn't going to last. Snuggling deeper into her jacket and shifting closer to her dog, she closed her eyes and tried to let her mind go blank. Just for one minute, because that was likely all she'd get.

She got two before Fife's words had her eyes flying open.

"Brian and Lacey are in sight. Slow their descent. That's it."

"Hawk, stay." Hawk opened one eye as Meg climbed down, then he closed it again. "Good boy. You rest. Stay." Meg picked her way over to Fife, staying well behind him so she didn't get in the way. "Doing great, Brian."

"Yay, us."

Meg could hear the relief in his voice that they were nearly there. Behind him, Lacey looked tense, her legs slightly splayed and her gaze shooting from side to side. She was always a slightly more anxious dog than Hawk, and while she wasn't being disruptive, she clearly was uncomfortable dangling in the dark.

"Coming up behind you," Meg said as she sidled past Fife. "Let me get to Lacey when they're down. She looks scared."

"Sure. Ben, stop the descent."

Meg climbed to where Brian was planting his boots and making sure he was balanced, but she went directly to his dog. "Lacey, love, you're doing great. What a good girl." She ran her hand over the shepherd's head, holding her anxious gaze. "Almost there, Lacey, then you can hang out with Hawk." Lacey's ears perked forward at Hawk's name. "Good girl. Brian, you're stable?"

"Yeah."

"Let me help you with the carabiner. I've had gloves on for a few minutes and can feel my fingers again. Fife, can you lift Lacey?"

"Give me one second." Fife was silent for a moment as he got his hand into position. "Got her."

Slipping around to stand in front of Brian, she yanked off her gloves, jammed them under one arm, and made quick work of the climbing cord and slings. "You can put Lacey down."

Brian immediately turned and dropped down to Lacey's level, wrapping his arms around her, stroking, and praising. He glanced up at Meg. "She did *not* like that."

"She's never done something like that before. Hawk's at least done it before during the Mannew case, but this was all new for Lacey."

"And you did great, didn't you, my Lacey-girl. Even though you were scared."

"Let's get out of the way so they can keep going. Who's next, Stacey or Corey?"

"Corey, and it should be faster, as they slowed the process down for the dogs. Stacey is going to rappel down like Ben. She knows there's no help for this taking as long as it is for safety's sake, but both she and Ben want to get to the survivors as soon as humanly possible. That's their fastest way down."

"Makes sense. Come over here. I have a spot set up for Hawk to rest and Lacey can join him."

Hawk's head was already raised as he waited for Lacey, his tail thumping happily in anticipation. Lacey hopped up on the pad at Brian's command and immediately beelined for Hawk's water dish.

When Brian moved to stop her, Meg grabbed his arm. "Let her be. You'll need to top up the bowl, but there's no harm in her using it. Hawk's food dish is there if you want to use it too." She patted the empty spot where she'd previously sat. "Hawk, come here. Let Lacey have your spot."

Hawk climbed to his feet and shifted to sit down where Meg indicated, and Lacey lay down in his spot, letting out a canine sigh of relief.

"Hawk's spot is still warm, which probably feels good. You get her food; I'll get her harness off. My fingers are no doubt warmer than yours."

"Wouldn't take much for them to be. My kingdom for a pair of gloves."

With both dogs fed, watered, and lying down together on the pad, Meg and Brian moved off a few feet to sit down, while Brian had some water, an energy bar, and a chance to warm up and rest.

"How's your headache?" he asked.

"About the same, now that you mention it. Which isn't bad, because I'd have thought the stress of doing that"— she pointed at Fife near the base of the rock wall—"would have reasonably made it worse. You?"

"I think it might be easing off a bit. Maybe the drugs are doing their thing."

"That was Todd's hope. Which reminds me, I have time now to update him and Craig while we're waiting for Stacey and Ben."

"You have time. Stacey and Corey are concerned about any weapons still in play, and don't want anyone in the group to be separated unless necessary."

"Works for me. Gives us and the dogs a chance to rest."

"Maybe grab a power nap. This middle-of-the-night climb is kicking my ass."

"Ditto." Meg pulled out her satellite phone and sent off a text to Todd. **We think we spotted the forward section of the plane. You would have been proud. I just roped down a 200' rock wall with Hawk attached to my climbing harness.** She followed it with an emoji of a face with giant, bulging, terrified eyes.

"Think he'll get back to you?"

"You're asking if the firefighter who's used to going from REM sleep to standing on his feet in under two seconds when the firehouse alarm goes off will wake up at three AM to the sound of a text coming in?" As if in answer, her phone dinged.

"Not anymore, I'm not." He pulled out his own phone. "Not sure Ryan will answer so quickly."

"Ryan isn't the person who will sleep through a car crash happening right outside his window. That's you."

"Good point." Brian bent over his phone and started typing with both thumbs.

Meg turned to her own phone to find a text from Todd. **Good for you! That must have been scary as hell for you.**

That's not the half of it. Waiting for everyone else to rope down so we keep moving as a group. We're basically in a mountain valley between two peaks. We think the plane is here. We saw a light.

There must be some kind of emergency lighting. No way the plane still has power after crashing.

Leave it to a firefighter to immediately analyze a disas-

ter site. **We think some kind of emergency flashlight. Probably LED to be bright enough to cut through the clouds up here. Visibility is lousy.**

Headache?

Not worse. Might be a bit better. Going to catch some downtime while we're waiting. Maybe a fifteen-minute power nap to recharge.

Good idea. Take care of you and our boy.

Guaranteed.

Meg sent another quick message with an update to Craig, ending with her goal to power nap so he wouldn't text back unless he needed info. She put her phone into her pocket just as Brian finished texting Ryan. "You got him?"

"Yeah. And he says to keep the updates coming, but I told him it would be a while if we're about to be dealing with dead or injured passengers and potentially a killer hijacker." He slid back to lean against the rock wall behind him, tipping his helmet against it. "I'm so tired, this is actually comfortable." He patted the open space beside him. "Take a lesson from our smart dogs. Come nap with me."

Meg took in the dogs, who were curled together on the pad, pressed back-to-back, sharing body heat. "They're no dummies."

"They're not. Come on." A little of the old Brian humor glittered in his exhausted eyes. "I promise not to cop a feel."

"Ha! Like you'd be interested."

"I'm very interested . . . in your body heat. Come on, share with me. I'll share with you."

"I'll take that deal." She climbed onto the rock and drew her boots up so her thighs pressed to her chest, keeping her legs off the cold stone. She pressed against Brian, felt his arm come around her shoulders, pulling her in, and she tipped her head back, angling her helmet to tap against his. She felt his chest rise and fall on a long sigh as his muscles relaxed. She closed her eyes, her limbs suddenly weighted with lead.

As they did in everyday life, they propped each other up, making a shared space on the cold, rocky slope. As one, they slid into sleep.

CHAPTER 12

First Ascent: The first successful ascent to the top of a new climbing route.

May 7, 1:51 am
Pyramid Peak
Aspen, Colorado

Twenty minutes out and they both felt brand-new upon waking.

Meg hopped off the rock, stretching muscles stiffened by cold, but she knew they'd loosen as soon as they started moving again. "I needed that."

"You and me both. Now I can definitely say the headache is getting better. Let's go see where we are." Brian took in the dogs, still peacefully sleeping. "Let's leave them as long as we can."

"Agreed."

They made their way to where Carlisle and Newall stood with Fife. The climbing cord running down the hill was now doubled and Carlisle still wore her climbing harness, which had considerably more hardware attached than the one Meg had worn.

"You made it down safely," Meg said to Carlisle. "Was it tricky on your own?"

"Not at all. Standard stuff, really, for someone who's climbed as much as me. It'll be a cakewalk for Ben." The cord ends twitched and Carlisle followed them up to where they disappeared into the cloud. "We should see him soon." She eyed the handlers. "You got a little rest? Feel better for it?"

"Yeah." Brian tapped his helmet twice. "Head's better too."

"Good. That's an extra challenge for you. Not to mention, your day began two hours earlier than ours simply because of the time zone difference."

"We're ready for the next round."

"Good." Carlisle looked to the rock wall, now lit by a ghostly glow. "Because here comes Ben." She unbuckled her harness. "Let's get ready to move out. We've left them waiting long enough."

A few minutes later, all the climbing gear, but the two ropes, was repacked and everyone had their trekking poles assembled. With Hensley leading the group, they made their way rapidly down to where the saddle bottomed out into a wide, mostly flat section. Far from the walls of the saddle, they took a moment to stow their poles and remove their helmets, now there was no risk of rockfall. They reattached their headlamps around their caps, pulling them down lower, needing the warmth as the brutal wind gusts felt more like January than May as they roared through the open end of the saddle and toward the peak.

"I thought the smell might be stronger here, but the wind must be blowing it away from us and over the peak." Carlisle adjusted her jacket to allow for easy access to her service weapon. "Keep the dogs near you and be ready for anything. Ben, how far ahead do you think it is?"

"Somewhere in the five-to-six-hundred-feet range. Do we want to announce our presence?"

"Normally, I'd say yes. This time I'm going to say no. If

the hijacker is alive and on scene, and is still in possession of a weapon, he could pick us off as soon as we appear."

"The headlamps are a problem," Newall pointed out. "They'll see us coming. Granted, they won't necessarily know we're law enforcement."

"The hijacker would be an idiot not to assume law enforcement was sent out with the rescue teams. Even if he doesn't know the flight attendant got word through, the plane disappeared from radar shortly after taking off. If he's going to be prepared for everything, he'll be prepared for that."

"My recommendation is for us to not wear the headlamps, and instead use them like handheld flashlights. We can't cover this rock field without some source of light, not without injury or without it taking so long we might as well wait until sunup. But we'll better be able to minimize the light." Hensley looked down at the GPS unit in his hand. "There's almost no incline here, but it's scree the whole way, so be careful in the lower light."

"Hopefully, they're still using whatever light source we saw from the ridge," Brian said. "That way we'll see them before they see us."

They headed across the saddle, carefully picking their way over small rocks with the capacity to roll, taking an ankle with it. They passed a cluster of pines in the middle section, skirting the western edge where the rock base transitioned to soil that had collected deep enough in the middle of the trough for the massive trees to root.

Holding her headlamp in her extended hand, shining the light for both herself and Hawk by her side, worked well, but Meg still had concerns. "They're still going to see us coming," she said quietly to Brian beside her. "There's no way around it."

"I agree. The dogs know how to drop and cover, if needed."

"Yes. And let's face it, someone with a gun is not going to be aiming for our knees. They'll go center mass." Meg took a step onto a rock that shifted under her weight and she had to quickly tilt left to keep her balance, the beam from her headlamp swinging wildly, drawing looks from Hensley and Carlisle in front of them. "Sorry," she called softly. "It would be better if I didn't wave a light at them as a heads-up," she muttered to Brian.

"It would be better if none of us did, but this is like strolling across a field of ball bearings." As if to illustrate his point, Lacey stumbled, and Brian reached out to steady her shoulder, then leveled a look at Meg that said, *See?*

When they were about two hundred feet from the estimated location, Carlisle asked them to try moving with only one headlamp between them, held out and pointed down and back, and they found while it slowed them down, if they bunched up tight enough, it provided sufficient diffuse light in the mist of the cloud to keep them moving.

Only a few minutes later, it was too much light.

"Ben, cover the light," Carlisle hissed.

Then they were in total darkness.

"Did you see something?" Meg kept her voice down, aware even in this wind their voices might travel.

"Smelled it. We're getting close. Does anyone see the light?"

Five seconds passed. Ten. Fifteen.

"There." Fife's voice came out of the dark. "To our right. I caught a flash of light."

"Do we think that's emergency lighting, or could that be someone trying to signal for help?" Brian asked. "Am I just being hopeful?"

"We're all being hopeful. We need to get closer and we need to do it without being fish in a barrel," said Newall.

"Let's try this." Hensley paused for a moment,; when his light shone again, it was muted. "It's inside my watch cap, so it's shining through the knit. This is as low as I can make it without leaving us in the dark."

"Then that's how we run. We'll move in that direction, but, Corey, you and I will lead, then, Ben, you and Fife, Meg and Brian follow behind with the dogs to minimize their chances of being hit if shots are fired. I don't know what we're walking into, and don't want to take any chances."

They reorganized, with Hensley still holding the lamp but shining it straight down, giving just enough light for Carlisle and Newall to see in front of him, while Meg and Brian could still navigate as well.

They knew they were on the right track when a trough appeared in front of them, the loose rock spraying out from it in an arc as wide as they could see and studded with mangled pieces of debris. They angled slightly to follow the trough just outside of the loosely thrown scatter, letting it lead them. If they had any doubts they were following the crash path, the sight of twin tires, shock absorbers, and struts from one of the landing-gear wheels—likely one of the rear pair from the size—ripped from the fuselage disabused them of that notion.

The plane had hit hard and left a path of destruction as testament to that force. It was amazing to think that even one person might have survived.

They crept ever closer. Now there was no mistaking the pungent, acrid odor of charred plastics and electricals.

As Meg detoured Hawk around the remains of a seat cushion, she concentrated on the light that had given her hope, that even in the midst of the path of debris, there might be at least one survivor. Beyond that, she had to hope some of what she was smelling wasn't charred flesh.

Possibly, one made it off the plane alive, one died during the flight, and two more were found dead in the tail section. That still left twelve others whose fate was unknown.

The air temperature rising was a clue to Meg they were getting closer. It was clear there'd been a massive fire after the crash—and possibly a slow-burning one since—and that might have been a godsend for any possible survivors, as the heat from the charred wreckage would stave off hypothermia.

A yellowish glow materialized out of the mist. They'd arrived.

Carlisle pulled her weapon from its holster, Newall following her lead, opting for his handgun in close quarters rather than his rifle. "You guys stay here. Corey, I'll go right and identify myself. Stay to the left and back, in case of attack; you'll surprise the hijacker if he's focused on me."

"Got it. If you can't find cover, stay low so he aims above your head if he tries for you."

The two FBI agents separated, slowly moving over the tumbled rocks beneath their boots, disappearing into the mist.

There was a full ninety seconds of silence, then Carlisle shouted, "FBI, put your hands where I can see them!" echoed by Newell announcing his designation as well.

A scream sounded, and then silence dragged on for long minutes. Meg and Brian exchanged concerned glances before Newall's voice came to them from the direction of the crash. "It's clear. Come on in."

Everyone snapped their headlamps on to light their steps, and only realized as light rose from the rocky ground how close they were. And the severity of the damage.

They were about thirty feet from what was left of the front section of the G-800, and even though Meg had anticipated the devastation, it still nearly knocked her back a step.

Metal torn as easily as if it were paper. The shattered fuselage; the top burned almost entirely away; the sides charred, with the windows darkened with soot. The outer third of the one visible wing, bent upward at a thirty-degree angle, with a large chunk of metal ripped clean away. Debris spread everywhere.

Now they were nearly on top of the wreck, the caustic scent of the burned materials was so thick, Meg could feel the particulates in the air as fine grit between her teeth.

Her gaze sweeping across the devastation, Meg found Carlisle and Newall about thirty feet away across the scree, and ten feet above as the slope rose up the saddle toward Pyramid Peak. They'd both holstered their weapons and were crouched down in front of a woman who lay on a blanket flipped back over her to provide additional warmth and protection. Meg only caught a glimpse of a pale face, but she sensed a critical immobility, indicating serious injury. A woman swathed in another sky-blue blanket sat beside her, dried blood running in jagged tracks over her left cheek from a gash on her head. She clutched an emergency flashlight in one hand. Beyond, two men— one wearing a suit jacket and clutching his left side, one with his tie loosened and hanging at a drunken angle, with his left shirtsleeve saturated with blood—sat off to one side, both with the faraway gaze of the shell shocked.

As Brian, Hensley, and Fife came to stand beside her, and their combined light spread wide, Meg felt the full human impact of the disaster. But through the blood and soot, Meg's first thought was so many more people than she expected had survived.

On the far side of the supine woman, three people huddled together under a shared blanket. The man in the middle sat hunched, his face in his filthy hands, his shoulders shaking, while the other talked to him. The woman to his left, sitting with one leg awkwardly extended, only had eyes for the rescuers. To his right, another man held a wadded mound of blood-soaked material to the right side of his face, covering his eye, nose, cheek, and most of his mouth.

Beyond them, three blanket-covered bodies lay near the shattered nose of the plane. Meg didn't linger there. The rescue teams knew there would be death at this site; they were lucky it wasn't more.

To Meg's right, a man in a long-sleeved white dress shirt, open at the collar, rose shakily to his feet from where he huddled near another fallen man, still mostly in shadow. As he stepped forward into the light, the epaulets of four gold bars against a field of black marked him as the plane's pilot. He cradled his left forearm in his right hand.

Carlisle looked over her shoulder, squinting in the bright beams. "Hijacker ran, and one of the survivors went after him. Everyone else is here. Ben, I need you. This woman is critical." As Hensley broke off from the group and headed toward her, she continued, "Fife, can you call this in? Then we need to triage everyone."

"Got it." Fife pulled his radio out of its harness and immediately contacted command, giving an initial rundown of the situation, and giving their specific location for the teams.

"Let's split up." Meg pointed at the three survivors. "Brian, you take them. I'll check out this one here. Hawk, come." Meg cut off to her right, the change in position suddenly lighting the men in the gloom. A man lay on his back, his face lax and his eyes closed, but it was the blanket saturated with blood covering his legs that captured Meg's attention.

So much blood. Could he still be alive?

"Thank God you found us." The pilot stepped unsteadily toward her, his eyes alight with relief and hope that help had arrived.

"Sir, don't move. We'll come to you." Not wanting an obviously wounded man to fall and complicate his injuries, Meg and Hawk quickly covered the distance between them.

"I'm Captain Hugh Laumbach, and that's Jon Slaight, my copilot," the man said. "We took the hit hard in the cockpit. I came out of it better than I expected, if a bash on the head and a broken arm are it, but Jon's in bad shape. It took three of us to extract him from his seat in the cockpit. Thank God he was already unconscious because he would have been in agony. His femur's broken."

"Hawk, come here and stay out of the way, boy." Once she had Hawk perched on a boulder about eight feet away, Meg knelt down beside Slaight. "You can tell from the position of the leg?"

"I can tell from the bone sticking out of his leg."

That would do it. "Has he come to at all?"

"Not really. Floated a little closer to the surface, but never came all the way awake. Better for him this way."

Fife joined them. "Every team is diverting to this location. Closest team is about an hour out."

"We can hold them until they get here." Meg motioned to Laumbach. "Captain Laumbach, Rob Fifer. Jon Slaight, the copilot, has a broken femur."

Fife bent over Slaight's blood-swathed right leg. "What did you guys do for him?"

"What little we could. There's bone protruding. We didn't want to mess with that, but he was really bleeding, so we tried to get it to stop."

Fife opened his mouth, then snapped it shut, his gaze shooting to Laumbach and then back to Meg.

Meg looked at him expectantly, brows raised in question.

Fife unbuckled his pack and set it on the ground. "There's no point in sugarcoating this. This is a bad injury. One of the worst you can have up here. Significant blood loss into the tissues and out of the body, immense pain, shock. We need to stabilize him and we need a chopper ASAP. Which isn't a possibility currently." He looked down at the unconscious man. "Without it, he's not going to make it."

CHAPTER 13

Spotter: A person who is positioned under the climber, ready to catch them in case of a fall, with the particular goal of protecting the climber's head and neck from impact with the ground.

May 7, 2:13 am
Pyramid Peak
Aspen, Colorado

"Even if a chopper could get in the air in the next few hours, he has to actually survive that long," Fife said, his words punching sharp while stress radiated from his stiff posture. "I've been trained and have supplies, but I've never dealt with anything like this in the field. Which isn't great when we have someone who's been in crisis for over twelve hours."

Meg understood Fife's frustration. For them to come this far, and for this man to have survived a plane crash only to die hours later, simply because they couldn't get him the help he needed? It was maddening.

He flicked a glance toward Hensley, then unzipped his pack and started to dig through it. "On top of that, I don't like the look of him, but Ben has his hands full with a more immediately critical case."

"Don't count us, or him, out yet. I have a plan." Meg unbuckled and set down her pack, then dug her satellite phone out of her jacket pocket. A quick check of the battery—still at eighty percent—and she placed the call, putting it on speaker.

It rang twice, then Todd answered, sounding fully awake. "Meg? Everything okay?"

"Hawk and I are fine. But we need your help."

In the background came the snap of the bedside light turning on. "Whatever you need."

"We made it to the plane and we have survivors. Some of them are in bad shape. I'm here with Rob Fifer, one of the Mountain Rescue Aspen guys, and the copilot sustained a femur fracture in the crash. They got him out of the cockpit before the plane burned, but he's in bad shape and has been for about twelve hours. Fife has been trained on this kind of injury, but has never dealt with it himself in the field. We could use your experience."

"You have it. Is he carrying an emergency med kit?"

Meg looked at Fife, who pointed to the bursting red bag he'd pulled from his pack. "Yes."

"Then let's do this. Can he hear me?"

Meg circled around Laumbach to kneel on the other side of Slaight, tipping her head down slightly to light the leg. "You're on speaker, and he's here with me."

"Hey, Rob. I'm Todd. I'm a firefighter/paramedic with DC Fire and Emergency Medical Services."

"Just call me Fife. And it's nice to meet you." Fife grimaced. "Sorry to get you out of bed at four AM, your time."

"No problem. Middle-of-the-night calls are what we do."

"Theoretically, I know what I'm doing, but normally in a case like this, we'd have a much larger team and I'd be guided by someone who's managed something like this before." Fife unzipped the bag as he talked, opening it out into four compartments, every nook and cranny jammed with supplies. "But we're shorthanded, currently."

"I can talk you through what you need to do," Todd assured him. "If needed, Meg can send me photos. Actually, Meg, go ahead and do that."

"Can do. Put your phone on speaker and I'll text you photos." Meg opened the camera app and snapped the first few shots of the blanket in place over the leg.

"Sounds good." A few seconds passed before Todd's voice returned with the slightly distant aspect of a speaker call. "Fife, talk me through what you can see, in case the images don't capture it."

"They used a blanket to stop the bleeding and keep it covered in an environment full of smoke and other debris. Uncovering it now."

"Do it carefully. There's been more than enough time for the blood to congeal and act like glue. Do you have any sterile fluids?"

"Saline and povidone-iodine solution."

"Excellent. Soften any stuck blood with saline."

Fife pulled on a pair of black nitrile gloves and carefully peeled the blanket back.

Laumbach stood off to the side, clutching his arm, his worried eyes locked on his copilot. "I didn't want the blanket to stick to the wound, so one of the women rolled up my jacket and propped up the blanket with it. We had to use the blanket for pressure on the wound, but once it slowed down to a minimal ooze, we tried to leave it clear. It's"—Laumbach cleared his throat—"a mess."

"Todd, that's Hugh Laumbach, the pilot, speaking," Meg clarified. "He and two others were able to extract Jon from the plane before the fire."

"Well done. And these injuries are always a mess, but we can help him. Fife, how's it going?"

Fife folded back the blanket, his expression telegraphing his relief that no material stuck to the wound. "We're clear."

Meg couldn't help the hitch in her breathing when the leg was revealed. The injury was grotesque, with about three inches of the upper part of the bone terminating in a jagged end jutting out of the viciously ripped flesh of his thigh. A swath of bloody muscle surrounded the lower half of the protruding bone. Torn skin oozed wet blood, and the blanket under the leg was soaked.

"Jesus . . ." Fife whispered.

"As I said," Laumbach said, his voice tremulous, "a mess."

"It's a mess, all right. Let me get in there and get some shots so he can see what we're dealing with. Todd, photos coming your way from a couple of angles." Swallowing hard to keep her gorge down, Meg got in close and took a number of shots, then sent them to Todd as a group. "Sending now. You should have them soon."

After a brief delay, Todd's voice returned, calm, as always, under pressure. "That's a compound fracture, no doubt about it. How's his foot?"

"He has shoes on," Meg said. "Want me to take it off?"

"Take both of them off—just work fast if it's too cold and you're worried about exposed skin."

"Actually, the temperature's not bad here. You'd be surprised how much heat a formerly burning plane gives off."

"I've overhauled buildings, so, no, I wouldn't be. That's good in this case, though I guarantee your air quality is lousy. We want to make sure blood flow is getting to the foot and you can compare both sides. From the blood loss in the photos and the fact he's still alive, I don't think the femoral artery was nicked, but that's going to be the issue with transport. You nick it, he's going to bleed out in front of you in about ten minutes."

Meg laid the phone on the ground between Slaight's legs and circled around to make quick work of both shoes and socks, being careful not to jog either limb. "What am I looking for?"

"You won't have the equipment for an ankle-brachial index to monitor blood flow, so we're going old school. Start with color. Do you have enough light to tell if the injured side is paler than the uninjured side? Are the nail beds blue? Are the feet the same temperature?"

"Light shouldn't be a problem. These LED headlamps are bright." Meg made sure her headlamp was focused equally on Slaight's feet. "Color looks good, no difference between them. Nail beds are pink." She pulled off her gloves and dropped them in her lap. "His feet are equally cool, but not surprisingly so for someone unconscious, injured, and lying outside, even if it's not cold enough for frostbite."

"One more test. Compress the end of the same toe on each foot. It will turn white, but then the color should bounce back. Time it."

Meg pressed a toe on the uninjured side first, then the same toe on the injured side. "Two seconds. Same for both."

"Good, so that's one less worry. Cover the feet again so he doesn't lose body heat. Fife, you guys are carrying oxygen to treat high-altitude illness?"

Fife nodded, then caught himself as if remembering it was a phone call. "Ben has it, but yes."

"Can you grab it?"

"I can," Meg offered. "He needs it?"

"Considering the blood loss, he has to be hypovolemic and hypoxic. And then there's the altitude, which adds stress to the system. The oxygen will improve his status for sure."

"I'll get it. Hawk, stay."

Meg climbed to her feet and headed for Hensley. As she left, she heard Todd say, "Let's get a baseline check of pulse and respiration so we can look at how shocky he is. Then run me through what you're carrying in your med kit."

Meg crossed the scree as fast as possible to find Hensley kneeling by the supine woman, securing a bandage around her head. She'd been moved to an inflated sleeping pad to get her off the cold rock, swaddled in a shiny silver space blanket, and her feet were elevated on a rock to help combat shock. "Ben, can we grab the oxygen?"

His hands busy, Hensley cocked his head toward his open backpack. "Portable oxygen kit is in my bag. Look for the light blue plastic case."

"Mask inside?" She pulled out the rectangular case.

"Yeah. Fife knows what to do with it." He looked across the clearing to where Fife riffled through his emergency pack. "Yours is bad?"

"Compound femur fracture."

Hensley cursed. "That's an injury none of us wants to see. Fife's okay with it? I know he's fully trained, but I don't know if he's ever done one in practice. I'm stuck here for now, but can come over in a few."

"Fife's holding his own. We have my paramedic fiancé on my sat phone and he's talking us through it. He also suggested the oxygen because of the combination of blood loss and altitude."

"Good call. Bring it back when you're done. We'll need it later."

"You bet." Meg hurried back as fast as she could without twisting an ankle. "How are we doing?"

"Good," Todd said. "Fife has everything we need to stabilize until morning. Fife, get that oxygen going, fifteen liters per minute."

Fife climbed to his feet and grabbed the case from Meg. "Will do."

"You think we'll be able to move them out in the morning?" Meg asked.

"That's going to be up to the chopper pilots, but I've been looking at your weather," said Todd. "I think you're going to have a window opening around dawn when you're going to be able to get the injured out. Of course that's a decision for those in the know. I could be wrong. But we need to stabilize him for as long as it takes. I'd like to give a bolus of fluids with wide-spectrum antibiotics, because that wound is infected by this point, but we don't have the materials for that. Ask for a med chopper if you have that option, and they'll start fluids and antibiotics the moment they have him."

"I'll pass that on to Ben. I'm sure he's in touch with Mountain Rescue Aspen command."

"They're sending more people your way?"

"They're all incoming. Though, depending on where they are, it could take them hours to get here."

Fife knelt at Slaight's knee. "Oxygen is flowing. And the closest team could be here within the hour. They'll have additional medical supplies. We're triaging the worst first, so the others are waiting. Speaking of which . . ." He pulled a compactly folded cloth rectangle out of the pack and extended it to Meg. "Can you help Captain Laumbach into this sling? He'll be more comfortable, and we'll look at his arm as soon as we've stabilized the criticals."

"Can do. Captain, please come with me."

"Just 'Hugh' is fine."

She led Laumbach to sit beside Hawk, so he was out of the way, but still near his copilot. "Sit down here with Hawk on your good side so he doesn't accidentally bump your injured arm."

Laumbach settled about a foot away from Hawk. "Thank you for calling your fiancé, even though it's so late."

"Very early in the morning for him. He's in DC."

"Even worse."

"It's okay. It's worth it to him to hear my voice. He worries when I'm on deployments like this. And I'm sure he's not the only one worrying tonight. Can I get the sheriff's office to contact anyone for you?"

"My wife. She must be going crazy. Or is sure I'm dead."

"When I have my phone back, I'll get your information and we'll make sure word gets through to her. By the way, Hawk is my search-and-rescue dog, but he's also a damned good therapy dog."

"I could use that right now. Hi, Hawk. I'd love to say hello properly, but no free hands."

Hawk's tail wagged as he kept his bright eyes on Laumbach.

"He's not going anywhere," said Meg. "At least until daybreak."

"You're going after the hijacker?"

"That's why we're here with our dogs. We need to get everyone stabilized, then we need to hear what happened up there." Meg shook out the sling to find an open tube of material, with a thick, adjustable webbing strap at both ends. "I'll try my best to be gentle. You think it's broken?"

Laumbach's rough laugh answered her question before he spoke. "Oh yeah. It was one reason why it took three of us to get Jon out of there. I wasn't much help. I tried to use it and almost went to my knees with the pain. Even just letting it dangle is excruciating. A ten for sure. Holding it like this"—he looked down to where he cradled the middle of his forearm in his palm—"keeps the pain at about a six."

"You're doing great. I'll ask Fife if he has some painkillers in his med kit." Meg loosened the straps as far as they could go. "I'm going to slip this over your thumb and hand." She slid the open end of the tube over his hand, carefully guiding his thumb into the small loop for support. "That's it. Now, this is the tricky part. I'm going to need you to let go of your forearm while I support your wrist, and then you take over there while I get the sling around your elbow. Go ahead and move your hand."

The groan of pain that rumbled up from Laumbach's chest when he let go spoke eloquently to the pain he was masking. Meg moved as quickly and carefully as she could, tugging the pocket of the sling over his elbow, seating the full arm gently into the body of the sling. "Keep holding for a moment." She slipped the strap over his head, then snugged it up. "How's that?"

Laumbach released his wrist, held still for a moment, and then his shoulders relaxed. "So much better. It still hurts like hell, but not nearly as bad as it was. Thanks." He turned on the rock so he faced Hawk. He offered a hand to be sniffed and then ran it over the Lab's head and down his back. "What a good boy." He looked over his shoulder at Meg. "We're a long way up, based on our altitude when we crashed. Did he have trouble managing the climb?"

"The worst part was getting down here to you. We needed to rope down. I'm going to see if I can help Fife. You stay here with Hawk. Hawk, visit."

To Laumbach's clear delight, Hawk lay down and rested his chin on Laumbach's thigh. He stroked his free hand along Hawk's silky fur, and Meg could see some of the stress ease away in real time.

Meg turned to where Fife knelt beside Slaight, using a miniature bottle of sterile saline to wash debris from the wound.

"That looks good to me." Fife eyed the wound and then splashed on a little more saline for good measure.

"Great," Todd said. "Now you're going to use your povidone-iodine solution to pack the wound. You have sterile gauze in the kit?"

"Yes."

"You're going to do a wet-dry dressing. Crack open the gauze packaging, and soak it with povidone-iodine while it's still in the wrapper. Then pull out the gauze and layer it over the wound. It's going to take a few rounds to cover it. Then you're going to cover it with dry gauze. Then we'll split it and wrap it with a self-adhering bandage. That's as stable as we're going to get it until you can air-lift him out."

"He's lost a lot of blood. I'm concerned about fluid levels."

"Me too, but you're not equipped to set up an IV in the field. If he comes to and can manage it, small amounts of fluids with electrolytes will help there."

"Let me help." Meg circled around to the med kit. "Tell me what you need."

"Can you get out the four-inch gauze?" Fife pointed to one flap of the kit where sealed squares of gauze were held down by a wide elastic. "And I need the bottle of povidone-iodine solution. That's in the middle section."

As he named items, Meg pulled them out of the pack and lined them up. Then, as Todd instructed, she opened the gauze, saturated it with povidone-iodine, and extended it to Fife for application. As he layered pieces on, she prepared the next one.

The grotesque wound was slowly covered with wet brown gauze. Fife meticulously wound the gauze around the protruding shaft, slowly covering every inch of exposed muscle and bone. Then he packed it with dry gauze.

"Fife, you said you have a SAM Splint?" Todd asked.

"Yes."

"Good, that's going to be our stability. Then you'll use the self-adhering bandage to wrap it up." Todd instructed

Fife to open the flat, folded, foam-covered aluminum, and then walked him through how to make a trough out of it to fit under the thigh. "Meg, we need you to glove up and help. Do you remember how Berk helped me with Mary's fractured tibia under the bleachers at Deep Creek? How he held the leg for me while I wrapped it? I need you to do Berk's job."

Meg had a sudden flash of herself and Todd, huddled around the broken body of a young girl—a child, really—who had fled from a brutal sex-trafficking ring in the middle of Hurricane Cole's landfall in Virginia. Mary had been found unconscious under the bleachers at a middle school, with a compound tibial fracture, where she and Todd had been assisted by Officer Berkeley, of the Norfolk Police Department, in stabilizing the girl.

"I remember. What do you need me to do?"

"You're going to need to hold the leg up just enough to get the splint underneath, then lower it into it. And you're going to have to keep it level. There's a shattered shaft in there that could slice the femoral artery."

"No pressure," Meg muttered.

"Then it all gets bound in a self-adhering bandage, and that's as stable as we can make it out in the field, with what you have. Are we ready to apply the splint?"

"As we'll ever be." Meg moved to straddle Slaight's un-injured left leg so she could kneel as close as possible, then blew on her fingers to warm them a bit and increase her dexterity before pulling on the nitrile gloves Fife handed her. "How much clearance do you need?"

"Two inches is more than enough. I'll try for less."

"Here we go then." Meg leaned in, willing her hands to be absolutely steady and sure; the last thing they needed was her nerves about what could go wrong in this procedure causing her hands to shake. She slid them under the thigh. "Todd, I'm giving the fracture about two inches of space on either side. I could do more above the break, but it's too close to the knee below for my hand to move much farther down."

"That will work. Just make sure you're moving slow and careful."

"Oh yeah, that's not a problem." She adjusted her hands slightly, spreading her fingers wide to balance the weight as best she could. "Tell me when I can stop lifting. On three. One . . . two . . . three." She carefully lifted the thigh, wincing when the balance of weight in her hands made it clear there was no solid long bone supporting the limb. Half an inch off the ground . . . one inch. She felt the edge of the splint bump against her wrists and pushed up higher on her knees so she could roll her forearms forward, straightening her wrists to give Fife more clearance.

Fife adjusted the splint slightly, settling the support into his hands. "I'm ready. You only have to lower the leg slightly and then slide your hands out so you don't disturb the break."

Meg lowered her hands so her fingers were caught between the weight of the thigh and the splint. "I'm trying," she said between gritted teeth as she attempted to move so slowly there was no chance of jolting the lower femur. Then the majority of the weight settled into the channel of the splint and she could pull her hands free. "I'm clear. Did I kill him?"

"No matter what happens, you didn't kill him." Todd's voice held a firm insistence. "If we don't stabilize him like this, he's going to die of hypovolemic shock now or infection later. Nothing you do here is worse than leaving him be."

She knew he was right, but it had been a day of high stress and the exhaustion was dragging her down. When other teams arrived, she needed at least an hour down before sunrise. After sunrise they'd be on the move for God only knew how long. "I hear you. Now what?"

"Now lift the splint so Fife can wrap the leg. You'll have lots of support for it now, just hold it steady."

Ten minutes later, the leg was wrapped in a self-adhesive bandage and carefully lowered to the ground, the bloody blanket discarded. As with the woman Hensley and Carlisle tended, they'd slipped a space blanket under him and then used its slick surface to get Meg's inflated sleeping pad under him, to get him off the cold ground. He remained deathly still, but Fife said that while his respiration was so far unchanged, his heart rate had started to stabilize.

It was only a tiny bit of progress, but in a day where total devastation was expected, Meg was willing to take it.

"Great work, guys," Todd said. "And that should be enough oxygen for now. You'll want to make sure there's enough for whoever needs it before backup arrives. Keep an eye on his heart rate and respiration. If he begins to deteriorate, give him some more then."

"I can sit here and watch him if you need to check out the others."

"Thanks." Fife coiled the tubing leading to the oxygen mask and packed it into the box. "Todd, thank you for this. You probably didn't go to bed thinking you'd be on duty in the middle of the night."

"Not really. But that's okay. We're all first responders. We know how this goes."

"We do. Meg, let me know if you have any concerns, and I'll come back to check on him shortly."

"Will do." Watching Fife walk away, Meg took the phone off speaker. "It's just me now. Thanks for that. Ben said Fife had been trained, but he'd never had to use that training himself because he's a little newer on the team.

Ben has more experience, but he's over there with one of the more critical injuries."

"Luck of the draw on a team like that as to who gets what injury on a call. It takes a lot of force to break a femur, so lesser breaks are no doubt more common. Do you need help with the other injuries?"

Twenty feet away, Hensley was holding still over the woman he treated, but his face and stance looked more relaxed as he talked to the other woman, who crouched beside them. Just beyond, Carlisle knelt in front of the man with the bloody arm as the man next to them waited, one hand still wrapped protectively over his left side. Farther away, Brian and Newall worked on the group of three—Brian was applying a gauze pad to a head wound as Lacey sat between two of the survivors, and Newall was evaluating the woman's ankle. The man who'd been comforted previously sat stone-faced between them, but he seemed calmer. "I think Ben has the worst of it. It's a miracle, but most of the injuries aren't nearly as bad as I thought they'd be. No one who survived is untouched, but there are fewer criticals than I expected."

"They design planes to be able to withstand tremendous forces."

"The proof of that is right in front of me. But if there's anything else we need your help with, are you okay with me calling back?"

"Always. How many did you lose?"

Meg's gaze inadvertently slid to the shrouded bodies. "It's bad, but it could have been so much worse. As far as I know, out of the sixteen alive at takeoff, one died during the hijacking, two died when the plane hit, broke apart, and lost the tail section, and two died in the main cabin, though we need to talk to the survivors to find out what really happened. Currently we're in triage mode."

"Deal with the injuries, then figure out what happened. That's the way to do it. So you have eleven survivors there?"

"Nine."

"That math doesn't add up."

"We're short two because the hijacker took off up the mountain and one of the passengers went after him."

"After a plane crash and in the middle of the night? Assuming they can walk at all, won't they walk off a cliff?"

"It's a possibility, as is dying of exposure. But they're out there somewhere, alive or dead."

"And that's where Hawk and Lacey will come in."

"Exactly. But not until sunrise. We need to get everyone as stable as possible and then hopefully catch some sleep. If we're going after them later today, we both need some rest, even if it's just an hour or two. Same for Brian and Lacey. We're all exhausted."

"I'm sure you are."

He paused for a moment and Meg could hear his unease in the silence that stretched between them. She let the silence breathe, knowing she needed to move on, but wanting a few last seconds with him.

"I know I said this before you left, but I need you to be careful out there."

"We're being careful." There was no defensiveness in Meg's tone, just assurance.

"As hard as it was to get up there, it may be equally hard going down. And if the hijacker spots you tracking him, you know he has a weapon. He could take to higher ground and simply pick you off. You're exhausted, which could affect your reaction time and reflexes, putting you at an even greater disadvantage."

She refused to lie to him. "I know."

"Working your way down will help keep you safe from the high-altitude illness, but it could put you in great danger. I know you know all this. I just . . . need you to come back to me. Both of you."

She felt for him, felt for the helplessness he must be feeling nearly two thousand miles away, waiting in the dark for any word from her, imagining the worst might be happening at that moment, and he was powerless to assist or to stop it. "I need that too. More than anything. And I will."

"I'm holding you to that." The sound of a heavy exhalation came across the line. "Don't hesitate to reach out again if you need me. I'm not on shift tomorrow and can always sleep late or catch a nap if I'm tired. If I can help you, that's more important. I'll keep my phone close; you keep yours charged."

"I have my battery pack in my bag. It's insanity to be out here with a dead phone, so I won't let that happen. Thanks again. Watch for my texts."

"Always. It was good to hear your voice."

"Ditto. Talk soon. That's a promise." Meg ended the call and then looked to where Laumbach sat with Hawk. She'd go to each survivor and get their emergency contact information to send to the sheriff's office.

Then it was time for the survivors to tell the terrifying tale of what exactly happened on flight BA0649 that ended in so much death and destruction.

CHAPTER 14

Beta: Tips, tricks, or information provided to a climber before a climb to assist in finding the safest or easiest route.

May 7, 3:09 am
Pyramid Peak
Aspen, Colorado

Just under an hour later, two more teams had arrived to relieve Team Four, pitching overnight camp for themselves and the survivors, as well as monitoring the critically injured. First Officer Slaight was holding on—he was still unconscious, but his condition hadn't deteriorated, which everyone considered a win—as was Eliza Sheard, the woman Hensley had stabilized.

Laumbach wanted to stay with Slaight, but Carlisle had asked that he and the more calm and stable survivors of the crash meet together to discuss what had happened. It was late, and they were all exhausted, but the agents wanted this information before they started the search in a few hours, and by dawn they needed to already be on the trail.

Hensley set up his emergency stove—a compact single burner that threw an impressive amount of heat—and had soup warming. Slowly the group gathered around the stove.

"Do I smell chicken soup?" Newall stepped into the light of the stove, his nose in the air like Hawk scenting the target.

Carlisle joined him. "It wouldn't be a rescue with Ben without chicken soup. Everyone with Mountain Rescue Aspen knows to pack for an incident with at least forty-eight hours of food, because you never know if you're going to get stuck on the mountain. Hot foods are a life-saver on a rescue like this. Some people pack coffee and a pot." She slapped a hand on Hensley's shoulder and he grinned up at her. "With Ben, it's always chicken soup."

"It's hot, and it has fluids and salt," Hensley defended. "Exactly what you need at a time like this. And who doesn't love chicken soup?"

"You have a point," said Newall.

Meg and Brian sat on the far side of the stove from Hensley, sharing Brian's sleeping pad to cushion them from the uneven scree; Meg's sleeping pad remained with Jon Slaight. They'd given both dogs the command to greet everyone around the fire, and Hawk and Lacey were making the rounds, comforting the survivors, cheering tired rescuers. Sleep was an oncoming locomotive Meg couldn't stop, and she figured she had about another thirty in her before she lost consciousness. As it was, she and Brian were half-slumped together, propping each other up.

She must have looked as exhausted as she felt.

"You guys look all in." Carlisle looked from Meg to Brian and back again. "Your dogs have more pep than you do."

"The dogs caught a power nap. We've hit a wall." Meg glanced at her fitness tracker. "It's been a twenty-two-hour day for us after all."

"Topped by a strenuous mountain climb and managing an eleven-thousand-foot-plus altitude change," Brian said, so tired his words slightly slurred. "We're going to need some downtime if we're going after someone tomorrow." He paused, as if making connections. "Today. Going after someone later this morning."

"So let's try to get you there. Us too. My second wind is beginning to feel a bit tenuous." Crossing her ankles, Carlisle dropped into a cross-legged sit beside Hensley as she scanned the group, including three of the survivors. "You've had something to eat? Some water?" Murmurs of agreement all around. "Good. We'll get some soup into you to warm you, and then we'll get you bedded down for the night. It's our hope the weather will be clear enough later today to get a chopper in here." She turned to Hensley. "Think we can get one into the saddle if the ceiling rises?"

"That's going to be up to the chopper pilot. He needs a minimum one-hundred-by-one-hundred-foot clear space without an angle greater than five degrees. According to the map there's a location near the middle of the saddle that fits that requirement. Even if the ceiling isn't an issue, the winds still will be. He'd have to get over the ridge and then down into the saddle. It can be done under the right conditions, but that has to be the pilot's call. Command is on it, and once we have light in a few hours, we can advise." His gaze tracked to where the two critical survivors lay, surrounded by rescue personnel. "Needless to say, we want them moved ASAP."

"That's the goal then. Still feels like we're inside a cloud, though." Carlisle glanced at Brian, who hid a giant yawn behind his hand. "Let's get into it. Captain Laumbach—"

"Hugh," Laumbach corrected from where he sat bundled in a blanket, his now-splinted arm set carefully in his lap. "After what you've done for us, we hardly need the formality."

Carlisle smiled her acknowledgment. "When we first arrived, looking for the man who hijacked the plane, you informed me he'd disappeared right after you crash-landed."

"Yes."

"We're also missing one of the passengers."

"Yes. He went after the hijacker. We've seen neither since then."

"You can hardly blame Eli."

All eyes swung to the woman Meg had first seen sitting beside the critically injured female. Meg placed her in her midfifties, and while her navy business suit was filthy and her dingy blouse was missing buttons, she'd tried to straighten herself. She'd even made the attempt to finger comb her short-cut blond hair into place. A white bandage rode her left temple next to a smear of blood running along her hairline. From her stiff posture to her clipped words, she exuded control.

"Eli? Eli Barron? The COO of Barron Pharmaceuticals?" Carlisle clarified.

"Yes."

"Why?"

"Because his father had just been executed in front of him." The woman met Carlisle's gaze unblinkingly, her jaw set and eyes sharp. "Two shots, right to the head."

The other survivors winced or groaned quietly, but Meg's eyes stayed locked on the woman. There were no tears in her voice, simply fury. They'd apparently found the steady hand in the group.

"The flight attendant told us there was a death."

Laumbach sat up straighter, then lost most of his color

and hissed with pain as he inadvertently jostled his arm. "Talia? Talia got word out?"

"Did she tell you about one execution or two?" the woman asked bluntly.

"There was more than one?" Carlisle asked. "In the air?"

"Two in the air. First he killed the security guard, then Kenneth. Didn't faze him one bit. Like swatting a fly."

"Got a straight shooter in this one," Brian murmured low enough only Meg could hear him.

"A little too straight," Meg responded, her eyes on one of the men, who'd turned his face away as if in pain. "Why don't we back up?" Her voice raised, Meg held up one hand. "I feel like we're getting ahead of ourselves. Or at least ahead of us because we're so tired." She looked at Carlisle. "Let's go around the group, making introductions. For those on the plane, tell us who you are, your role at Barron Pharma, and where you were sitting. Then we'll get into what happened in chronological order."

"Agreed, that would be helpful." Carlisle tapped her breastbone. "I'll start. Special Agent Stacey Carlisle, out of the FBI's Denver field office. Special Agent Corey Newall"—Newall raised his hand in greeting—"and I deployed after Ms. Russel contacted one of the Denver air traffic controllers to tell us of the hijacking. Ben?"

"Ben Hensley." Hensley jabbed a thumb toward Fife, on his left. "Rob Fifer. We're Mountain Rescue Aspen. When the call went out about the crash in the mountains, we responded. Meg?"

"I'm Meg Jennings and this is Brian Foster." She shoulder-bumped Brian. "We're from the FBI's Human Scent Evidence Team out of Washington, DC. They sent us to Colorado yesterday afternoon when there were concerns a search might be needed to track the hijacker. We see now that was the correct call. We'll begin that search as soon as day breaks." She scanned the circle to find Hawk, pressed against the man with one arm wrapped around himself, clutching the ribs on his left side. "That's Hawk, my black Lab, and"—she found Lacey across from her being stroked by a dark-skinned man with a gauze patch covering his right eye—"that's Brian's Lacey across the way. They're search-and-rescue dogs, but they also understand people under stress and know how to make them feel better. Right, Hawk?" She surreptitiously gave him the hand gesture for "speak" and he complied with a sharp bark, making everyone laugh.

There was so much tension in the group, a little levity to break the heavy mood was good. The surviving passengers needed to be able to settle in and tell them what happened.

The man with Hawk went next, his smile at the dog's response relaxing some of the harsh grooves that pain had cut into his face. "My name is James Worland. I sit on the board at Barron Pharmaceuticals, and when everything went to hell, I was seated in the main cabin, toward the front." Pain edged deep again, but this time Meg got the impression it wasn't possibly broken ribs, but emotional agony. "I was sitting near Kenneth." He looked to the woman to his left.

"Hannah Jewitt, Barron Pharmaceuticals Board of Directors. I was sitting midway back because Kenneth made sure he was surrounded by only supporters for the flight. He didn't want to talk business and he knew if he sat beside me, we'd be wasting no time."

She turned her laser-sharp gaze on the remaining survivor in the group, who hunched into himself slightly under the blanket. The youngest in the group—Meg placed him in his late thirties—he wore khaki slacks with a blue button-down and suede oxfords, all showing the wear and tear of what he'd experienced. He looked battered and beaten, but the gauze covering his right eye appeared to be his only medical intervention.

"Andrew Blenn," he said, under the weight of Jewitt's gaze, "Barron board, and I was sitting closer to the back."

"What was the setup of the plane?" Newall asked. "Private jets can be configured in multiple ways."

"Big leather chairs facing each other, with a table in between so passengers had the option to work during the flight," Laumbach said. "One run of seats on one side, two on the other, with the aisle between them. Lavatory at the rear of the plane, as well as the kitchen area with the flight attendant's jump seat for takeoff and landing. Jon and I were up front."

"Did the cockpit door lock?"

"Not on that plane. A door that closed to give the passengers privacy, but there was nothing to stop anyone from coming into the cockpit." His face went hard. "And didn't."

"Let's start at the beginning so you're telling a coherent story rather than jumping in partway through," said Carlisle. "You boarded the plane at the Peyton Airfield. From the passenger manifest, it was all seven of the board of directors, Kenneth and Eli Barron, CEO and COO of Barron Pharmaceuticals, CFO Eliza Sheard, junior assistant Nora Gleason, and two security guards—Patrick Connolly and Sid Drubek. As well as Captain Hugh Laumbach, First Officer Jon Slaight, and flight attendant Talia Russel. Who took control of the aircraft?"

"Sid," said Blenn.

Carlisle locked on Blenn's words. "Sid Drubek was the hijacker?"

"No one saw it coming. Sid was always the friendly one. Always said hello, always was pleasant." Blenn's brows drew together in consternation. "He remembered the names of my kids and asked about them specifically. And then he goes and pulls a gun on us?" Outrage goosed his final question.

Meg pulled out her satellite phone. Brian leaned in to watch as she called up her contacts, selected McCord, and started a text message to him.

"Sending McCord out on search?" he murmured.

Meg glanced sideways to find Brian only inches away. "You know he's going to want to be on top of this. And he already has the lay of the land. All I'm doing is pointing him in the right direction. Though I'm going to be nice and send it as a giant text message that will get split up into multiple messages all at once rather than a series of alerts while I'm typing it in, to keep him awake for the next thirty minutes."

"Not to mention, he'll ask questions you won't be able to answer. You're giving him everything we know right now. He won't be able to help himself."

"That's how guns got onto the plane?" Newall asked, bringing Meg and Brian back to the main conversation. "If you'd gone through a regular commercial airport, firearms wouldn't be permitted. But in a private facility, Barron and his son would have been in control."

"Them being in control was bringing their own security," said Worland. "We weren't involved in the day-to-day operations, but we knew about the death threats."

"From who?"

"They always came in anonymously, but there were multiple threats. Kenneth and Eli reported them to the authorities, but knew if there was a real risk, law enforcement couldn't be present enough to protect them, so they used private security, contracted by a reputable local company."

"Until that private security turned on them," Jewitt said crisply.

Worland stared at her in disgust. "Do you have any compassion at all? People are dead. *We* nearly died!"

"Because of their carelessness." Jewitt's words lashed. "They allowed that man on the plane and we nearly died."

Worland took a breath, as if to shoot back a rejoinder, but the pain in his ribs had that breath catching in agony.

"Are you okay?" Carlisle asked.

"Ribs are on fire. Other than that, I'm great," Worland wheezed, the sarcasm unmistakable even through clenched teeth.

"Rest for a minute and we'll come back to you." Carlisle turned to Blenn. "So the two security guards had firearms. Anyone else?"

"No."

"Hugh, were you aware there were weapons on the plane?"

"Yes. We'd fly with Barron, or Barron and his son, at least a few times a month. For the last nine or twelve months, they were accompanied by security guards who were always armed. That was the point. They were there for protection."

"Was it always the same two guards?"

"No. During that time Patrick was always there, but they had a couple of different guys, and then they had Sid. He's been there for months now."

"You need to speak to Gloria Seghers, Kenneth's executive assistant," said Jewitt. "She organizes everything for him. Normally, she would have been on this flight, but she's eight and a half months pregnant. Her doctor told her she was too far along to risk something going wrong while they were in the air, so she did all the organizing and then sent a junior assistant to make sure everything went off without a hitch at the annual meeting." For a brief moment sorrow flitted across her face. "And the poor girl died, simply because they told her to sit at the rear of the plane near the galley so she was out of the way. When the plane broke apart, she and the flight attendant were in the tail section that ripped away." She sighed, and for a moment her hard edges softened, but then she snapped them abruptly back into place.

Armor, Meg thought. *It's her protection to get her through this experience. She's not as hard as she appears.*

"Anything you need to know about this trip, Gloria will have the information," Jewitt continued. "She can give you the work histories of everyone on the plane. She can tell you how they hired their security guards. I'm sure they came via some firm recommended to them by someone they trusted. They wouldn't just hire anyone off the street when their lives were on the line."

"And look how that turned out," Blenn muttered. "Kenneth is dead and his son may be, too, by this time."

"Let's keep things in order instead of jumping around," Newall said. "How long were you in the air before things went sideways?"

"About ten minutes," said Laumbach. "It was a low ceiling, with high winds, but Barron insisted we get off the ground on time. We were on our way to a cruising altitude of thirty-two thousand feet, where the flight would have been smooth above the clouds. We stayed in the pattern longer to gain altitude before taking a western heading toward the mountains. When I heard the shot and the first screams, we were only just over eleven thousand feet."

"You checked your altitude?"

"Whenever something goes wrong, the first thing you do is prepare for an emergency landing, just in case. You check your altitude, speed, and location. All subsequent decisions come from the scenario and those factors."

Carlisle looked at the three passengers. "What happened in the main cabin? And where was Drubek?"

"We were settling in for the flight," Worland said. "Still belted in as we were climbing. Drubek and Connolly were at the front of the cabin, closest to the door and the cockpit. I'd flown with them before, and once they'd checked the plane before boarding, they were the last ones on and the first ones off, so they always sat in the pair of chairs nearest the door, and the rest of us were behind them." He paused, his eyes narrowing in thought as his lips compressed into a flat line. "The way they were sitting . . . the chairs were facing each other, but Drubek was sitting facing into the main cabin so he could see everything but the cockpit. He would have been able to see down to the galley at the far end. Connolly was facing him, so he'd only see the cockpit."

"So Drubek knew where everyone was and that they were belted into place."

"Yes."

"What did he do?"

"I didn't see it directly." Worland looked from Jewitt to Blenn. "Did anyone else?"

Both shook their heads.

"I hadn't reviewed last year's annual meeting minutes," Jewitt said, "so I was using the time of the flight to review that document before the upcoming meeting. I heard the gunshot, but didn't see it."

"I think he just pulled his gun out and shot Connolly. There was no argument; they both seemed in good spirits getting on the plane, with us and with each other. He just . . . executed him."

"I saw the wound when we dragged his body out," said Blenn. "One shot center of the forehead. Would have died instantly."

"They're still seated at that point?" Newall asked.

"Yes. We had to unbuckle Connolly's body to move him."

"So Drubek kills Connolly, then what?"

"By the time I looked up," Jewitt said, "he was standing, so he must have already unbuckled his belt in preparation. He told us to stay seated and belted in. He pulled Connolly's gun and then opened the cockpit door. He stayed in the doorway, pointing one gun at the pilots and the other at us with his left hand so we wouldn't try to rush him."

"He opened the door and put the gun to my head," said Laumbach. "Told Jon to deactivate the ACARS so we'd vanish off the radar, and then told me to set the autopilot for the current speed and altitude." He reached up with his free hand and rubbed the back of his head as if still feeling the pressure of the barrel.

"Would that have knocked out the Wi-Fi?" Worland asked.

Laumbach looked at him sharply. "No, they're totally different systems. Was it down?"

"Yeah. I was scrolling my phone. When we were on the ground, no problem, I was connected to the local cell tower. But once we were in the air, I tried to connect to the plane's Wi-Fi. No go."

"The plane normally has a Wi-Fi connection for the passengers?" Newall asked.

Laumbach nodded. "It's an air-to-ground Wi-Fi system. We've never had a problem with it, which makes me think it was sabotaged, considering the timing."

"Would Drubek be able to do it?"

"Yes, for a couple of reasons. His habit before any flight was to check the plane over before Kenneth and Eli boarded, while Connolly stayed with the Barrons. All part of the process, he'd say. The first few times I'd bring him on myself, but after that, he'd come on and do the check solo and then give the all clear."

"Did he do that today?"

"Yes."

"Could he disable the air-to-ground Wi-Fi in the time it took for him to do his check?"

"Absolutely."

"And he'd know how to do it? Where to find it and how to disable it?"

"The first time I brought him on, he expressed real interest in the plane. Asked all kinds of smart questions about it. It was months ago, so I don't remember him asking about Wi-Fi specifically, but it would've been the kind of question he'd have asked. Where it was and how it worked. He could have found out in other ways how to disable it, then could have done it last minute this morning while he was alone on the plane. No one would have noticed until we were in the air. By then, it was too late."

"But it meant no one could alert anyone on the ground about the hijacking via that system," said Fife.

"We wouldn't have known about it, if it wasn't for Ms. Russel," said Carlisle. "Otherwise, you would have quietly disappeared from radar and no one would have been the wiser until reports of the crash came in or you were missed at the airport in Napa." She scanned the faces of the survivors. "I think that was the point. He wanted you all to die, and didn't want any outside force getting in his way. And if that meant his own life, then so be it."

CHAPTER 15

Running Beta: Information provided to the climber during the route.

May 7, 3:23 AM
Pyramid Peak
Aspen, Colorado

"Back to the sequence of events," said Carlisle. "Drubek came into the cockpit with a gun and had you set the autopilot."

"Right," said Laumbach. "I argued we were too low and the winds were too strong and we needed to be higher, but when he nearly rammed the muzzle of the gun through my skull, I did it. That was when I knew we were screwed. He didn't care if we lived or died when he had me set the altitude for twelve thousand five hundred feet, with us heading into the Elk Mountains. Then he herded us into the main cabin. Kenneth was screaming at Drubek, but Drubek pushed us past him, then shut him up by pointing the gun at his head and asking if he wanted to end up like Connolly."

"What was everyone else doing at this point?"

"Mostly sitting shocked, but I could see Eli and Ajay were coordinating something between them. The plane was being tossed around by the turbulence and they were probably hoping Drubek would lose his balance, since he was standing while the rest of us were sitting. If he'd gotten off balance, Eli and Ajay would try to take him down."

"Ajay Varma, who also sits on the board?" Newall turned to look behind him to the passengers who hadn't joined them. "Where's he?"

"Getting bedded down with the rest of the survivors," Hensley said. "Grade-three concussion and upper-arm through-and-through GSW. He lost a moderate amount of blood, so he's resting instead of being here, with us. I think he'll be clearer if you get his story later."

"We'll do that. So they were making plans to jump Drubek?"

"That's what I think," said Worland. "They're the two youngest among us, and Ajay is the athletic type. But Drubek cut that off quickly by putting his gun to Eli's head. He was seated across from his father, and that stopped Kenneth in his tracks."

"Drubek then asked Kenneth how he could live with himself," said Jewitt, "knowing he was killing people by the thousands. Kenneth denied it, but Drubek insisted his drugs were responsible for all those deaths and for ripping apart happy families."

"There has to be personal experience, personal pain, behind that," Brian pointed out. "There's no way Drubek did this because of someone else's loss. When we dig into this guy, we're going to find he lost someone and blamed it on Barron Pharma. And the Barron family, personally."

"He asked Barron why he should spare his son's life, and Barron pleaded with him to put the gun down and they'd talk it out," said Blenn.

"Sid let Kenneth carry on for a couple of minutes," Jewitt said. "You could see he was enjoying Kenneth's desperation. Kenneth was trying to diffuse the situation, telling Sid he could have whatever he wanted, all the money he wanted, as long as he'd remove the gun from his son's head and let the pilots return to the cockpit."

"It appears Drubek went to an immense amount of effort to set up this scenario," said Meg. "It sounds like he couldn't be bought off with offers of money."

Blenn's laugh had a razor-sharp edge to it. "Definitely not. He said no amount of money could fix what Barron and his company had done."

"He said a fish rots from the head down, and the only way to fix it was to chop off the head," Jewitt stated. "That's not the attitude of someone you can negotiate with."

"Chopping off Barron Pharma's head by taking out the executive officers and the board of directors," Newall stated. "Did Barron understand it wasn't just his son's life in the balance? Did his son?"

"They knew we were all going to die if we stayed on course," Laumbach said. "I made it clear when we went into the main cabin, so everyone knew the danger we were in. We only had minutes." He met Worland's gaze. "I know we were all thinking the same thing. Flight 93."

With those words Meg understood exactly what had happened onboard the Gulfstream. United Flight 93, the plane scheduled to fly from Newark, New Jersey, to San Francisco, California, before it was hijacked on September 11, 2001. Because it was the fourth and final plane to be hijacked, the passengers onboard had learned of the three previous hijackings and crashes, and worked together to fight back, dying in their attempt when the plane crashed near Shanksville, Pennsylvania. But, for their heroic efforts, they'd denied the hijackers their highly prized target in Washington, DC, possibly the White House or the Capitol Building. Their sacrifice had saved hundreds of lives and kept the country from potentially falling into unbridled chaos.

Clearly, the passengers on BA0649 regarded this as a similar *Let's roll* moment. Fortunately, they were successful, but they'd only had one hijacker to deal with.

"Yeah," Worland agreed. "If we were going to die anyway, we had nothing to lose in trying to survive. I could tell from the looks everyone was exchanging we were all on the same page. We needed to bring Drubek down so the captain could get back to the controls."

"I think he knew it," Blenn said. "He'd been enjoying Kenneth groveling for his son's life, probably reveling in the power and control, but then he swung the gun toward Kenneth and pulled the trigger. Twice." He shuddered. "Blood and brains everywhere."

"Eli lost it." Worland continued the story. "Was out of his seat and on Drubek and didn't care if he got shot in the attempt. Ajay had surreptitiously unbuckled by that time and leaped in to help in the fight for the gun. That's when he got shot."

"While they were struggling, I climbed over the seats beside them to get to the cockpit. Jon was right behind me. The plane was tossing like crazy, but we managed to stagger into the cockpit, turn off the autopilot, and then struggle to get our altitude up. We passed off the controls while we each buckled in." Laumbach's gaze slid to where his copilot lay. "Good thing too . . . I don't think we'd have survived otherwise."

"Could you see anything?" Carlisle asked.

"Nothing. It was like flying in pea soup. I had the controls, and the one goal under those conditions was simply to get up and over any mountain in front of us. If I'd had visuals, I'd have been able to fly through a gap, but there was nothing. And then a mountain wave downdraft caught us and slammed us into the mountain. We must have hit some kind of ridge, because the plane was ripped apart and then we were skidding down a slope. I knew the main cabin had ruptured from the sound, but didn't realize the fuselage had been cleaved in two until we stopped. The fact we lost the engines with the tail section might have helped our chances of survival, because artificial thrust stopped at that moment and it was strictly inertia and the slope carrying us down after that. The friction of the slide helped stop us."

"What happened in the main cabin?" Carlisle asked the board members.

"Eli and Ajay were struggling with Drubek when we hit," said Blenn. "The force of the strike was shocking, and rocked everyone. Everything not tied down went flying in different directions, but most of us were still belted in, so we stayed in place and tried to protect our heads from the briefcases and laptops flying around. Jin must have taken off his seat belt, getting ready to help Eli when we hit, because he was thrown against the ceiling. I think he must have died instantly. Eli and Drubek ended up wedged under a table, between two chairs, but Ajay went flying. That's probably when he got his concussion."

"Then we were skidding along a level surface," Worland said, "until we finally came to a halt. I was still trying to piece together what had happened, when Drubek stumbled by and then went out the gaping hole in the rear of the plane. He'd taken advantage of the chaos and run. Or limped. Some of us are more badly injured than others, but none of us are untouched. There's no way he is."

"Honestly, I'm surprised there were only three deaths in the crash," Brian said. "We kind of expected the worst."

"Us too," muttered Blenn.

"Modern plane design seems a little miraculous to me, even though I fly one regularly," Laumbach said. "They have to be designed so all passengers can evacuate in no more than ninety seconds. For larger planes it's multiple egress locations and slides. For smaller planes it's the same stairs used to board, which we got down on the far side of the plane." He looked toward the wreckage of the plane, now lit with emergency lighting, the lingering cloud giving it a ghostly glow as light bounced off moisture in the air. "Though we had a new exit location with the loss of the tail. But planes themselves are designed to be able to withstand an amazing amount of force and the aftermath of a crash. Seats that can withstand sixteen g's, a strengthened fuselage, landing gear designed to break off when a plane hits the ground, nitrogen pumps in the fuel tanks to suppress flames and prevent explosions, flame-resistant cabin components, and better exit lighting on the floor to lead the way out. It's meant to keep people alive inside the aircraft, slow the inevitable fire, and get passengers out quickly."

"How much time did you have before the fire started?" Newall asked.

"Started or got out of hand? It would have started pretty much immediately. A spark and some spilled fuel would be all it would take. But then it would spread to what was left in the tanks. And considering we hadn't gone far, they were practically full. We had maybe four minutes. Enough time to get the stairs down for a second exit, gather blankets and emergency flashlights, move the injured, and then those who were most mobile returned for the dead. Everyone was moving fast; no one wanted to be onboard if it turned into an inferno or, worse, exploded."

"Was Eli Barron helping you?"

"As soon as Eli realized Drubek was on the move, he was after him," Jewitt said. "Jumped out of the plane and went after him as fast as he could."

"Do you think it was his intention to catch him?"

"I think it was his intention to kill him," Worland said. "He picked up a gun from where it had landed under one of the seats before he exited the plane. His father died before his eyes. Knowing Eli—he'll be looking for retribution."

Carlisle eyed him sharply. "He's the eye-for-an-eye sort?"

"Oh yes. You don't cross Eli Barron without paying the price for it." Jewitt's tone was biting. "He takes after his father that way. Ruthless businessmen, inside and out."

"I'm sure you had low visibility, but at least it was daylight. Did anyone see where they went?" Meg asked. "The dogs will follow the trail, but you'll save time at daybreak when we start if anyone saw them go."

"I did." Blenn pointed past the nose of the plane, due south, up the saddle. "That way. Last I saw of Eli, he was heading toward that ridge, but then he disappeared into the fog. I guess they never made it down, or you'd have known more about the crash site."

"We certainly didn't see either of them," Hensley said. "But by the time we came, it was dark and the visibility was near nil. If I'm judging the route placement properly, they were to the south of us. But none of the other teams farther to the south reported spotting them."

"I don't know how they could have safely managed a climb in these conditions. Maybe they didn't get very far," Blenn suggested.

"Does anyone know if either of them are climbers?" asked Newall.

Blenn shrugged. "I doubt Eli is. He never seemed to leave the office. The job was his life, just like it was his father's. Kenneth always said Barron Pharmaceuticals was his legacy."

"It will be now, in more ways than one," muttered Jewitt.

Carlisle stared at her. "Clarify something for me, Ms. Jewitt. You're extremely negative about this company and the people in it. Yet *you're* a part of it."

"I've been a part of this company's board since they formed one. It's a private company; they didn't have to. That was back in the days of old Mr. Barron, Charles, Kenneth's father. Private companies aren't required to have a board of directors, but some have them because it shows accountability to their investors. Charles wanted that investment and put together the first slate of directors. I was on that board."

"And you're still on it because it's a paid position? What form is that payment?"

"For me it's money. Some people took stock options. I would have made more, had I done that, but I don't need the retainer income I get from the company. I'm independently wealthy, and taking stock options was a buy-in I wasn't comfortable with in the last decade."

"If you weren't happy with the company, why didn't you quit?"

"I stayed on in Charles's memory, may he rest in peace, these last fifteen years." Jewitt's face softened as she said the elder Mr. Barron's name before smoothing out into neutral lines. "When something is broken, if you want to fix it, the best way to do it is from the inside. I'm sure Kenneth was never fond of me, because I was always the voice trying to check his plans. Had I left the board, he would have had almost no pushback. I wasn't entirely successful, but had I not been there, how much worse would it have been?"

"You were aware of the issue around the narcotics Barron Pharma produced?"

"Yes."

"And benefited from the sale of them?"

"No. I would have, had I taken stock options." Her icy gaze passed over Worland and Blenn, her meaning crystal clear. "I did not. My remuneration did not change, no matter how well the company did. Or poorly."

Hawk wandered to Meg, who ran a hand down his back, but kept her eyes on Jewitt, mentally readjusting her internal read on the woman. She came off as brash and abrasive, stiff and exacting with her armor. But maybe she'd been the only clear-eyed one in the bunch, and that stiff spine had allowed her to speak her mind and call the shots as she saw them. It had also carried her through this crisis.

"Drubek and Eli Barron." Newall brought them back to the immediate situation. "What are the chances they survive the night?"

"That depends," said Fife. "How prepared were they? I'd assume not at all, but what were they wearing? It also depends if they could find some sort of shelter. Assuming, of course, they didn't die before nightfall from a fall, and we haven't found their bodies yet."

"Drubek was wearing a black winter jacket when he got on the plane, which he didn't take off," said Worland.

"He always wore heavy black boots, with black pants and a black Henley-style shirt," Laumbach interjected. "Kenneth didn't want his security guards to blend; he wanted them to look big and tough to dissuade people from bothering him. No suit and tie to blend in with the business crowd, just basic black. And no concealed carry; he wanted the fact they were armed to be front and center. I don't know about his son though."

"Eli was casual, at least for the travel part of this meeting," said Worland. "Jeans, I think?"

"Jeans and a Stanford University hoodie. Sneakers,"

Blenn added. "But Eli's not stupid. Aggressive and competitive, but not stupid. He grabbed someone's winter jacket from the chaos in there before he left. No idea whose. Likely, not his own. It was red; too colorful for Eli."

"But it sounds like no gloves or hats for either of them," Fife said. "And it's cold here tonight. Hasn't hit freezing yet, but it's close. And the winds are biting. Come daylight, we may find neither of them made it."

Meg remembered what Todd had told her about the limits of temperature on the human body, when they were looking for survivors following the collapse of Talbot Terraces, and how between extreme hot and cold temperatures, the human body could survive cold much longer than heat. If the clouds cleared later today and the temperatures rose with the sun, they might make it after all.

"Alive or dead, the dogs will track them. And that's our cue. Lacey, come." Brian pushed to his feet. "We need to bed down for an hour or two, or we won't be useful to you once the sun rises."

He held out a hand for Meg, who hurriedly ended off the text message to McCord, letting him know she and Brian would be sleeping for the next few hours. She slapped her hand into his, and he hauled her to her feet.

Brian grabbed his sleeping pad and tucked it under his arm like it was a surfboard. "Ben, where do you suggest we go for a little shut-eye?"

Hensley pointed to the far wall of the saddle. "Don't go far, but I understand if you want to pull back from the noise and lights a bit. I'd say circle around to the far side of the plane. Everyone is on this side; it's darker and quieter over there. We need to get some rest, too, so we'll join you there shortly. But I want you to do something first. I know you're exhausted, and have managed the change in altitude way better than I thought you would, but I want you each to do five minutes of oxygen therapy. As well as you're doing, your oxygen is low, and this will push it higher while you sleep, which will then be more restorative. Then another five tomorrow morning before we head out." His gaze dropped to the dogs. "We don't have a canine mask for them, but I'd like to see the same treatment for them."

"We'll see if we can get the human mask to work. We may lose some of the oxygen with them, but it's still better than breathing this air, right?"

"Right."

"We'll do that now. Thanks for the suggestion."

A couple of Mountain Rescue Aspen rescuers from the new teams helped them with their oxygen therapy, and, while Meg and Brian were being treated, jury rigged a mask cover for the dogs' muzzles, using plastic bags, which they had Meg and Brian hold in place while their dogs took their turn. Neither of them liked the hiss and airflow of the pressurized oxygen, but both sat quietly under their handlers' touch and praise.

Their treatments finished, Meg had to admit she felt more at ease. She hadn't thought she'd been struggling in the low oxygen atmosphere, but bringing her level up made her realize her body had been under stress from the atmospheric conditions. Added to that, the fire-fouled air had only compounded the situation.

"Let's get settled so we're out of the way when everyone else comes in," Meg said to Brian and then led the way around the rear of the plane to the darker side, away from the misty glow of the emergency lighting.

"Hopefully, they won't wake us when they settle down around us."

"I don't think that will be a problem for me. I'm practically asleep on my feet. The mountain could fall and I'd sleep through it."

Meg led Hawk a short distance away from the crash site proper, Brian and Lacey trailing behind. No spot would be truly comfortable to make camp for the night, not on a giant field of scree, but some spots were better than others, and they found a flat span of fairly level rock near the rim of the saddle large enough for two sleeping bags side by side.

"This work for you?"

"Standing straight up and leaning against the ridge wall would work for me currently." Brian slung his backpack off and unzipped it, looking for his sleeping supplies. "We've been awake for almost a whole day at this point, and if I don't get some shut-eye, I'm going to be useless to-morrow. Correction, today." He dragged out and unrolled his sleep bag. "You gave the copilot your sleeping pad. Want to share mine?"

"It's hardly big enough for you, let alone you and me. But thanks. Fife got me another one from one of the new teams and showed me how to inflate it with the pump sack." She inflated her sleeping pad, then pulled out her sleeping bag and bivouac sack and made quick work of unrolling both, fitting the waterproof, yet breathable, Gore-Tex bivouac bag around the sleeping bag and laying it out over the pad.

Brian eyed her sleeping arrangement. "That thing looks like a waterproof coffin."

"As long as it keeps me and Hawk warm and dry, while still letting us breathe, then I don't care what it looks like. I might be uncomfortable if I was trying to get eight hours in this thing, because there will be next to zero room, but we're only in it for the short term." Pulling a spare fleece shirt from her pack, she rolled it into a makeshift pillow. She unzipped the sleeping bag, then sat to unlace her boots and pulled them off, stuffing them into her pack to stay dry in case of precipitation, and slid into the sleeping bag in her socks. "Hawk, come here, boy."

Hawk wound around Brian, who was setting up his own sleeping bag and bivouac sack next to her, to stand beside Meg.

"This is going to be cozy in the extreme." Meg lay down on her side and patted the space in front of her. "Come here, Hawk. Lay down."

Hawk gave her a tilted-head look, clearly expressing his confusion, but did as commanded, lying down on his side against the curve of Meg's stomach so his head fit neatly under her chin. She tugged the sleeping bag zipper around him until it was nearly at his head, leaving room for him to breathe. Then she pulled the bivouac up, ready to shelter them.

Brian climbed into his sleeping bag and arranged Lacey beside him. "You good?"

"It's not the Ritz-Carlton, but as I'll be unconscious in about forty-five seconds, it doesn't have to be. What time are we getting up?"

"Better aim for at least a half hour before sunup. Enough time to eat and get ready for the next challenge."

"Works for me. I'll set an alarm on my phone. Night, you two." He flipped the top of the bivouac sack over his head.

"Night." Meg snuggled in a little farther and covered herself and Hawk with the top of her own bivouac, then zipped it up to just leave a few inches open for air exchange over their heads.

She pulled her dog in closer, his fur so cold, the chill had to go right down to his bones. But their combined body heat built quickly in the enclosed space and soon Meg felt her muscles relaxing, though the spot of her back where the rock had struck still ached dully. Hawk let out a long, exhausted sigh, his body going loose. She stroked a hand over his side a few times, making sure he was comfortable and resting easy.

The first raindrop struck the bivouac, sounding like a pebble hitting the Gore-Tex, snapping her eyes open. It was quickly followed by a patter of drops and then a steady stream. In the background Meg could hear rescuers working to get everyone into dry shelters.

I guess Sheriff Cox's left knee was correct after all.

The rain lulled, and, warm and dry with her dog, Meg let sleep take her.

CHAPTER 16

Switchback: A location on a route where the path turns 180 degrees.

May 7, 5:13 AM
Pyramid Peak
Aspen, Colorado

Meg and Brian were up as the first fingers of dawn lightened the sky.

The clouds had lifted—not away, but higher—and even though it remained overcast with a biting wind, as light filtered through, they got their first real look at where the plane had crashed. Walking across rocks still wet from showers that had ended sometime in the last half hour, approaching the gaping hole of the plane's main cabin, they could now see the details they'd missed the night before in the dark and dense mist.

It was impossible to miss where the plane had been driven into the ridgeline. A huge bite was taken out of the edge of the cliff, a deep curve carved through stone, opening into a ragged trough that cut down the slope of the saddle, spraying rock as easily as if it were a wake behind a boat skimming over the waves. Debris was strewn around the trail—

twisted bits of metal and wood, scattered electrical components, and crushed mechanical machinery.

"What's that?" Meg pointed to a glimpse of white against the gray landscape about ten feet away.

"What?"

She stepped carefully over the scree and bent to pick up the single, saturated piece of paper, gently loosening it from where one edge had been caught under a rock. She held it between thumb and forefinger, water dripping rhythmically onto the rocks below. Minus the rainwater, it looked essentially untouched, except for the torn edge in the top right corner, exactly where a staple would be. Across the top it read: *Barron Pharmaceuticals Annual Meeting,* followed by a date the previous May and *Meeting Minutes*. She dropped the paper back onto the rocks.

"This must have been part of the document Hannah Jewitt was reading. It got sucked out of the plane after the tail broke off, so it avoided the fire that gutted anything left inside the cabin."

"Speaking of which." Brian turned around and headed for the rear of the fuselage.

Even twelve hours after the fire, the wreckage still vaguely smoked and reeked of burned chemicals and electronics. Inside, the devastation was unmistakable.

Fire had ripped through the cabin, destroying everything it touched. The walls were stripped down to the soot-covered metal struts and shell of the plane, though now a long gash in the roof of the cabin running from the missing tail section almost all the way to the cockpit let the weak morning light trickle in. The windows remained intact, but were thick with soot the rain hadn't been able to wash away. The rough conformation of the cabin setup could still be discerned, though the foam, fabric, and leather of the custom chairs was burned to ash, leaving only the heat-twisted metal frames. The tables between the sets of the seats were destroyed, though in some places the hint of the floor mount poking through the rubble remained. Far ahead of the passenger compartment, the cracked windshield of the cockpit revealed a similar devastation.

Brian whistled. "Not a thing left to salvage here."

"No. They had fuel to get them all the way to the Pacific, so once the tanks caught, it must have been a hell of a blaze." Meg peered at the clouds overhead. "If the ceiling had been a bit higher, we'd have been able to pinpoint the crash site from the light given off by the flames. But it was socked in and visibility was too limited."

"Kept them warm, though. That likely saved a few of the more badly injured survivors. Obviously, from the rain, it didn't go below freezing last night, but I think it came within a degree or two of it. Cold enough for hypothermia, which would have been even more deadly for them."

"I suspect you're correct." Meg raised a hand to cover her mouth as she coughed several times, the acrid fumes of the spent fire irritating her lungs. "This wreck reeks." As Meg turned away, her satellite phone sounded an incoming text. She pulled it out. "It's McCord."

"Responding to last night's info?"

"Yeah." She led Brian and the dogs away from the wreckage and into clearer air. "He's worried he's waking us. He knows he's two hours ahead, but wanted to catch us before we start out on the search. Let's make this easier." She dialed McCord's cell phone.

McCord answered on the first ring. "You're up."

"Brian's with me and you're on speaker. We're up. We got a solid ninety minutes down, which was a huge help. As was another oxygen treatment."

"You're not having difficulty with the altitude?"

"We are, but we're managing. So are Hawk and Lacey, because they're troopers. But no sign of the serious symptoms Todd's worried about, so that's good. You got my text landslide from last night?"

"Sure did, thanks. It woke me when it came in. And then, since I was up and it was just before six, I got to work, so I've been at it for a while. And have hit a bit of a wall."

Brian's raised eyebrows mimicked Meg's surprise. "You?"

"Even us superstar investigative reporters can hit walls. But I'm good at climbing over them, given enough time."

"What's the wall?"

"You sent me everyone's name and position in the company. Then you outlined what happened during the flight. The obvious first place to start was with Sid Drubek. Only one problem there—Drubek doesn't exist."

"Weren't the Barron Pharma security guards contracted out by an outside firm?" Brian asked. "And wouldn't you think that outside firm would do its due diligence to make sure the people they hired for *security* are who they say they are?"

"You would think so. On the surface Sid Drubek seems to be a real person. In reality he probably either is, or was, a real person. But the Sid Drubek who works for Barron Pharma doesn't appear to be. He's a construct with just enough information to pass a basic scan, but that's about it. At least that's what it looks like so far, but I'm just getting started. I wanted you to know where you're looking for motive to explain this, it's probably the wrong place."

"It's clear Drubek . . . or whoever he is," clarified Meg, "carried a real grudge against Barron Pharma. Enough of a grudge he was willing to die to take the Barron executives and the board of directors with him. In fact, I'm not sure that would qualify as a 'grudge.' More like 'retribution.'"

"That's someone who's suffered real loss," Brian said. "He's willing to go down with the plane to make sure the job gets done. It's someone who has nothing left to lose."

"Or live for," said McCord. "But now he's on the run. Which makes you wonder if he even knows who lived or who died during the crash."

"It sounds like he didn't stay long enough to find out."

"You have to wonder if he'd circle back to find out."

"Maybe." Meg turned to study the survivors of the crash. Some of them were still bedded down, but a few of them were now up and about, getting cookstove coffee and being given some basic MRE supplies to stave off hunger until the day's rescues were fully planned. "But that might depend on whether Drubek knows he was followed by Eli Barron. If he knows someone is after him, escape is likely his only thought."

"Not to mention," Brian said, "if he has any reasoning skills, even if he didn't know the flight attendant had made contact with the ground, he'd have to know someone was going to notice a missing aircraft at some point and a search would be launched."

"Also, any plane hitting the ground wouldn't do so quietly," added McCord. "The reason you guys are physically where you are is because people reported the sound of a crash high in the mountains. They might not have known what happened, but they knew it was something unusual. Drubek has to be weighing his options—come back to finish the job and risk his life in jail if he gets caught, or set his sights on escape."

"There's one other aspect to any escape plan you aren't thinking of, because you aren't here," Meg said. "It's not just a matter of circling back around a few city blocks and taking another stab at it. Every step up here puts your life at risk. I can't see him returning, because he'd never make it. I see two options for him. Either he wants to take himself out on his own terms, in which case he can simply step out into thin air at numerous locations and it's over in seconds. Or he's going to try to escape and start over, knowing he at least had the satisfaction of terrorizing and then ending the man he held most responsible for . . . whatever it is that's driving him."

"So it's the usual division of labor for us," McCord said. "You guys get the bad guy. I'm going to figure out what made him tick. I'm sure the FBI will do the same, so if you hear anything useful, let me know. But I'll be trying to suss out what happened through channels they'd never use. Do me a favor?"

"Sure."

"Be careful up there. I have plans to attend a wedding in less than two weeks, and I'd really like for those plans to remain unchanged."

"I think we can all safely say that," said Brian. "Let me assure you, we're doing our best."

"All any of us can ask. Keep in touch with someone when you can. We're sharing info as it's coming in. I'll let Todd, Cara, and Ryan know you're heading out on search."

"Thanks. Talk soon, McCord." Meg ended the call. "Let's find the teams and get organized." She considered the slowly lightening sky. "They're going to be on the move. We need to be as well."

CHAPTER 17

Exposure: The empty space surrounding a climber at high altitudes, especially if there is a high probability of injury from a fall due to steep terrain.

May 7, 5:47 AM
Pyramid Peak
Aspen, Colorado

When Meg and Brian returned to camp after talking to McCord, they found Carlisle and Newall standing with their full packs at their feet, waiting for Hensley and Fife as they met with the other Mountain Rescue Aspen rescuers. One of their teammates was on a radio, passing on information to command and to the other members of the team.

Brian raised a hand in greeting as they approached. "Are we ready to head out?"

"We are," Carlisle said. "You need to get your gear together still?"

"No." Meg pointed toward the plane. "We left our bags where we bedded down last night, but we're packed and ready to go. What about Hensley and Fife?"

"They're getting the update from Mountain Rescue Aspen command this morning." Newall studied the clouds.

"Hensley is hoping they'll get a chopper, if not two, here this morning. At the very least, Sheard and Slaight need to be airlifted out as soon as possible. If they can only manage one chopper, assuming the weather holds, it can make multiple runs. Some of the passengers and the rescue teams can make it down on foot." Newall seemed to sense Brian's question and cut him off. "Not the way we came up." He pointed down the saddle to where Sievers Mountain rose in an unimpeded view. "They'll take the saddle north and then go northwest and down again. Fife says they have just under two thousand feet to go to get down to Maroon Creek Road, and most of it's a long, slow, steady decline. They might need to rope them down the last four hundred feet or so, but other than that, it's the long way for distance, but the safest route."

"That's really all that matters." Meg eyed the group of rescuers. "But Fife and Hensley stay with us?"

"Yes."

"While we're waiting for them, let me update you on McCord's latest intel."

"That's your reporter?" Carlisle asked.

"Yes. I sent him the info we learned from the survivors last night. He's been researching and has learned something important." Meg briefly caught the two agents up on McCord's findings concerning Drubek's identity.

"That's definitely something we need to know," Carlisle said when Meg finished. "We would have arrived at the same conclusion ourselves, but he's saved us that time."

"As we said, you won't regret working with him."

"Sure sounds like it." Newall's gaze was fixed on Hensley and Fife as they approached. "We ready to move out?"

Hensley settled his pack on his shoulders, buckled the waist strap, and yanked it tight. "Yes."

"Is air rescue coming?"

"Flight For Life Colorado is sending a helicopter."

"The ceiling is high enough?"

"For now, it is. Richardson is riding the stick for this flight and says he can make it."

"The pilot makes a difference?" Brian asked.

"Absolutely. The pilot has go/no-go power. And while the ceiling has lifted, the winds are still brutal. But Richardson is a tough son of a bitch—an ex-Marine who flew Hueys in Afghanistan, so he's flown through some extremely challenging conditions. He says he can do it and will get them directly to St. Anthony Hospital in Lakewood, which is just west of Denver. He should be taking off shortly. It'll be a tight fit, but he'll take Slaight and Sheard, as they're critical, and will come back for the other more injured survivors if the ceiling and winds hold. The ceiling looks good for the day; the winds will be the issue. They're going to put the drone up, too, as long as the conditions are stable, but they'll bring it down if the weather worsens. They can't risk losing it. Those search runs will likely be at a lower altitude, so the upper-level winds shouldn't be as big of an issue."

"Once we begin the search and get a feel for where they may have gone, can we get them to focus on that location? Not that I don't trust the dogs, but it could save us some time. And give us a way to send in more teams via the sheriff's office to trap Drubek between us."

"Everything is on the table for now."

Brian's gaze was fixed on the shrouded bodies lying in front of the nose of the plane. "What about the deceased?"

"Air rescue, not Flight For Life. They could all go in one flight if we can get one up here. Richardson is going to have body bags, so they'll be able to properly package the bodies for transport, but right now, their concern is getting the living down in one piece. They may have to leave the dead for now and return tomorrow when there's no risk to anyone's life to retrieve them. No one dies to recover a body. It seems harsh, but they're already gone. We won't leave them here; we'll come as soon as it's safe, but safety is the priority."

"Totally understandable."

"Are you guys up to speed on your doses?" Hensley contemplated first Brian and then Meg. "You look okay."

"I'm feeling okay. Not like I could win an eight-hundred-meter dash—I'm definitely fatigued, but less headachy than yesterday." Meg dropped a hand down to Hawk's head. "And best we can tell, the dogs are doing okay too. We're all due our next doses by midday."

"I think we got lucky," Brian said. "Todd's advance warning that got us dosed before we left DC likely saved us, and the oxygen treatments did the rest. It's affecting us, but because we're in good shape as a baseline, we're managing."

"We're okay too," Carlisle said.

"That was a concern?" Brian's surprise showed in his tone.

"It's not as common for someone from the Denver area to get high-altitude illness, because we're starting at just over five thousand feet. But when you're going up to twelve or fourteen thousand feet, that's still a seven- or nine-thousand-foot jump. It can happen to us too. It's less likely than someone starting at sea level, but not impossible."

"Glad that wasn't an issue then. Bad enough it's slowing me and Meg down a bit. We don't need anyone else being affected." Brian looked down at the two dogs, taking in their bright eyes and waving tails. "The dogs are ready. Let's grab our bags and find the scent trail."

By shortly after six o'clock, they were ready to begin the search—helmets and packs securely strapped on and armed with their trekking poles. They didn't have a specific scent article from either man to give the dogs to set them on a direct trail. But, as Meg expected, when they took the dogs to the area Blenn had indicated as where Drubek had fled, both dogs quickly zeroed in on the combined scents and only stopped immediately following the trail when Meg and Brian told them to hold.

"How do you want to play this?" Meg asked, perched on a boulder fifteen feet from the floor of the saddle, Hawk and Lacey five feet above, Brian just below. "Yesterday you led us, taking the safest route straight up. But this time we need to follow the dogs."

"The dogs will follow the scent trail? Exactly?" Fife asked.

"Yes."

"Then we're looking at a trail a human has already taken."

"Unless it's leading straight down," Brian muttered. "We're not following that trail."

Hensley's shifted gaze told Meg that Brian wasn't so quiet he wasn't heard. "Is there a risk the dogs would follow that track?"

"No." Brian and Meg spoke in unison, then Brian extended a palm to Meg. *Go ahead.*

"The dogs are trained to take risks, but they know if anything is questionable, they don't move without our permission. They trust us to tell them what they can manage and what they can't. If either of them feels unsafe, their first reaction will be to freeze. Then we make the call on how to proceed."

"That should work," said Hensley. "Let's have you two and the dogs go first, at least for now. When the path starts to get narrow and is single file, how will you handle it?"

"The dogs are used to working together and with us," Brian explained. "If Meg gives Lacey a command, unless I counter it, she'll follow it. The reverse is the same with

Hawk. When it gets into a single-file area, the two dogs will go first, followed by us. Whoever is in front will have a better view of the risks and will make the call. The dogs will obey. And, if it's a crisis situation, if we're worried about their safety, we'll use their 'don't mess with me' names."

Newall and Carlisle exchanged puzzled glances.

"Their what?" Newall asked.

"Their 'don't mess with me' names. Both dogs are trained to two names, with their primary names being Hawk and Lacey."

At the sound of their names, the dogs, still holding above them, fixed their gazes on Brian, their ears perked, but at ease.

"But when we do this . . ." Brian turned to his dog. "Athena, come."

"Talon, come," Meg echoed.

The dogs instantly became laser-focused on their own handler, moving quickly, though carefully, down to stand at their knee, heads high, eyes unblinking as they awaited the next command. The intensity was unmistakable.

"Good boy, Hawk." At the sound of his common name, the dog relaxed, his energy moving from single-minded focus to energetic attention.

Brian echoed the praise and Lacey similarly morphed back into her normal aspect.

Newall whistled. "That was like flipping a switch on, then off."

Meg bent to stroke Hawk's side. "There are circumstances when you don't have time to take a decision to committee. You demand instantaneous and singular attention and obedience. So, if they get into trouble up there, we can issue commands they'll follow with no hesitation."

"Do you have to use it often?"

"No, thank God. It's only used in extreme circumstances, and we try not to get into those, if we can help it. We'll send the dogs first, then Brian and I will follow. Hensley, if you or Fife come next, then you'll be able to hopefully foresee any difficulties the dogs might have on their current path, and how to circumvent that. We don't want to follow the trail to the point where it goes downhill and they can't stop that descent. Or get cliffed out, to put it in climbing terms."

"We definitely want to avoid that, especially for the dogs," said Hensley. "I know they're well-trained, but I can't explain things to them. Even you can't, for a complex task."

"They're damned smart, but there are limits." Brian pointed toward the ridge. "Lacey, find."

"Hawk, find."

The dogs headed up the field of scree, scrambling over tumbled rock and boulders, starting with a gentle incline for the first two hundred yards. They ran side by side, their noses down most of the time, occasionally raising them to scent the wind as it skimmed down the ridge, past them, and into the saddle. A few times the dogs took different paths, separated by ten or fifteen feet, each handler following their own dog, but their steps converged again shortly thereafter.

"It's mostly a common trail," Meg called, "but as you can see, the two men didn't take the exact same path, though their paths keep coming together in the end, back to the best route."

Meg kept her eye on Hawk: He was moving freely, his energy practically snapping after a solid rest and a high-energy breakfast, his head high when he was nose-up air scenting, his tail waving proudly. He exuded happiness in doing the job he loved best, with the woman he loved most, and with the canine companion to which he was practically bonded.

It made Meg happy to see him in his element like this. She wanted him to wring every bit of satisfaction and success out of these short years as possible. With Todd's blessing she was delaying parts of their lives together—namely, their joint desire for children—for a few years because once she was sidelined with a pregnancy, Hawk might be sidelined forever. They were a matched team, and when one member of the team couldn't work, the team as a whole couldn't. It's not like either of them could be farmed out to a new partner without requiring months of acclimation.

But seeing Hawk like this, Meg didn't regret a day of their working life together. There was time for the other aspects of her life with Todd; right now was for Hawk. Thank God Todd understood that better than most men.

The dogs followed the greater incline for about another hundred yards, and then the walls of the ridge rose on a steep incline. In front of them and to their right, the scree fell away and solid rock rose at a nearly ninety-degree angle. Above, all but hidden from view from the saddle, Pyramid Peak rose another 2,500 feet above them in a series of rocky peaks. To the left, leading to the outer edge of the saddle, the slope was only about forty degrees, though it was still a scramble across loose scree until the last few hundred feet, where a channel cut through solid rock leading up to the ridgeline.

Beyond was only low clouds, rolling thickly over each other in the sharp wind. And a long, *long* drop.

Dampness broke out across the back of Meg's neck, and her hands went clammy.

She'd been fine in the saddle. More than eleven thousand feet up, but safely cradled in the high walls of the saddle. Nowhere to fall.

That was about to change.

The walls of the channel narrowed, and the dogs moved

into single file, with Lacey in the lead and Hawk following behind.

"How about I go first," Brian said loudly, with a meaningful glance ahead, then back to Meg.

Translation: How about I go first so you aren't blazing the trail twelve thousand feet up? This way you can watch me, and I'll watch the drop.

"Owe you one." Meg kept her voice low so only Brian could hear.

"Nah." Brian planted his trekking poles firmly, using the poles to propel him higher as the dogs scrambled ahead of him.

Soon the dogs crested the ridge, Brian right behind them. As Meg climbed to the ridgeline, Brian let the dogs find the scent trail, but then stopped them about fifteen feet along the ridge to wait for the other climbers to catch up.

Unless she stared at her boots, there was no way for Meg to miss the panorama around them. Yesterday they'd climbed in the dark and in the clouds. Today, in daylight, there was no avoiding the height.

The view would have been breathtaking if she could appreciate it. Scratch that, it *was* taking her breath, but for all the wrong reasons.

Hunter Peak ranged across from them in a series of long ridges and valleys—couloirs running from the ridgeline down, down, *down,* to East Maroon Creek below—all leading to the jagged central peak rising more than thirteen thousand feet into the air, just visible below the roiling clouds. The mountain itself ran as far as Meg could see from north to south, a colossal hulking mass of snow-tipped rock. Verdant green—both evergreen and deciduous trees—ran up the rocky face of the mountain, carpeting the dull rock in vibrant spring color.

Meg couldn't help her gaze skimming down the mountain, across the faint track of the creek, only visible from this great height as a twisting break in the trees, and up the slope of Pyramid Peak. At this angle the blur of green climbing toward them seemed a long way down. To their right a narrow stream of water ran from the peak above, burbling over rocks at an eye-watering speed, runoff from the snowy heights above. She couldn't take her eyes off its progress as it helplessly tumbled downhill, gaining speed with each additional drop. . . .

Meg's stomach rolled as her heart rate kicked into overdrive. She felt her head spin as if overcome by a wave of vertigo. She planted her poles firmly, her fists white-knuckled around them, and pulled in a ragged breath, forcing air into lungs that had forgotten how to expand.

Hands closed over hers, locking her in place. "Look at me." Brian's voice, close, drew her gaze. "That's it. Just look at me."

Brian's green eyes filled her field of vision, he was so close. "I made a mistake," she whispered. "It was pure arrogance to come here. I never should have agreed."

"Bullshit." There was no meanness in Brian's tone, simply utter surety. "I've seen you walk train trestles and the Ocoee Flume. Those were drops that would have killed you when you fell from a height, with nothing to catch you. Yes, it's higher here, but it's not a straight drop. I know you—if you slipped and fell, you'd fight with everything you had to survive. To catch yourself. Remember the Conasauga River in the Cohutta Wilderness?"

A series of images shot through Meg's mind: *Tumbling down the hill. Being catapulted into a raging river. Shooting the rapids without a boat, the risk of being crushed against the rocks increasing with every second. Hawk's head breaking the surface just as her strength was flag-*

ging, dragging her to shore. Escaping first a sunbathing rattler, then a pack of coyotes who considered both woman and dog to be the perfect meal.

A shudder ran down her spine, and she was sure Brian felt the ripple through her clenched hands. "Yeah. I wouldn't have survived without Hawk."

"I disagree, but even if true, you have him here today. You have me and Lacey too. We got this. Is Hawk the right dog for this deployment?"

Brian's abrupt left turn had her replying without thought. "Yes."

"Then you weren't wrong to accept the assignment. Stop doubting yourself. You can do this." He made sure she was steady, then released her. "Now, keep your eyes on me, Hawk, or the ground in front of you. Nothing else. If you need to know something, I'll make sure you do." His gaze shot over her shoulder as he released her hands. "Great, we're all here. We'll start the dogs again."

Carlisle pushed a loose strand of hair that had escaped her helmet behind her ear, but the swirling wind immediately yanked it free again. "It's pretty windy up here. The dogs will be able to track them through this?"

"It's going to make it more of a challenge and will lighten the trail," Brian replied, "but in this rocky ground, skin cells and scent will pool in the crevices, below the wind gusts. The dogs will be able to follow."

"Good. Onward and upward then."

"Hopefully, not upward," Meg muttered, making Brian grin as he turned away from her and commanded Lacey to find, Meg echoing the command for Hawk.

There was no sign of either man, but Meg didn't expect there would be. They had enough of a head start that unless the drone spotted them—which was akin to finding a needle in a haystack, especially when they had no idea how high up the mountain the men were, let alone how far along the length—scent was their only option, unless they got extremely lucky. They were fortunate the aviation forecast called for the ceiling to stay high. It needed to hold off for at least a few hours if the rescuers had any hope of more than one Flight For Life rescue.

They followed the ridge, covering territory south of where they'd climbed the mountain in the first place. Meg wondered if either of the dogs might have indicated if they'd found fresh scent, had their paths crossed, but in mapping the safest path up, Hensley's route had put them due north and fully upwind of the scent trail.

When the ridge angled toward the peak, both dogs unerringly turned east, starting downhill into scree that wanted to roll underfoot and required care to not tumble down the slope. The dogs didn't head straight down, but angled across, hugging a solid rock wall that rose at a nearly ninety-degree angle, staying so close Meg could reach out to rest a hand on the wall as they climbed down, making her feel more secure.

They had helmets and trekking poles, but Drubek, leading the way, had neither, and, at least while he had daylight, would have tried for the safest route down. He was also likely injured in some way following the crash, though clearly not enough to keep him from attempting escape. Yet, despite his head start, Meg felt they had to be slowly gaining on him. Or, rather, on *them,* as there was no sign of Eli Barron either. One thing was sure—the two made their escape before the teams had disbursed to section off the mountain in the dark. Had they fallen down to the creek level, their bodies would have been seen. Granted, that left a lot of ground in the two thousand feet between their current position and the creek, with many outcroppings to hold a body. The teams had been spread across the eastern face of the mountain before they had been redirected to the crash site, yet no one had reported any sign of human life or activity.

As if Carlisle read Meg's mind, she called, "I don't see anything below us that looks human. Remember, Drubek was in black, so he may be harder to spot, but Barron is wearing red. He'll stand out."

"Not a great thing if the guy you're chasing in black has a firearm and you're a big red bull's-eye," quipped Brian.

Their path led them down nearly fifteen hundred feet, and the creeping headache Meg had noticed began to ease off slightly.

They were partway down when a distinct low thrum filled the air.

"Hawk, Lacey, hold," Brian commanded.

Meg planted her poles and her boots and then twisted around to look upslope to where a bright orange-and-yellow Eurocopter AStar helicopter was approaching from the north.

"That's Flight For Life," Fife called. "This is going to be the tricky part."

"Getting over the ridge and into the saddle?" Meg asked.

"Yes. The winds are unpredictable, but Richardson is damned good."

The group went quiet, watching the helicopter bob and weave slightly as it crossed the barrier into the saddle, then it slowly and steadily dropped from view.

"Knew he could do it." Hensley's grin showed his confidence. "As I said, a tough son of a bitch."

It seemed like a miracle, but from what felt like certain death, they had a chance at life.

Now they needed a chance at justice.

CHAPTER 18

Traversing: Following a climbing route that moves horizontally instead of vertically.

May 7, 7:36 am
Pyramid Peak
Aspen, Colorado

Twenty minutes later, as they continued their descent, they paused to watch the chopper rise into the air and head toward Denver. It gave each of them a boost. So much of the crisis could have gone wrong in so many different ways. Time and again, luck had been on their side, from most of the passengers surviving the crash; to getting the critically injured through the night; to the cloud cover lifting, allowing air rescue; to the dogs picking up the trail . . . it had all gone so right.

Part of Meg wondered how long their luck could hold.

They hiked for another two hours before Meg and Brian called for a break at a spot in the trail where the dogs were going due south, running along a cliff edge topping a nearly vertical drop.

No easy way down from here, so Drubek had continued at 10,500 feet, looking to descend the last thousand feet. If only he'd realized he'd missed an easier way down a half mile to the north. Or perhaps he knew the area well enough to know civilization and paved roads lay to the north. Help would come from the north. More importantly, law enforcement would come from the north. He had no choice but to aim away from anyone who could give him aid, because there were too many who looked for him. Considering what he'd done, he knew it could very well be a shoot-first-ask-questions-later scenario, especially if they suspected he was packing his own firepower. He'd shown no compunction in killing his fellow security guard; it was simply a means to an end. And he'd certainly been willing to kill everyone on the plane, including the innocent crew, when it crashed. He would likely assume—correctly, in Meg's opinion—that after a string of federal and state crimes, law enforcement would be unlikely to show mercy, especially at the first sign of aggression from him.

They took ten minutes to hydrate, refuel, rest muscles tired from a difficult descent, and for the mental break. Meg purposely sat with her back to the cliff edge to give herself a respite from the constant reminder of height and pulled out her satellite phone, shooting off texts to Todd and then Craig with updates—health and status for Todd; case, health, and status for Craig.

"Anything from McCord?" Brian asked around a bite of energy bar, which he then washed down with water.

"Nothing so far. McCord works fast, but even he's unlikely to have definitive answers in under three hours." Meg ran a hand over Hawk's fur, where he lay beside her. He'd inhaled both a bowl of water and his high-energy kibble, and now lay beside Lacey, his respiration slowly quieting.

The dogs were doing great, but Meg was relieved they now hiked at a lower elevation. It didn't do much for her nervousness around heights—a thousand feet above the creek still gave plenty of room to die—but her concern for Hawk and, to a lesser extent, herself was easing.

Score one for Todd. His alarm at their deployment and quick-thinking solution might have saved their lives.

Hensley had an update as well—the first Flight For Life had arrived at St. Anthony Hospital. Sheard was stable and Slaight was already in surgery, his outlook encouraging, news that gave everyone a boost.

Ten minutes was all they allowed themselves, then the search was on again.

"You're sure this is the right way?" Newall asked from directly behind Meg in the closer conformation this landscape allowed. "If they're off the trail . . ."

"They're not," Meg said, turning her head slightly—toward the peak—so her words would carry. "I wouldn't think Hawk is off the trail, even if he was the only dog, but with Lacey here, there's no chance. We can tell from their attitude. They're energetic and focused. They haven't lost the trail since they picked it up."

"Even in this wind?"

"Even in this wind. You've never worked with dogs before, have you?"

"Not directly. It kind of seems like magic."

"Not so much magic, just a lot more physiology and neurons devoted to smell. I like to compare it to our sight; that's where our neurons are concentrated. Their sense of smell is the Technicolor we see. They can pick out a single-known scent out of hundreds, or follow a trail that's days or even a week old, depending on the conditions. This trail is less than a day old. Trust them."

The first sign of someone running into trouble came a little over a half mile farther south. The more level ground they'd followed melted away as the cliff disappeared, leaving nothing but a steep slope covered in scree and spotted with trees and low scrub that somehow managed to thrive seemingly without soil and against gravity. But when they came to a shallow, rock-filled couloir, the dogs split, Lacey arrowing down, following a narrow disturbance in the scree. Hawk, meanwhile, took the couloir straight across and then started up the far side.

Meg followed him, but stopped at the top of the gully. "Hawk, hold." She stood with him as he waited, panting. "Brian, what's down there?"

"Lacey, leave it." Brian crouched down, examining the rocks Lacey had been sniffing. "Someone took a spill here. There's a smear of blood on the rocks. Not a lot, but someone was injured. Maybe hit his head."

"Or was already injured in the crash," Carlisle suggested, "and exacerbated an existing wound."

"That would also explain it." Brian straightened and looked up the slope. "You may not be able to see it from your angle, but from mine you can clearly see where someone slipped and slid or tumbled down to here where he managed to catch himself. I'm going to bag this rock, keep it as a scent source." Brian unbuckled and slid his pack off, opened it, and pushed through the contents for about twenty seconds before pulling out a zippered plastic bag.

"What's that for?" Hensley asked.

"Hawk and Lacey have been doing air scenting to follow the men, but to really trail an individual subject, we need something we know he's worn or he's come into contact with. Or some sort of bodily fluid that's come from him. We always carry plastic bags in case we find some trace of a subject. If we do, we bag it and let the dogs use it as a scent source. The dogs are trained to recognize a person from skin cells, sweat"—Meg watched Brian pick up the rock with the bag inside out so he didn't touch it, and then close the bag around it—"or blood. Brian's offering the rock to Lacey to sniff. She's now going to search for that specific scent. The track has clearly split here, so we won't offer the same scent to Hawk. He'll continue to track whoever went this way."

Lacey cast about for scent, and took several steps south, staying about twenty feet below the rest of the team. "Lacey, hold. He kept going from here," Brian called.

"Second scent trail keeps going from here," Meg said.

"And that's why we have two dogs. Split the teams?"

"Makes sense to me." Meg turned to Carlisle. "Stacey, you'll stay with me, and Corey will go with Brian?"

"Yes. Fife, you go with Brian; Ben, you stay with us. We'll stay in touch via satellite phone. If we need to contact Mountain Rescue Aspen, both teams have radios. Is there any way to tell how long ago they both came through?"

"Not with any accuracy. If you give the dogs two scents, they can tell the fresher of the two, as it will be the stronger scent, but they can't tell us if they passed through four hours ago, that kind of thing."

"They likely passed through here fairly close to each other. Let's push on. Day's young and I'd like to track them down today. The more time we give them, the better chance Drubek makes it to civilization and finds a way to disappear."

The teams separated, crossing the narrow couloir, and moving into a section more densely packed with trees on the far side, a situation Meg definitely preferred, as it essentially blocked her view of the downward slope, even though she could tell from the terrain they were on how steep it was. Whatever it took to fool her brain was fine with her.

Brian, Newall, Fife, and Lacey hiked a little farther downslope as they moved south, Brian looking up frequently to make sure the two groups were running in parallel, until they disappeared into deeper brush.

A high-pitched whine came from a distance, growing

louder as it approached, raising the hair on the back of Meg's neck. She was all too familiar with that particular sound. "Drone's out."

Carlisle stopped, her head tilted, eyes unfocused as she listened for a few seconds. "There it is. How did you hear that so early?"

"I've had some bad run-ins with drones in the past. It's a sound I hear in my nightmares sometimes." She looked through the leafy canopy above, but could only see snatches of gray clouds. "This one is being used for good at least. They know where to look?"

"They know where we're headed and will try to see if they can spot anything," Hensley said. "But it's a big mountain. Drubek and Barron may not even be on it anymore if they managed to get down and off. Drubek would be a fool if he wasn't trying to get out of the mountains and find transportation out of this area."

"If he's being followed, it's possible he might get driven higher."

"Possible."

"The drone can only cover so much ground, though," Carlisle warned. "And the sound of the drone is its own early warning. So don't get your hopes up. They could be hiding behind rocks, be sheltered inside the trees, or simply not be in range."

"Thank God for the dogs." Meg smiled down at Hawk, scrambling over the rocky terrain in front of her. "The drone can only spot them if they're in plain view. They can't hide from the dogs, though, and they can't camouflage where they've been. For the dogs the scent trail is like a glowing path for them to follow, even though we can't see it."

The drone whined louder as it passed overhead and then slowly grew fainter as it continued its pass down the mountain. Only when the sound was gone did Meg relax.

It was a knee-jerk reaction, but after the Mannew case, she doubted she'd ever be comfortable around drones. For weeks that incoming buzz had been the harbinger of brutal death she'd seen up close and personal. It was hard to throw off the instant stab of fear that whine induced.

Meg's satellite phone rang ten minutes later. "Hawk, stop. Hold." She dug the phone out of her jacket pocket to see Brian's number and put it on speaker as soon as she answered. "Where are you?"

"I think we're still essentially running parallel to you, but Lacey went a little off course around a tree. I think my guy spent the night here, probably propped up against it. Mostly out of the wind, which would have increased overnight survival. It also would have helped keep him dry in last night's rain. There are traces of where he relieved himself too. The trail continues on south from here. It's possible he could have briefly rested here, but I suspect this was where he stopped when he ran out of light."

Carlisle leaned in toward the phone. "This is the same guy who took a spill. He's hurt, or more hurt when you take into account any injuries from the crash. He'll be exhausted, chasing or being chased, it's dark, and he knows he's going to kill himself in a fall if he continues in those conditions. Maybe he didn't even sleep, just laid low while it was dark. But the trail continues?"

"Yes, in the same direction we're already going."

"Then we know whoever it was survived past this rest stop."

"If they're not that far apart," Hensley said, "then we're either going to find another spot where the guy we're following stopped, or chances are good that we'll find the body at the bottom of the slope."

Ten minutes later, Hawk led them to a spot in a clump of underbrush that bore the marks of a body resting there for a period of time.

"This could work for us, though not as well as Brian's bloody rock." Meg pulled out one of her own plastic bags. "A used piece of clothing would be much better, something with ground-in skin cells and absorbed sweat, but I'm hoping some of the scent of whoever spent the night here will have transferred. Mostly through scattered skin cells." Turning the bag inside out over her hand, Meg crouched down and pulled off crushed bits of plant matter. When she was satisfied with her collection, she pulled the bag up to cover the greenery and then offered the open bag to Hawk, who leaned in and sniffed in a short series of inhalations. "Hawk, this is Drubek or Barron. Find him, Hawk. Find."

Hawk put his head down, cast about for a few seconds, and then trotted south, his nose down, but his tail high and his steps sure.

"There's enough. He's found that specific scent trail." Meg jammed the bag into a side pocket of her pack so it would be easily available if needed, slung her pack on, and followed, buckling her pack as she went. Even with the trees, Meg realized, the footing was rocky and difficult, but at least for the humans, a hand could be put out against a tree to keep one's balance. Hawk occasionally slipped a bit and had to scramble back to the scent trail.

It was gloomy inside the trees, the sun's brilliance already filtered through thick clouds and then farther through the pines and aspens. Meg surmised each man must have stopped as soon as proceeding became a dangerous endeavor; starting again only when there was enough light to see a clear path. Anything else would have been suicide.

It took the better part of forty-five minutes to maneuver through the forest and across several narrow, scree-filled couloirs, one containing fast-flowing spring runoff. There'd been no help for it, but to carefully wade through, though Meg was grateful the water didn't flow over the top of her waterproof hiking boots, keeping her socks dry. Wet socks on a long search were the best way to get debilitating blisters that would significantly hamper the team's effort.

They paused on the far side of the narrow waterway for Meg to pull out a towel to dry Hawk's feet so he wouldn't get chilled. The water was icy, possibly just a few degrees above zero, and Meg was glad she could chafe some warmth into Hawk's pads.

Brian, Newall, and Fife broke through the trees, with Lacey about 150 feet below. Straightening, the towel slung over her shoulder, Meg kept watch as they traversed the stream, then waved back when Brian saw them. Another wave, once Lacey was dry, then Meg offered the bag to Hawk to scent again, and both teams disappeared into the trees.

One last couloir carried them onto a plateau about one hundred feet wide, with a gentle incline that rode the top of a steep slope. Looking down, they found Lacey leading the trio up a sharp incline toward them.

"Looks like their paths converged here again," Carlisle said. "Let's wait for them and keep the group together."

"Agreed." That one quick look down the couloir had been enough for Meg, so she turned to look up the mountain, her gaze attracted by a smudge of white high on the peak above, which she then realized was two smudges. "Are those . . . goats?"

Carlisle and Hensley turned to look upslope.

"Sure is." Carlisle chuckled at the two goats nimbly managing what looked to Meg like an invisible path hanging over a fatal drop. "This is their mountain, really."

"They live here?"

"All over these ranges. You can spend eight grueling hours summiting a fourteener, practically drag yourself to the top, and a goat hops up behind you looking fresh as a daisy, as if they don't have a care in the world, and is all,

'Hey, what are you doing here?' They don't get close, but they're used to people on their mountain. And people don't get close, because who wants to get kicked off a summit or a narrow ridgeline by a goat?"

"Makes sense to me." One goat leaped to the level above. "They're amazingly agile."

"They are. You'd think you'd find goat carcasses strewn around the bottom of the mountain the way they carry on, but I've never seen one slip. They're incredible." Carlisle turned to the newly arrived group as they puffed their way up one hundred feet of slope to join them. "Welcome back."

"Thanks. Lacey, stop. Hold." Brian bent over and braced his hands on his knees and let himself breathe hard for a moment. "I'm in good shape and this is hard. I can't imagine how two regular guys managed this."

"Even if it feels easier at this lower altitude, you're still fighting against the lower oxygen levels and so are they," Fife said. "They have to be struggling. I think we must be gaining on them." He scanned the top of the rocky cliff face that spread out for what had to be a good three-quarters of a mile in front of them. "I don't see them, though. And Barron's red jacket should stick out. You're sure we're on the right track?"

"I'm sure both dogs are on the right track." Meg offered the bag again to Hawk. "Find them, Hawk. Find Drubek and Barron." Hawk immediately continued south. Meg slapped Brian on the shoulder. "Up and at 'em, old man."

Brian straightened, tossed her a sour look, offered Lacey his bag, and commanded his dog to find. Grinning, Meg fell into step beside him.

They crossed along the short plateau, giving the slope below a wide berth and instead following along the base of the upward slope. The rocky terrain was covered with dense, low scrub with only the odd tree, telling Meg how shallow the scant soil was here.

The dogs stayed focused, leading them along a lengthy, slow incline, carrying them up to almost eleven thousand feet. They broke for twenty minutes for rest, lunch, more meds for Meg, Brian, and the dogs, and to update the Mountain Rescue Aspen command team, various FBI special-agents-in-charge, Ryan, and Todd.

McCord hadn't contacted them yet, but Meg wasn't surprised. He worked fast, but even McCord had his limits. Maybe by end of day he'd have an update.

They resumed the search, the dogs finding the trail and leading them farther along the plateau.

Meg admitted to herself she was tiring much too easily. This part of the search wasn't terribly rigorous, though everyone had to be careful of a slip and fall, or, worse, a slide, but her limbs felt leaden, her muscles straining, and her breath coming much too hard as her muscles screamed for oxygen. She could see Brian faced a similar challenge, but they both bore down.

If the dogs could do it, so could they. She could see that Hawk, while determined, wasn't keeping pace quite as quickly as usual. But she didn't rush him; they had no idea how much farther they might have to go, and a slip and fall could be fatal.

They left the trees to a long stretch of downward slope that extended the decline, allowing for a shallower angle. Both dogs scrambled down the slope, sometimes on a separate path, sometimes coming together for sections where the safest way down was a common route.

Ahead of them, three rivers tumbled down from different directions to meet in a slender depression. They drew Meg's gaze up. And up and up and up, all the way to the peak rising above them, the southernmost peak of the mountain. While it didn't have the height of Pyramid Peak, Meg guessed it to be well over thirteen thousand feet, a rocky crag, its upper third still covered with snow. Thus leading to the spring runoff and the trio of streams, tumbling down more than three thousand feet to East Maroon Creek far below.

Trees lined the streams, but the main body of the slope was either jagged rocks or low ground cover. The dogs picked up speed, clearly glad to be free of the treacherous scree, and Brian and Meg let them pull away slightly, no longer as concerned about the dogs tumbling to their deaths due to uneven footing.

"Shoot." Brian looked down to where his left hiking boot was untied. "Stay with them. I need to tie this up before I wipe out and somersault down the hill. I'll catch you in a second."

"Sure."

Meg stepped ahead as Brian crouched down and quickly retied his bootlace, the two rescuers and two FBI agents passing around him.

Suddenly, from far above, a muffled *whumpf* sounded, followed by a low roar.

Meg froze in her tracks, her head whipping around to stare uphill in horror as the slab of snow above them fractured in real time, starting to slide as an intact slab before crumbling and rolling, tumbling over itself.

"Avalanche!" Hensley's bellow was startlingly loud, snapping Meg out of her shock and into action.

"Talon! Athena! Run!"

The dogs took off as fast as they could, arrowing for the trees on the far side, leaping gracefully from one rocky surface to another. Meg pounded after them as quickly as she could, knowing one misstep, one slip off a boulder, one miscalculation of distance on a jump, could cause a fall, and the snow would be on her before she could get up.

Get up . . .

Brian.

Brian, who'd been down on one knee to tie a badly-timed loose bootlace.

Meg slowed on a long, flat surface long enough to turn and look behind her to see Brian—face ashen, eyes wide—wobble to his feet, then get his bearings. *"Brian, run!"*

Eyes locked on hers, Brian sprinted after them.

Meg had no choice but to turn away. She was in front—she had to keep the dogs safe. For Brian. For both of them. Because they'd be lost if anything happened to either dog.

She'd be lost if anything happened to Brian.

She heard pounding boots behind her, knew the whole group was moving as fast as they could for the trees.

They'd seen how an avalanche could toss mature trees around like matchsticks. The forest was no match for the power of an avalanche. But it might slow it down if it spread that wide.

A quick glance uphill showed the snow coming at a breathtaking rate. Could they make it?

She wasn't sure they would.

The ground beneath her boots started to shake. It was coming closer . . . closer.

Already low on oxygen, her breath sawed in and out, her lungs burning. Ahead of her, Hawk stumbled, but she found enough air to scream his name even as he found his footing, falling behind Lacey by less than a yard.

"Faster!" Hensley yelled.

With everything Meg had left, she dug deep and poured on every last bit of speed she had as the earth trembled and a tremendous roar blocked out all other sound.

The force and speed of the approaching snow created its own wind, whipping clouds of flakes into a white blur around them.

It was nearly on them.

They'd been so lucky up to now, she should have known it couldn't last.

Their luck had run out.

CHAPTER 19

Strategic Shoveling: The process used to extract an avalanche victim as quickly as possible, increasing the probability of victim survival; uses victim burial depth and the number of rescuers to prescribe digging locations and the role of each rescuer.

May 7, 12:14 PM
Pyramid Peak
Aspen, Colorado

Dig deeper. Find more.
With a groan ripping from her chest, Meg pushed harder, driving the dogs in front of her, aiming for the trees, looking for shelter when she knew, deep down, shelter didn't exist from this monster.

She wanted to look back, find Brian, find the others, but didn't dare. The time lost doing so might cost her life.

Not now, not when there's so much to live for.

Todd . . .

The dogs hit the trees and shot between them, Lacey stumbling in exhaustion, but then finding the reserves to not only find her balance, but to keep going. Meg followed close behind, hearing other footfalls behind them. "Talon, Athena! Run!"

The next few seconds could be the difference between life and death.

They were thirty feet inside the forest when the roar went by, a deafening tumble of roiling chunks of leaden, water-drenched spring snow splintering wood as the icy slide effortlessly pulled down trees at the forest's edge.

Then it sped downhill and the sound died away.

"It's past us!" Hensley bellowed.

"Hawk, Lacey, stop!" Meg pulled up herself, the dogs slowing and spinning to face her, waiting for their next command.

Heart pounding, exhaustion running through every fiber of every muscle, Meg turned, bracing one trembling hand on a tree to steady herself as her body swayed with panting, ragged breaths.

Carlisle stood behind her, Newall off to one side, bent over, his hands braced on his knees, breathing hard. But as her gaze passed beyond them to Hensley and Fife, and both turned to look back, her blood went cold.

Nothing but a field of white spread wide behind them.

"Where's Brian?" Meg pushed between Carlisle and Newall, following Hensley and Fife, who were already jogging into the slide path. *"Brian!"*

They broke from the trees to a wash of snow covering what had been a slope of grasses and underbrush. And not a person to be found.

The air froze in Meg's lungs, and all she could do was reach out for a stranglehold on Hensley's arm while visions of Brian shot through her mind like a series of slides.

Brian standing with her at Arlington Cemetery beside the open grave, his fingers intertwined with hers as they gazed down at a dead woman who looked horrifically like Meg. Surfacing from the black to Brian's desperate whisper to come back to him after being thrown by the Gettys-

burg explosion. The determined glint in Brian's eyes above their locked hands as she hung suspended over a deadly drop when the second floor of a hurricane-pummeled house collapsed, nearly taking her with it. Cradling her devastated partner in her arms as they waited in the vet's office while Lacey was in surgery after nearly being killed by the cougar who had tried to take out Brian. The joy in Brian's eyes when Meg had asked him to officiate their wedding.

He *would* officiate their wedding.

This couldn't be the end.

"Prepare for a search!" Hensley clearly didn't think this was the end either. He turned to her, met, and held her gaze. "We can find him. Get out your transceiver and set it to search." He shook off her hold and turned to the rest of the group. "All transceivers to search mode!"

Meg unzipped her hip pocket and pulled out her transceiver, nearly dropping it as her hands shook. She blew out a breath and centered herself for one second, then concentrated on the task at hand—unlocking the dial and turning it from TR to SE.

"We're going to spread out across the slide and walk down it in parallel. Space yourselves out. It's about a hundred feet across. Leave about twenty feet on the outside and spread out across the space. Hold your transceiver at waist height, parallel to the ground." Hensley glanced down at his transceiver. "I'm not picking up a signal from Brian's beacon. Whoever gets it first, call out your number and then keep calling out every ten meters. A reminder, the measurements are in meters, and there are three point three feet or thirty-nine inches in a meter. Keep that in mind when you're calculating distances. It's not in feet. Now spread out."

On autopilot, Meg moved to follow Hensley's instructions when Hawk bumped against her legs. She dropped a hand down to him, about to command him to come with her, when he bumped her again.

Meg snapped out of her terror-induced fog, thinking like a handler again. "Ben, we need a two-pronged plan of attack. Are there enough of us to do the search without me?"

"The search could be done with just one. Five is a luxury."

"Then you four do it." Meg studied Lacey, who stood anxiously passing her weight from foot to foot, held by Meg's command, but clearly wanting to break away. "I'll take the dogs. They know Brian. They know his scent. We might get lucky." Her gaze passed over the field of white running downhill for hundreds of feet.

It was likely an impossible task. While the dogs had been trained for underwater detection—the closest associated skill to this—that scenario required scent particles to slowly disperse up from the watery depths to the surface, where the dogs would be able to detect the incredibly diffuse scent from a boat above. Here, where the snow was packed like solid cement, there would be no diffusion in the minutes following the slide. But there had been enough snow mixing that a trace of Brian might have rolled to the surface.

"I'll take lucky," Carlisle said. "Head down the slide, we'll start here. Ben, we need to move."

"I know." Hensley pointed at Meg's transponder. "Keep it on search mode and glance at it occasionally. Can't hurt." He turned to the rest of the group. "Spread out!"

"Hawk, Lacey, come." Meg crouched down, stroking a hand over each dog. "Find Brian. Brian is missing." She looked deep into Lacey's eyes, seeing the same fear that slid like ice through her own veins. She straightened. "Find Brian!"

For dogs who had worked together this long, they didn't need any more direction from her. They spread out across the pile, working a zigzag pattern, winding back and forth across the snow, meeting at an invisible line in the middle that only they could see to not cross, so they efficiently worked the whole area. An advantage of the avalanche was it left a rough, uneven surface the dogs could cover faster without fear of slipping.

Studying the two dogs—Hawk on the north end of the slide, Lacey on the south—Meg noted subtle differences in stance that made her think that while Hawk was sensing nothing, Lacey was detecting a subtle trail. It was in the set of her head and tail, the intensity of her search, but Meg was willing to bet Brian was on the south side. If he'd been at the edge of the slide when it caught him as he ran to follow them, that positioning would make the most sense.

Walking down the middle between them, Meg glanced at her transceiver—the lights indicated search mode, but no directional arrows or distance showed.

Hang on, Brian, we're coming.

She checked her fitness tracker. About three minutes had passed since the slide went by. Fife's words rang in her head: *Thirty minutes is all you have. Really, your best chance of survival is in the first ten minutes.*

Seven minutes to save a life.

Her heart pounded like a drum, no longer from the exertion of escaping the avalanche, but from pure terror.

Imagine how terrified Brian must be. He has to be panicking, locked under this field of snow, as minutes tick by and his air is slowly exhausted.

This isn't the end. It can't be.

Find him.

Turning around, Meg saw everyone else had spread out, with Carlisle on the southerly end, then Hensley, Newall, and Fife on the northerly end, with about fifteen feet between them. They walked forward in unison, with their heads down and their eyes fixed on their transceivers.

Even though they were moving at a good pace, Meg had to clamp down on the need to tell them to hurry.

They knew a life was on the line. They didn't need more pressure from her.

Meg turned back as Lacey stopped to scent a large clump of snow, when Carlisle's voice sounded behind her.

"Signal! Thirty meters!"

Finally.

Turning around, Meg found Carlisle, then followed the slope down to where Lacey still paused. She wasn't sitting—her alert signal for a live find—but she'd halted her search.

Something, some trace, was there, Meg would bet her life on it. Would bet Brian's life on it. But was that where he was?

"Lacey may have something!" Meg called uphill. "Something that might put her in range of Stacey's distance. It's just not enough for a full alert."

"Twenty meters!" Carlisle called. She glanced at Meg long enough to meet her eyes and give her a reassuring nod. *Hang in there. We got this.* Her eyes dropped again as the numbers fell.

Meg checked on Hawk, who continued his zigzag pattern, but still with no indication of finding a scent trail.

Lacey had something; Meg was sure of it.

She let Hawk continue, but jogged to Lacey as the dog continued to circle one spot, catching a trace of something, but not enough to be sure. "Do you have something, Lacey-girl?" Meg asked, calling the dog by Brian's affectionate nickname for her as encouragement. "What do you smell?"

"Fifteen meters!" This time it was Hensley, still in his own lane, but picking up Brian's beacon.

"Ten meters!" Carlisle countered.

Meg stepped away from Lacey, wanting to stay out of the way of the technology, which would help Brian more than his own dog this time.

"Five meters!" Carlisle was closing fast on Lacey. "Three." She walked past Lacey. "Point nine." Three more steps. "One point seven." She turned around and hurried back to the spot showing the lowest value. "Point nine." She dropped to her knees.

"You remember how to bracket?" Hensley asked, striding to Carlisle.

"It's been years, but you don't forget."

Meg called Hawk to suspend his search and come stand with her. Telling the dogs to stay, Meg stepped forward as Carlisle dropped an open gloved hand flat on the ground at the point of the lowest number, holding her transceiver over it, the screen reading "0.9." She began a series of passes, bouncing the transmitter forward as far as she could reach with her hand planted, then to each side, then back, calling out values. "Point nine. One point one. One point three. Point seven." She set her hand on the spot with the lowest value and started the bracket over. "Point seven. Point nine. Point eight. Point five." She moved her hand to the lowest value and started again.

While she was reading out numbers, Fife had his pack off and had drawn out what looked like a folded series of sticks. Holding the end of one piece, he tossed the other pieces away from him, simultaneously pulling on a small handle on the end. With a clatter, the segments seemed to magically align, locking into a long red pole with measurement markings down the side.

"Point five. This is the lowest." Carlisle patted the snow under her hand. "That's our burial depth."

"That's just a few inches under two feet," Meg said,

dropping to her knees about a foot away from the spot and leaning into the snow. "Brian! If you can hear us, we're coming. Hang on! Brian!" Beside her, Lacey let out a high-pitched double bark and Meg stared at the shepherd. "Can you hear him, girl? Is he answering? Speak! Tell him you can hear him." Lacey barked again.

"Let me in." Fife stepped in as Carlisle drew back, and inserted the pole at the spot Carlisle had indicated. The pole dropped to the sixty-centimeter mark, and Fife pulled it back out.

"Nothing?" Meg asked.

"Not yet."

"You can tell the difference between snow and a person?"

"Snow is hard," Carlisle said, stripping off her pack and unhooking the shovel from it, while Fife inserted the pole in a concentric circle around the spot. "Bodies are squishy. You can definitely feel the difference."

Fife must have felt that difference at the third insertion, because he left the pole in place, buried to just over forty-five centimeters, and yelled, "Strike!" He jumped to his feet and stepped back to his pack to grab a compact shovel Meg hadn't seen him remove.

There wasn't any discussion, but Hensley, Fife, and Carlisle fell into position as if they'd trained for this for years.

Because they had, even if Carlisle was a little rusty.

Hensley and Fife stepped downhill one pace from the pole and started digging furiously, using the metal blade of their short-handled shovels to first chop the hard snow and then used them almost as if they were paddles to sweep the snow off to the side. They worked in a blur, their movements coordinated and lightning fast. One extra pace below them, Carlisle unlatched her shovel off the handle, snapped it onto a notch at the other end so it was perpendicular to the shaft instead of in-line, and then used her shovel to chop the snow and then hoe it farther downhill with her perpendicular blade.

Meg checked the time—seven minutes, and closing in fast on the ten-minute mark.

She couldn't have asked them to work faster. Experienced rescuers, they shoveled quickly and efficiently, with minimal discussion among them as each understood their role and how to get the job done.

Sixty seconds later they hit pay dirt.

"I'm through!" Fife called. "Let's get an airway established."

Staying on the uphill side of the digging, Meg crept closer as the shovels continued to fly, keeping her weight flat and distributed so it didn't imperil Brian's nest in the snow below, while the small hole that looked like it was Brian's knee expanded.

When a single hand shot out, Meg was there to catch it in both of hers. "Brian, we have you. Hang on a little longer."

His fingers wrapped around her hand in a death grip, hard enough to grind her bones together. But she didn't care. If he needed to hold on for dear life, she was happy to be the lifeline he clung to.

"Hang on," Hensley called, and all shoveling stopped as he bent down and peered into the widening hole. "Brian?"

"It's about damned time."

Brian's words weren't loud, but they filled Meg with overflowing relief, simply to hear his voice. She'd been so terrified they'd lost him, to hear his voice released all the tightness in her frame. She had to refrain from collapsing onto the snow in relief. Better yet, to hear Brian's typical sass filled her with joy.

Lacey had a similar reaction as she gave three sharp barks, and Brian's grip loosened at the sound of his dog so nearby.

The strained expression on Hensley's face relaxed as his smile broke wide. "Well, we discussed stopping for coffee before trying to find you, but your dog overruled us."

"That's my girl. Kicking ass and taking names."

"How hurt are you? Can we move you?"

There was the sound of fabric rubbing over snow. "I'm probably bruised to hell and back, and everything aches, but I don't think anything's broken. And wearing this helmet probably saved me from a concussion."

"Give us a couple of minutes and we'll clear a path out of there for you." Hensley picked up his shovel again, and he, Fife, and Carlisle made quick work of clearing a platform in the snow for him.

With a double squeeze to Brian's hand, Meg released him and slid back far enough to stand without her weight being directly on top of him. "Hawk, Lacey, come."

With the dogs flanking her, she circled around to stand downhill, out of the way of the flying snow, but close enough to see into the hole. She laid a hand on Lacey's head; the dog vibrated with need to be with Brian when they were separated by twenty feet. She'd heard his voice, she knew he was alive and safe, but until she could be with him, she didn't absolutely believe it.

Meg knew how she felt.

They finally got a first look inside the path of the avalanche. Brian lay inside on his side, his knees pulled high in a fetal position. His gaze shot between the diggers to find her, and then dropped to Lacey.

Then Hensley and Fife moved in, blocking Brian from view as they extracted him from the snow. Ninety seconds later, after some low conversation and adjusting, they pulled back a little farther on the platform.

Brian sat propped against the snowbank on one side of the platform, his legs stretched out in front of him. He looked not so different from less than fifteen minutes before, except his helmet was now off to lie faceup on his thighs.

Brian held out one hand and whistled softly. Lacey took off like a bullet shot from a gun, galloping across the snow, and practically landing in his lap. Brian gave her a good twenty seconds to leap around him, licking his face and making keening sounds as if he had returned from a two-year military tour, not ten minutes inside the packed snow left by an avalanche. Then, with a quiet word, Lacey calmed and sat beside him.

Meeting Meg's eyes, he grinned and held out a hand again.

"Hawk, come." Meg slipped in between Hensley and Fife and dropped to her knees in front of Brian and caught him in a hug. "Think I'm going to come when you whistle for me like you would your dog?"

"Would you?" Brian's voice was directly in her ear as she held on tight.

"Fat chance."

He shuddered once and whispered, "I knew you'd find me. I hung on because I knew you wouldn't let me die here, all alone."

"Never. And neither would the rest of the team. It literally involved every one of us. Besides, I owed you one. You just got paid back." She gave him one more squeeze and then released him to ease away. "You gave us one hell of a scare."

"Yeah. Me too."

"Don't do it again."

"I can heartily promise I will never purposefully do that again."

"It must have been terrifying."

"Surprisingly, I was pretty calm in there. I knew you

wouldn't let me go." Brian stroked Lacey's fur. "Neither would Lacey. The thought of the two of you searching for me blew away the worst of the debilitating fear."

"You had faith."

"In you two? And Hawk? Always. I called for Lacey, and she heard me. I could hear her barking."

"She could hear you. We couldn't"—Meg motioned to the group behind her—"but she could."

Brian blinked up at Hensley and Fife, and Carlisle and Newall, who had crowded in behind them. Newall was grinning like a loon, while Carlisle simply looked relieved.

Meg suspected Carlisle recognized exactly how close they'd come to losing Brian altogether.

"What caused that hellish slide?" Brian asked. "Did we miss them? Were they right above us and they caused it?"

"No way." Meg looked down at the dogs, Lacey sitting so close to Brian, she was practically on top of him, Hawk hovering close to Meg's other side, as if unwilling to risk she, too, might disappear as Brian had. "Think about what the dogs were doing when it started. They were angling down toward the creek." Meg looked down the long expanse of snow that ended about one hundred feet above the creek, surrounded by the vibrant green of spring. "They were headed down. If not all the way down, then at least lower. If it wasn't them, then what started the avalanche? Other climbers?"

"Could be." Hensley studied the terrain above them. Snow still rode the peak, but in the upper area of their couloir, a ragged depression marked where part of the snowpack had broken away to tumble downhill destroying anything in its path. "But it's doubtful in this weather, especially when the main entrance to this mountain is blocked by a massive disaster response. In this case it's going to be caused by the weather. It's just warm enough today to be a problem, especially when you add in the additional water volume from last night's rain."

"That rain didn't melt the snow. Trust me, what came down was solid as hell."

"What was on top was definitely solid. The problem is what was underneath. This looks like a wet slab. You have a layer of snow on top, but as the air warms and it starts to melt, water collects under the top slab of snow. If you get enough water under there—like what happens as the temp warms in the spring or if there's significant rainfall, like we had over the weekend, then more last night—it cuts the connection between the slab of snow and the rock beneath it, and the weight of the slab brings the whole thing down."

"So that whole nightmare was a 'wrong place, wrong time' kind of thing?"

"Unfortunately, yes."

"Lucky me." Brian rolled his eyes at Meg. His gaze wandered past her to the edge of the trees, now nearly a straight edge compared to a previously meandering line. If it was possible, Brian lost a little more color. "Did that tree line . . . move?"

"Yes. The avalanche wiped out about ten or fifteen feet of mature trees, all the way down."

Brian looked a little green around the edges. "Jesus . . ."

Meg gave him a visual assessment from wool cap to hiking boots. "Which makes me wonder how you came through in essentially one piece. Nothing is broken, you're conscious, your spine is intact, you have all your faculties . . . well . . . as much as you ever had." She winked at him.

He blew her a saucy kiss in return, but then his face went serious. "Ben's quickie lecture yesterday probably saved my life. It was top of my mind and I did exactly what he suggested. I was nearly at the trees when it caught me, so I was lucky it was the edge and not the center mass of that monster. I kicked, I flailed, I did the backstroke. A couple of times I made it to the surface and could grab another lungful of air before I had to clamp my mouth shut to keep snow from getting in. When the slide slowed, I fought the snow as it tried to close in on me and managed to make a good-sized air pocket so I could breathe. I punched out, but I kind of lost which direction was up." He looked at the snowy coffin that had nearly encased him for his last breath. "Looks like I was about forty-five degrees off."

"Everyone else was looking for your transponder, but I had the dogs looking for *you*. I think Lacey picked up your scent, but the best trail she could scent was about six feet off and likely where some of the snow you kicked off landed. Had you broken through the snow, she'd have found you in seconds." Meg reached across to stroke the shepherd. "She did great." She lavished praise on her own dog. "They both did great. Really gave it their all in a landscape where finding scent was almost a pipe dream."

"But my Lacey-girl did it." Brian pulled his dog close and gave her a smacking kiss on the head, earning a long lick in return. "Give me a hand up."

"Are you sure?" Meg looked him over again. "What if there's internal bleeding or something? Maybe we should get Flight For Life for you?"

"Don't need it. If there was something broken or internal bleeding, I'd be in agony. I feel like I've been hit by a truck, but that's about all. Get me on my feet—then if you need it, I'll strip off a few layers, and you can do a once-over to make sure there's no blood seeping through anywhere."

"Are you sure you can continue?" Carlisle asked. "No one is going to think less of you for stepping back after what you've just gone through."

"I'm sure. I didn't like this guy before because of what he did to everyone on that plane. Now I'm additionally pissed because of what just happened to me, and what nearly happened to all of you. God forbid what could be happening to anyone else who showed up to help today. None of us would be here except for what he did. He needs to be stopped and he needs to pay for the lives he took, the lives he attempted to take, and anyone affected because of the rescue. As long as I can walk, I'm still in this hunt."

Meg gave him a single nod, got to her feet, and extended a hand.

Brian slapped his palm against hers and let her haul him to his feet. He wobbled for only a second or two, then got his boots planted, took a breath, looked up at the avalanche path, and flipped it the bird.

Then he met Meg's eyes. "Let's do this."

CHAPTER 20

Working a Route: The process of working out the best way to proceed through a route with the end goal of completing it without errors.

May 7, 12:36 PM
Pyramid Peak
Aspen, Colorado

It was a relief to get off the snow and back onto rock and grass. Not only was it less treacherous, but Brian needed the distance from the constant reminder of what had happened to him. Meg had been correct, and when the dogs had once again picked up the scent trail about 150 feet lower in the trees, it led them down to East Maroon Creek.

Hensley and Meg had checked Brian out before they were willing to continue, but Brian had told them the truth—while bruises were already blooming, there were no broken bones and no sign of bleeding. He was chilled, but argued the best thing to do was keep moving to warm him, something that would also keep his battered muscles from stiffening. Meg finally agreed they should continue as a group, but insisted Brian take three minutes to call

Craig and give him a personal update. They both knew Craig would fry their collective asses if they didn't keep him in the loop on something this big. However, Brian was coherent and convincing, and in the end Craig rubber-stamped the continuation of their search with Brian as part of the team.

Meg had taken the same time to have a quick text conversation with Todd, letting him know they were on the way down the mountain as the search continued. For now, she left the avalanche out of the update. She didn't have time to get into the minutiae with him—and she knew the first responder in him would want every detail of the rescue—so she'd save that for tonight. She'd assured him they were safe and taking a break before continuing the search.

If guilt poked at her, she pushed it away and told herself it would be worse for Todd if she dropped the avalanche bombshell, then disconnected and ran. Literally.

The dogs followed the scent trail down to the valley between Pyramid and Hunter Peaks, all the way to the established trail running along East Maroon Creek. The path was wide enough there for the dogs to trot side by side, followed by the handlers, and then the rest of the team.

"They still have it," Meg said, her eyes on the dogs. Each handler had offered their bagged scent to their dog—neither knew for sure which scent represented which man they followed, but between them, they were covered—and the dogs were sure on their mutual trail. Drubek had taken this path, Barron had followed, and the dogs knew it. They were both firmly in the zone, their energy boosted after the high of getting Brian back, combined with a short break for a snack and hydration.

"Yeah, no doubt." Brian's voice carried a hint of stress.

"You okay?" Meg took in the set of his mouth, the lines radiating around his eyes. "I'm not going to make you stop, so you can tell me. Would be better if you did tell me, in case we need to make some accommodations to the search."

"Not gonna lie, I'm sore." Brian glanced behind them, judging the gap between Hensley and Carlisle, who followed, and then Newall and Fife behind them. "For about forty seconds it was like being in a blender. I got pummeled but good. But, as I said, I was at the outer edge." His gaze rose to the peak falling behind them. "I think if I'd been in the middle of the path, you'd be comforting Ryan when you got back. I'm not sure how I'd have survived much more than that."

"If there's anything I've learned through the years, it's never to count you out. You'd have fought like hell to get back to Ryan and Lacey. We'd be airlifting you out with myriad broken bones, but I refuse to believe it would have taken you out."

"I like the way you think."

"I can tell you the way I'm thinking right now is, I'm beyond glad to be back on terra firma. The last eighteen hours have been crazy."

"You managed it great. No one suspected you were terrified. I knew, and most of the time I couldn't tell."

"Thanks. What say we try not to ever do a deployment like this again?"

"Your mouth to God's ears." Brian rolled his eyes. "Neither of us wants to go through this particular experience again."

They were making good time, the dogs taking advantage of the wide path and flat terrain, when about a half mile farther south, the path split, one side continuing to hug the creek bed, the other meandering west to follow the base of Pyramid Peak as it narrowed near the southern end. Instead of moving together, the two dogs separated, Lacey taking the creek path, Hawk the mountain path.

"Hawk, stop." Meg called a halt to the search when it was clear Lacey was tracking a different trail. "They separated here."

"You're sure?" Newall asked. "Or, rather, the dogs are?"

"Yes." Brian peered down a path that disappeared into the trees flanking the waterway. "Lacey didn't hesitate. Whoever we're following went this way."

"Back to split teams, then." Carlisle squatted down to study the ground where the paths diverged. "This ground is hard enough and rocky enough, there's no indication of which way Drubek went."

"Barron had a fifty-fifty chance, and picked the wrong path." Newall stepped around Carlisle as she stood and followed Brian's path. "We'll stay in touch."

"Us too." Carlisle took Hawk's path, Hensley behind her as Fife followed Newall. "Lead the way, we're with you."

"Lacey, find him." Brian offered the bag to Lacey again, who took a quick sniff, put her nose down, and cast about for the scent trail, finding it almost instantaneously.

Brian, Newall, and Fife followed Lacey as she trotted down the path, nose down, steps sure.

Meg offered Hawk her bag. "Hawk, find." Hawk didn't hesitate, continuing down his path from the fork.

"This split in trails is going to put a big damper on Barron's quest to hunt down Drubek," Hensley said.

"For sure," Carlisle agreed. "We don't know who took which path, but breaking off from Drubek's path probably cost Barron enough time that he lost Drubek for good, unless the two paths converge ahead."

"Losing Drubek could save Barron's life," Meg said. "Drubek brought down a plane, he won't hesitate to bring down one man following him."

"Or us, for that matter. Or the dogs." Carlisle adjusted her jacket, making sure her weapon was easily at hand, as if she thought they might be getting close. "We'll make sure we're ready. No one else gets hurt. I'm amazed Brian is still on his feet."

"He can be a stubborn ass." The affection in Meg's tone was unmistakable. "Sometimes it's a pain, sometimes it's instrumental in getting the job done."

They'd only gone another few hundred yards when Meg's satellite phone rang. "Hawk, stop. Hold." She dug out her phone, answered Brian's call. "Hey."

"Hey. So we hit a two-way trail."

"What's that?" Carlisle asked. "Another fork in the path?"

"Not exactly. This isn't about geography, it's about scent. Lacey hit a point where the same scent trail went in two directions. Meaning the guy doubled back and picked a different way. Brian, can you tell what happened?"

"Yeah. We hit a spot where Lacey was clearly conflicted. Two paths, and one not significantly fresher than the other."

"Meaning she can't tell which is the newer trail?" Hensley asked.

"Right," Meg said. "Some time has to pass between the trails for them to be able to tell. If it's only a matter of minutes, they'll smell the same. But an hour or more? They can tell you which is the more recent path. Brian, was it a short double back before taking a new route?"

"Yes."

"What made him recalculate?"

"That part is clear. Ben, you said it rained a lot over the weekend? And, as we know, it rained last night."

"Yes."

"We came to an area where the creek overflowed its bank. It's in a spot with a turn where the far side is a rocky rise, so there was nowhere for the water to go on that side, only on this one. And it really flooded the area. There's enough water it turned into a fifteen-foot muddy bog.

Shoe prints—not heavy boot prints to match the boots we were told Drubek was wearing—go about three steps into the mud, then stop."

"Can you tell why?"

"Sure can. There are no other prints. Whoever I'm following realized he's on the wrong path. No one had just crossed this area, and the bushes and trees around it were too thick to push through. Which also means we're following Barron. He's not blazing trails; he's trying to follow one."

"Which means Hawk's following Drubek. Good to know."

"Barron must have realized he took the wrong path at the fork and, instead of going all the way back, found a thinner area of underbrush and pushed through to meet up with the path you're on. At least that's the theory. We're making our way west now."

Meg scanned the area to the east of them, but couldn't see them yet. "We'll wait for you. If the paths converge, it would be better to stay as a group."

"Agreed," Brian said. "But there's one more thing. I don't think Barron is well. He didn't just turn around in the mud; he staggered. From the muddy prints left on the dry dirt, it looks like he's limping."

That caught Carlisle's attention. "Are those prints still wet?"

"Wet enough." Newall's voice sounded in the distance, and then came on stronger, as if Brian had handed him the phone. "You can see the mud came out of the treads of the sneakers he's wearing, and, at this temp, with no sun, they haven't totally dried yet. Stacey, I think we're only a few hours behind at this point. At most, at our pace. And as Brian said, this guy is clearly injured."

"He survived a plane crash. It's not a stretch he didn't come through unscathed. And Lacey's following his blood."

"If he wasn't hurt in the crash, he was hurt on the mountain descent. We're coming now. Probably only a few minutes behind you." Newall ended the call.

They didn't have to wait long. Meg spotted a flash of color coming through the thinning trees, then Lacey stepped onto the path and trotted toward them. She greeted Hawk like she hadn't seen him in weeks, circling and scenting him, tail whipping from side to side.

"Really, Lacey? You saw him fifteen minutes ago." Brian rolled his eyes at Meg.

Meg grinned down at the ecstatic dogs. "Hawk would spend every minute of every day with her. He doesn't mind if she wants to know where he's been. Of course he's been here, on this path, so there's not much to smell. Though I'm impressed with their energy." She held up a palm in the air to Brian.

He automatically high-fived her. "What's that for?"

"That's all the enthusiasm you're going to get from me right now. Welcome back. Now let's move. Hawk, find."

Brian chuckled and fell into step with her. "Lacey, find."

A quick reorganization of personnel and the party was on its way. They followed the established walking path for nearly a mile, and, in that time, the drone passed above their heads twice. As the day moved to early afternoon, the sky lightened, the clouds rising. Even with no sunlight breaking through the clouds, the temperature rose into the fifties, and the bitter gusts of the previous night decreased to a pleasant breeze in the valley.

Their path rose steadily as the valley marched south. Several meager streams of runoff tumbled down the south end of the mountain, gathering into a larger creek bed running parallel to the path to flow farther south. Ahead of them, a thick pine forest beckoned, rising around the waterway, while multihued shades of green climbed the sides of the mountains surrounding them.

Out of the long sleep of snow and winter, life woke and rose again. Even under the dingy light of the cloudy sky, it was a breathtaking sight. To their right, Pyramid Peak stepped down to earth. Turning slightly, Meg caught sight of the rocky summit of the mountain for the first time, free of the surrounding clouds. Past it, nearly all the way back its five-mile length and about halfway up the mountain, lay the crash site, hidden from view in the cradle hold of the saddle.

She was glad she was seeing the whole mountain only now they were off it—she wasn't sure she'd have had the courage to climb it, had she seen it in all its terrifying glory. It was a gorgeous spectrum of rugged beauty from below. From above, it was simply mind-numbingly high—too high for Meg to appreciate the raw landscape around her. She wished she could have.

To their left, the summit of Keefe Peak was just behind them, smaller peaks and valleys running south to meet the Teocalli and White Rock Mountains in the distance. But it was the terrain ahead of them that caught Meg's eye. Mountains rippled over the horizon, notably lower than the peaks surrounding them, but still reaching high toward the clouds . . . except for one spot that dipped low, showcasing the lightening sky and additional rocky peaks in the distance.

Brian noticed her focus. "What's wrong?"

"Why do you say that?"

"I know that furrow you get between your brows when you're fretting about something. You have it now. What gives?"

"I think I see where this search is going." Meg half turned to find Hensley and Carlisle behind them. "What's that low area there?" She pointed to the dip between peaks in the distance.

"East Maroon Pass." Hensley's gaze fixed on it; his eyes narrowed as if jumping ahead of her question.

"Is that the only way through these mountains, rather than over them?"

"It's not the only way, but yes, the easiest and closest."

"What's on the other side of the pass?"

"You're thinking Drubek is going to try to get through that way?" Carlisle interrupted before Hensley could answer the question.

"I'm looking at the geography through the eyes of someone who doesn't know the area," Meg replied. "We can't be sure he doesn't—with his fake identity, we know nothing about the real man—but he may not. If he's from the Denver area, then unless he's a climber, he may not be intimately familiar with the mountains. And if he's not from around here, but came to Colorado specifically to exact some kind of revenge on the Barrons, then this terrain might be all new to him, like it is to me. Traveling through this area, and having just experienced the difficulty and danger of a high-altitude peak, I'd want to avoid that. Also, speed is a factor. We're covering ground so much faster down here than we did up there." She threw out a hand toward Pyramid Peak. "I'd do everything possible to avoid climbing again. It doesn't look like there's an easy way out of this area from here, but that pass would be easier than anything else. The dogs will lead us, but my gut says Drubek is heading for that pass. And Barron, unless he's too injured to manage it, will make that same calculation, even if he loses Drubek's path. If Drubek had gone north, he'd have run into the overflow of the rescue group's base camp. Whether he spotted it from above and turned away from it, or simply had a fifty-fifty chance of choosing a direction and went south, he moved away from the easy road that would carry him into Aspen, where he could get lost or find transportation down to Denver, an even better place to get lost."

"Or to get caught," Brian suggested. "Instead, he may be trying to get lost in the mountains until things cool down. We also don't know if Drubek knows he's being followed. Has he spotted Barron in his red jacket? Does he know Barron is injured and is trying to lose him by escaping via a climb Barron can't manage?" He indicated the pass. "How high is it?"

"About eleven thousand eight hundred feet," Hensley said. "Where the lowest peak surrounding it is about twelve thousand five hundred feet."

"It's not just the altitude," Fife called from where he hiked behind them, clearly following their conversation. "East Maroon Pass has a clear and climbable path. Soil and rock, very little scree. Where Pyramid is a category-four climb, the pass is a category two at worst. Lots of it is category one. In the old days it was a trail used by mule trains carrying ore out of the mines. Unless Drubek wants to go way east to the Triangle or Copper Passes, I agree, East Maroon Pass is the path he'll take. From there, he has access to CO 317 into Crested Butte. But . . ."

When he paused for a long moment, Meg turned around to study him. The expression on his face told her there was more. "What?"

"I guess it depends on whether he knows the area or not, but going over that pass crosses him out of Pitkin County and into Gunnison County . . ."

"Where the Gunnison County Sheriff's Office isn't looking for anyone yet." Newall completed Fife's thought. "We can rectify that. I'll call in our suspicions, and raise the alert with the Gunnison Sheriff's Office."

"That's a good idea," said Hensley. "They won't be able to mount a massive search on our suspicions alone, but they can be ready to move on a confirmation. Pitkin is only a third of the size of Gunnison, but has the greater population, so the challenge for the Gunnison County Sheriff's Office is how spread out they are. Luckily, headquarters is only about fifty miles away from here."

"That seems pretty far," said Brian.

"You're too used to DC. Up here? Not so far." Hensley nodded at Newall. "Call them, get them ready. They can always stand down."

Newall pulled out his satellite phone. "Agreed."

They'd only walked another few minutes when Meg's satellite phone warbled an incoming text. "It's McCord. If we can take the time, he needs to update us. Can we pause for a minute? The dogs could use a water break anyway, so we can do that while checking to see if anything Mc-Cord has will help give insight into Drubek."

"Or whoever he really is . . ." Brian mumbled.

"Exactly. Is everyone okay with that?"

"Do it," Carlisle said.

The handlers told the dogs to stop and sit, then Meg texted McCord, telling him to call if he could talk now. The phone rang almost instantly. Meg answered and put the call on speaker so everyone could hear. "Hey, McCord, you're on speaker with the six of us." She handed the phone to Carlisle while she set up Hawk's water dish.

Carlisle extended the phone into the middle of their circle so everyone could hear.

"Perfect. How has the search gone so far today?"

Brian tossed a nonplussed look at Meg from under his eyebrows from where he knelt beside Lacey as she drank.

"Nothing special, just a nice walk on a mountain that wants to kill us."

"What?"

"Later, McCord, when we have more time." Meg cut

him off, not wanting to make explanations that would get back to Todd. "What do you have?"

"I think I have Drubek's real identity."

"Think?"

"I don't have enough confirmation to write it in stone, but I think you need what I have now. If I'm right, it will put you in the guy's head and will explain what he's done."

Carlisle leaned in. "Special Agent Carlisle here, Mr. McCord. We'll take it under advisement this is a work in progress and your information may not be complete. What have you learned?"

"I started at the security company that contracted out guards to Barron Pharma—East Colfax Security Services. I worked my way up the ladder there." McCord chuckled. "Nice to see the words 'Washington Post' continue to strike terror into the hearts of businessmen across the country. I ended up with the CEO, a Mr. Rupert Leonard, who didn't want to give me the time of day. When I explained that one of his employees had hijacked a plane, which then crashed in the Elk Mountains, killing numerous people, he loosened up considerably, especially when I told him his company had been part of the swindle and, surely at this point, he'd want to help, so I could shine a positive light on ECSS in my upcoming article. He got talkative then."

"Nothing like an insecure security company," Newall commented. "Anything negative you say about them will impact their bottom line, so it was in Leonard's interest to put as much of a positive spin on it as possible."

"That's it, right there," said McCord. "It took us a while, but he looped in an HR rep and we got the full story, as much as we knew it from their perspective. Drubek joined ECSS more than a year ago, working local jobs and proving himself to be indispensable and always willing to take on overtime hours when they ran short of bodies. So, when they needed someone on short notice to help at Barron Pharma, he offered to jump in, doing double duty until they could find someone to fill his previous role at one of the local financial institutions. Drubek not only had commercial security experience, he had bodyguard experience, which made him perfect for the Barron Pharma role, so they moved him there full-time."

"But Drubek doesn't exist," said Carlisle. "Is it fair to assume his entire résumé was fictional?"

"Yes. Before, when I said Drubek doesn't exist, I was mostly right. Sid Drubek does exist. She's been in a coma in Kansas for the last eighteen months."

"Did you say 'she'?" Meg asked.

"Yup. Sidney Drubek, female, aged forty-four, single. Has been in a coma since being struck by a car speeding through a pedestrian sidewalk in Topeka. He stole her identity and took her Social Security number for his own use, so when he used it at ECSS, Uncle Sam didn't blink, as it wasn't on file anymore in Kansas because the real Sidney had been released from her job, as she couldn't complete her duties. Being in a coma and all."

"How nice of them."

"Well, it worked for our Drubek," continued McCord, "as, by this time, the real Sid Drubek was only known by her immediate family and the hospital staff. I've done stories on identity theft before, so I've seen similar scenarios in the past. He likely got into her email. Used the 'forgot password' link on the website and then correctly answered her security questions."

"How would he do that if he didn't know this lady?" Fife asked.

"I found a copy of her résumé on LinkedIn, and he could have done the same. Listed things like where she lived, her high school and college, early jobs. From there I found her both on Ancestry.com and Facebook, and collectively found out more details about her. The name of her cat, her mother's middle name, et cetera, et cetera. That info was likely enough to do the job on the email. Once he had control of her email, he could go further, like straight into her bank accounts. He could do a similar password reset there because he had access to her email. Same thing for government websites without two-factor authentication, because he didn't have her cell phone. But a lot of people don't have two-factor turned on because it's a pain in the ass. Presto, he now had full access to her identification. He registered with ECSS as Sid, not Sidney, and no one blinked because it's a gender-neutral name. Leonard dug into the hiring process for Drubek and found, while three different email addresses had been given for reference, they only followed up on one. Leonard now questions if that email address and the company it came from were real. But whoever answered the email, likely Drubek himself, was very complimentary, and Drubek was hired. He managed to stay under the radar there for a full six months before Don Hull, one of the two regular guards posted to Barron Pharma, was jumped one night getting out of his car by an assailant with a tire iron who shattered both bones in his right forearm. That seriously put Hull on the DL."

"He's right-handed?" Meg asked.

"Yes. It's hard to wrestle someone to the ground with a broken arm, or pull your firearm in case of an emergency. Hull was cycled to a desk job while he healed and Drubek took his position. By the time Hull returned to full duties, Drubek was well established with Barron Pharma, so they put Hull somewhere else."

"Who assaulted him?" Brian asked.

"You know, funny thing, that. The cops never found

out who it was. The guy was wearing a heavy parka and a balaclava to hide his face."

The way Carlisle was shaking her head told Meg she'd already made the same mental leap. "The attacker could have been Drubek, ensuring there was a spot open with Barron Pharma."

"That's the way I'm leaning. Seems kind of convenient otherwise."

"Which means this guy's been playing a long game for over a year."

"I think so."

"But who is he really, McCord?" Meg checked her fitness tracker. "They started with an hours-long lead on us, but we were catching up before we stopped to chat. And the clock is ticking." She collapsed Hawk's water dish and slid it away.

"Right, sorry. To make a long story short, I started tracking down lawsuits and charges of opioid pushing against Barron Pharma. It's a long list, but then I started cross-referencing. I came down to a short list of four possibles, but I'm ninety-nine percent sure I identified your guy. His name is Rod Palin. Year before last, Palin's twenty-two-year-old son, his only child, was in a bad car accident, requiring reconstructive surgery of his knee. The recovery was hellishly painful, and he was prescribed and became addicted to Zelcone. When his doc wouldn't continue to prescribe it, he started buying it, or an equivalent, on the street. He OD'd two weeks before he turned twenty-three."

"Damn," breathed Newall. "That was when Palin made plans?"

"I don't think so. That happened when his wife decided she couldn't live without her boy and took an entire new bottle of depression meds with a whiskey chaser one day while Palin, who worked as a bailiff at the local court-house, was at work. He came home and found her body."

"That's the whole ballgame, right there." Carlisle's struggle with sympathy for the man was clear on her face. "He lost his whole family. Some men might have taken their own life to join them. He decided to bring down the family that stole his."

"The family, and the whole company," Newall corrected.

"Right. And you have to wonder if he didn't mind dying in this attempt because it would be to join his family. If his own death was what it took to find justice, he was okay with that."

"Note, though, he didn't leave anything to chance," Newall pointed out. "He took out Patrick Connolly for expediency, but then seemed happy to let the plane crash take out everyone else, except for Kenneth Barron."

"There always could have been a chance someone survived the plane crash, small as it might be. But he wanted to make sure Kenneth Barron not only suffered the potential loss of his son—a pain Palin knew well—but then died before the crash. Two bullets to the brain was overkill, but actually makes a bit more sense now. Zero chance of recovery."

"I thought this might give you a little more insight as to what you're looking at," McCord said. "From up here in the cheap seats, it looks like he set out to find justice for his wife, his child, and for everyone else who has perished because of these drugs, as well as everyone they left behind. And one other thing was a crucial piece to cement my bringing this to you now. I found some video news stories about the Barrons—court appearances and the like. They always travel with their bodyguards—one of the two men in those videos is a match to Rod Palin's Facebook page, which hasn't been updated since his wife's death, but is still online. There's a lot more I need to find out about this man and how he set this up, but at this point I knew I needed to loop you in."

Meg met Carlisle's eyes. "Thanks, McCord, you've given us something great to start with. I know it's preliminary, but it seems to click. We need to continue the search now. I'll try to catch you later today, if possible. Can you put those details in a document and send it to Craig? He'll disperse it to the Bureau people who need it."

"Can do. Safe searching."

Then McCord was gone.

Hensley, who'd been quiet for the whole conversation, scanned the faces of the agents and handlers. "So, what next?"

Carlisle puffed out a breath. "We continue. No matter how sorry we might feel for this man, for the agony he's gone through, the be-all and end-all is that he used illegal means to find his justice instead of going through proper legal channels."

"You know, I can't blame him." Fife's eyes were hard, his jaw set; it was clear he wasn't conflicted at all. "He lost his family. And we've all seen big companies like this, with their billion dollars of profit and barrage of lawyers, skinny out from under legal jeopardy by using every loophole they can find. He probably didn't think he'd live to see justice done."

Carlisle sent him a sharp look and opened her mouth to snap back, but then she paused and deflated slightly. "Goddammit," she muttered. "You know what, I can't completely blame him either. I think if that happened to me—if I lost my whole family because of a drug a company knew was addictive and deadly, but pushed it anyway in the name of profits—I'd lose my mind. Especially when I knew the people making the decisions were likely going to be protected from taking the hit they deserved. Honestly, I don't know what I'd do. But our path is clear here. He's killed multiple individuals innocent of anything that happened to his family, and wounded more. We have to bring him in to let the legal system deal with him." She met Fife's eyes. "I hear you. But we can't let him escape. His fate needs to be in the hands of a jury to make the call after hearing the evidence."

Fife hesitated briefly, then nodded.

Carlisle gave him an understanding smile and then turned to the handlers. "We need to find Palin and Barron. Let's get the dogs back on the trail." Her gaze wandered to the pass in the distance. "I think you're right; that's where we're going, but we'll let the dogs tell us for sure."

Meg and Brian offered the scent bags to the dogs and gave them the command to find. Once again the dogs immediately followed the trail only they could sense.

They covered the ground quickly, moving away from the slender waterway that hugged the base of Pyramid Peak into deep forest, the ground rising slowly beneath their boots. Everyone felt the need to end this chase while their prey was still on foot.

The pass, seen only in brief snatches through breaks in the canopy, came closer and closer, but Meg had learned that what appeared close was actually a much larger piece of the terrain, farther away than originally perceived.

They broke into a clearing about five hundred feet across. Meg could see small wisps of blue sky peeking through the cloud layer, and took heart from the brightening of the sky and the warming of the day. Combined with their constant activity for hours, both she and Hawk were comfortably warm.

Brian had fallen slightly behind, and Meg let him catch up to her. He was puffing harder than this exertion would usually engender, but considering all her partner had gone through that day, she wasn't about to point fingers. Had it been her, she wasn't sure she'd still be on her feet. "Hanging in?"

"Absolutely. I'm not about to—"

Crack crack crack! Three sharp blasts split the air, the sound echoing repeatedly off every peak and valley, making it sound more like a twenty-one-gun salute.

"Talon, down!"

Hawk immediately flattened himself to the ground. As she dropped, Meg slipped a hand inside her jacket, unerringly finding her holstered Glock, flicked off the elastic securing the weapon, and drew it out. She threw herself on top of her dog, sheltering his body with her own.

Had they caught up with Palin and he was firing on them, trying to kill them rather than be taken into custody?

CHAPTER 21

Crux: The most difficult section of a climbing route.

May 7, 1:41 PM
Pyramid Peak
Aspen, Colorado

As silent seconds ticked by, Meg cautiously raised her head to find Brian just slightly behind her. He'd also drawn his Glock and was similarly positioned over Lacey. A glance behind found everyone else belly down in the wild grass of the clearing.

Carlisle was on her elbows, gun gripped in both hands, scanning the surrounding area, ready to fire if necessary to protect the group. Meg couldn't see Newall clearly, but from the way his legs were shifting on the ground, Meg guessed he had his pack off and was unstrapping the Remington 700. He'd left it strapped to his pack all this time because until there was a threat, it was more important for him to have both hands free for climbing. Not to mention that a rifle dangling from a sling strap might not only be a hazard to him on the steep rocky slopes, it could also damage the rifle. It had been safer to keep the firearm securely strapped into place.

Not anymore.

Another gunshot sounded—not quite as loud and with an extended echo—and Hawk shivered under her. "It's okay, buddy, you're safe." She scanned the terrain around and above them, but could see no sign of movement.

Carlisle cautiously pushed to her knees, revealing New-all, stretched out in the grass behind her in a prone sniper's position, his right eye pressed to the scope, slowly panning with the rifle as he took stock of the rocky terrain above them. "That shot sounded farther away, maybe on the other side of the pass." Carlisle waited another twenty seconds, a small but clear target above the others in the grass. "Corey?"

"I don't see anyone, moving or down. I think one or both of them have crossed over the pass, because I can see most of this side of the slope."

"I bet he's not shooting at us, but at Barron as he cleared the pass. Trying to buy time."

"I asked before, but the question got sidetracked," Meg said. "What's on the other side of the pass? What's he headed toward?"

"Copper Lake," Hensley said. "There are a few associated campsites, but the state doesn't have bookings until the end of this month. They should be unoccupied. But there could be hikers. A few miles outside of the town of Crested Butte, there's a parking lot at the trailhead for Judd Falls, and then it's about a five-, five-and-a-half-mile hike to Copper Lake." Hensley's gaze rose to the sky, panning over clouds floating well clear of any peaks. "Weather is better today, so hikers could be a consideration."

"Assuming Palin's shooting, I think we're safe in assuming after everything that's happened, he'll do what he needs to avoid being caught—including shooting any innocent bystander who might be in his way." Carlisle got to her feet. "We need to pick up the pace. Can the dogs trail faster?"

Meg holstered her firearm and pulled out her scent bag. "It will eat away at their endurance and we'll run a greater risk of losing the scent trail, but if we're getting close to the end of the search and there's a chance we might lose the target or put anyone else in jeopardy, it's worth it. If he gets over the pass and finds that trailhead and steals a car, we may never find him again." She offered the bag to Hawk. "Hawk, this is Palin. Find Palin. Fast, Hawk. Find Palin fast."

Hawk took off so quickly Meg didn't stuff the bag in her pack, but folded and slid it into one of her jacket pockets, zipping it shut so there was no chance of losing the precious scent source now they knew Meg's bag contained Palin's scent, while Brian's held Barron's.

"Here we go!" Meg called over her shoulder as she drew her firearm again, then fell into step with Brian in a light jog. She gave her backpack a boost to adjust the weight on her shoulders, and then simply concentrated on her dog, on his pace, his stance, and his breathing.

Humans had the luxury of deep breathing during exertion, although, as Meg and Brian knew well at this point, deep breaths of air with little pressure to push oxygen into starved tissues was nearly useless. Lucky for them, now three thousand feet lower than the previous night, neither struggled for oxygen like they had since yesterday. Three doses of acetazolamide later, and they were both feeling stable, which was reflected in their mental acuity and athletic performance.

It was harder for the dogs, who were not only working strenuously under the same lower oxygen conditions, but were forced to breathe differently to accomplish their designated task. When they were tracking and trailing, they

employed a short series of inhalations to bring scent into
their olfactory recess—a specialized series of folds with
220 million receptors located between their eyes. But air
going into the olfactory recess never reached the lungs,
leaving oxygen-deprived dogs even more deprived. So far,
they weren't showing signs of strain, thanks to their own
doses of acetazolamide, but Meg knew that could change
quickly, especially as they were going to have to climb
again to traverse the pass.

The dogs abruptly left the path to cut southeast. Meg
could see sections of flattened grass ahead—while one
path was fairly direct, the other wavered significantly.
Lacey followed the undulating path, falling into place behind Hawk so she could stay on the exact trail.

Meg dropped back a few paces to give Lacey space to
work. "She's right on top of the trail. She has Barron dead
to rights."

"Can't hide . . . anyone . . . from her." Brian's words
were punctuated by heavy breaths, the intervening words,
coming rapid-fire.

"Is this getting too hard? You sound pretty breathless."

"I feel pretty . . . breathless, but I got it. Let me tell you,
when this . . . is done, I want . . . a fire . . . and a big glass
of . . . red wine. Think après-ski . . . without the ski."

"I'll drink to that." Meg gave him one more concerned
glance and then returned her gaze to her dog. "I need you
to tell me if you can't manage anymore. Promise me."

"It's fine—"

"Don't pull that on me, especially not when ninety minutes ago, I'd thought I'd lost you. Please."

He was silent for another four jogged steps. "I promise." Another ragged breath. "You can trust me."

His word was enough for her. "Always."

The dogs led them into the trees, following a path through
the underbrush clear as day to them, but only had minimal

markings to the human eye. Partway through, Lacey veered off from Hawk, staying between fifteen and twenty-five feet away for most of their remaining time over the level terrain. However, when they came to a narrow couloir, the paths converged, following the narrow depression uphill in a path leading directly to the pass.

The weekend rains must have run heavily downhill in this location as the soil lining the couloir was damp, even muddy in some locations, causing the odd boot slip, nearly taking Newall down before he managed to catch himself, one hand on the ground, one hand still gripping the stock of his rifle.

They set a pace as fast as they all could manage. Meg would have preferred a faster pace, but it was realistic for the team having already been searching for nearly eight hours today. Moreover, Meg was sure they were still moving faster than the two men in front of them, who had been on the move for approximately the same period of time, but without the stamina of those following. It took the team a full twenty minutes to travel the half mile uphill, the last third of that distance in an uncomfortably exposed position out of the protection of the trees, but as long as the dogs stayed on the trail, they stayed with them.

Meg knew they were close, and not only by the gunshots they'd heard. She could see it in Hawk's and Lacey's certainty on their respective trails. Following a trail less than an hour old, in conditions with a moderate breeze and with no precipitation, meant the trail was extremely vibrant from their perspective. Meg and Brian didn't need to repeat the command to pick up the pace; the dogs' own enthusiasm kept them going.

At 11,500 feet, they intersected a path from the west that led directly up to the pass. Then as they cut through a sparse thicket of trees, Lacey broke into a gallop, shooting up the path as it rose even higher.

"Stay with her," Meg panted, keeping one eye on Hawk, who didn't seem to feel the same urgency. "The wind must have brought her something new."

"On it." Somehow Brian found some store of energy from deep inside and powered after his dog.

Meg was twenty feet behind them when Lacey veered off the path, Brian following her. Then she saw the flash of red on the ground through the tree trunks to the west of the hiking trail.

Red. Barron had taken someone's red jacket. But if he was on the ground, it couldn't be good.

"Barron's here!" Brian's call came just as Meg made it to where their trail had diverted. But where Meg slowed for Brian, Hawk went another ten feet along the path before Meg commanded him to stop and to come with her.

Carlisle, Newall, Hensley, and Fife were directly behind her. With one look at the man on the ground, Hensley and Fife unstrapped their packs and moved in.

Eli Barron looked like he was in his late thirties. In good health, he was likely a tall, good-looking man, with symmetrical features, broad cheekbones, and blond hair. But the man on the ground was deathly pale, with a nasty bloody scrape down the right side of his face. Moreover, he seemed delirious. A dark bloom of blood soaked the left side of his jacket at waist level as he lay on the ground, clutching his head and moaning. Pink froth bubbled at one corner of his lips.

A Heckler & Koch HK45 pistol lay about two feet away from the body, as if flung from Barron's hand as he fell. At least they could now account for one gun. Still, how many guns did Palin really have? Had he brought additional weapons, perhaps in an ankle or shoulder holster, along with extra magazines, to ensure his takeover of the flight was successful? They couldn't assume Palin would exhaust one magazine and be left with no firepower. They had to assume he had at least one backup piece, as well as extra ammunition. If they were lucky, they were wrong.

After the avalanche Meg couldn't be sure luck was on their side.

Fife was digging through his pack. "I have the oxygen."

"I have the wound." Ripping open his first-aid kit, Hensley quickly pulled on gloves and then tore open a pack of hemostatic gauze. "This should help stop the bleeding." He unzipped the jacket, finding the slate-gray sweatshirt below saturated with blood just under Barron's ribs. Hensley pulled up the hem of the sweatshirt to reveal the regular margins of an entry wound, and pressed the gauze firmly to the wound. He carefully rolled the body slightly to find a ragged, gaping exit wound soaking blood into the dirt and rocks under Barron. "Through and through, may have pierced the spleen from the location. If we're lucky, it missed the stomach, intestines, and kidneys. Hand me another piece." Carlisle opened more hemostatic gauze and handed it to Hensley, who packed it against the wound, holding it with his right hand while applying pressure to the upper surface with his left. "We need air support." Hensley looked up at Carlisle. "Now, or we're going to lose him. We don't have hours for this one."

"Not if he has edema. Let me use your radio. It'll be faster."

As Carlisle stepped away, radioing Mountain Rescue Aspen command and telling them they needed Flight For Life immediately, Newall took off his pack and snapped a few pictures of the scene with his phone. Then he pulled out evidence bags and a pair of latex gloves—leave it to the FBI to be ready to process a crime scene, even out in the middle of nowhere—and, after safely removing the magazine and active round, bagged the firearm and ammunition, and tucked it into his pack.

Brian knelt down beside Lacey, who sat—her alert signaling she'd found her target—directly beside Barron's writhing body. He was mumbling incoherently and trying to pull off the mask Fife pressed over his nose and mouth. "What's going on? He's more than just shot."

"High-altitude illness. Grab his hands and keep him from flailing." Fife kept his head down as he repositioned the oxygen mask and double-checked the oxygen flow.

"Isn't he from around here?"

"Yes, but remember, being from Denver doesn't mean you can't get high-altitude illness up here; it's just less likely. His condition is probably exacerbated by the stress of the crash, followed by trailing Palin. He's progressed to HAPE—high-altitude pulmonary edema—which is an extremely serious issue. Fluid is collecting in his lungs, which is why there's pink froth around his mouth. He needs real medical help, not field triage. And he needs it now."

Meg remembered Todd's words of warning before she left DC: *A cerebral or pulmonary edema . . . can lead to a coma and death.*

Eli Barron was in serious trouble.

"I thought he was weaving on the trail because he was hurt. But maybe it was because of the high-altitude illness."

"He has to have been struggling for hours, with it getting progressively worse," Hensley said. "It probably made him a sitting duck for Palin; even here in the trees, he wasn't able to get out of the way of one of the four shots. Palin must be in bad shape himself, or there's no way Barron could have even remotely kept up with him in his condition. The shot took him down, but honestly, if he'd gone much farther, I think the edema would have taken him out." Hensley looked down at Barron, who had grown quieter with the delivery of lifesaving oxygen.

"It's kind of unthinkable he pushed himself this far," Brian said.

"Jewitt, Worland, and Blenn described him as being the unforgiving, hard-core personality type," Meg reminded him. "He was enraged at his father's killing, but also likely at the possible gutting of the company that's now his responsibility. And maybe he isn't ready for that responsibility, and that's another layer that could have generated more rage to keep him going."

"They're coming as fast as they can." Carlisle stepped back into the group, sliding the radio into Hensley's harness as his hands were occupied. "They understand they'll have to land about a mile away. Command said there's an area on the Copper Pass spur trail that's suitable for the helicopter to put down. They'll bring a basket and you'll have to package him and carry him out." She straightened. "We're going to have to leave you here with him." She turned to Meg. "Hawk's still following Palin?"

"I had to command him to stop. He'll pick up the trail again."

"Guaranteed he's left the area."

"Agreed."

"Will Hawk know if he doubles back the same way?"

"Yes. He could circle around and we could follow him, but I don't think Palin's that stupid. His only way out is on foot. He has to be hurt and exhausted, and must think his chances of being followed are pretty good after those gunshots. If so, he'd have to suspect we're gaining on him and will be looking for any way to get clear of us. He has a gun. If he makes it to the parking lot Ben says is five miles away, he may attempt to carjack a vehicle. His only goal then will be to get gone."

"It's going to be crucial to catch him while he's still on foot," Carlisle stated. "We already know he has significant expertise in adopting new identities. He gets his hands on a vehicle, he's definitely going to try to disappear for good."

"It's doubtful he knows we're trailing him with dogs. He likely thinks if he stays out of sight, he'll be fine. My bet is he'll aim for the forest, where he's hidden from view, especially from any drones or helicopters we might have in the air."

"That may be his downfall, as we'll be able to follow him. But the combination of his physical state and current firepower makes him an extremely dangerous man."

Brian peered up at Carlisle. "Because he'll be more likely to pull an Indiana Jones?"

"A what?"

"An Indiana Jones. You know, in *Raiders of the Lost Ark* when the guy swinging a sword challenges Indy, and instead of joining the fight, he pulls out his gun and shoots him, ending the threat immediately? That. Why go for something complicated when a simple kill shot will do the job?"

"Reference acknowledged. That's exactly what I mean. There won't be any discussion if he runs into anyone, just action. Good thing hiking is lousy right now and the campsites are unoccupied. It gives us a chance to end this without additional bloodshed, because, otherwise, someone else could be in the line of fire." She crouched down next to Hensley. "I'm sorry to leave you with him. We've lost a few minutes here, but we're in a spot where we can still catch up."

"Definitely. Good hunting. Let me know if you need us to come after you, once Barron is transferred. Get word to command, and they'll pass it up the line."

"Will do." Carlisle stood. "Let's get Hawk on the trail."

"Let's get them to the main trail where I stopped him. There's no scent for the dogs to find here."

With a few last reciprocal words of goodbye and good luck, the handlers led their dogs onto their previous path.

"We can use both dogs, now we're only tracking one

person." Meg pulled out the bag, offering it first to Hawk, then to Lacey. "Hawk, Lacey, this is Palin. Find Palin fast."

Neither dog hesitated, both of them instantly finding the previous trail and trotting uphill.

Meg followed behind, trailed by Brian, feeling though their short break to find Barron possibly on the verge of death had been full of tension, the brief respite from physical activity refreshed her on what was, hopefully, the last part of this journey. Brian, also, as his breathing had steadied.

There was no way they were going to lose Palin because Meg, Brian, or the dogs struggled with the geographic or atmospheric conditions. They just needed to hang on, to dig deeper and pull out their last vestiges of strength and stamina to stop a killer. There would be time for rest and recovery later.

It was three hundred feet to the pass, but their trail carried them across rock and dense soil, over a well-worn footpath that allowed them to move rapidly. Within fifteen minutes they stood at the top of the pass.

A lush green valley spread wide below them. Precarious Peak towered to their right, White Rock Mountain to their left, with a long, low-lying area cradled between them. The trail stepped approximately a thousand feet down to the valley floor, but, at about half that distance, a trilobed greenish-blue lake nestled against the pass's downward slope.

"That's Copper Lake?" Brian asked.

"Yes, with its associated campgrounds." Carlisle unbuckled and shrugged off her pack, digging through and quickly finding her binoculars. "Now the fog has lifted, they'll finally be useful. There's another pair in Corey's pack too." She lifted the binoculars to her eyes and scanned the valley below.

Meg carried her own binoculars, but it would be easier to retrieve Newall's than to unbuckle and remove her own pack to get them out. "Where are they?" Meg asked Newall. "I can grab them so you can keep your pack on."

"Middle front pocket, though they're likely down toward the bottom." Newall glanced down at the Remington 700 locked between his hands. "Go ahead and dig for them; my hands are full."

Meg opened the pocket, bringing out a pair of compact binoculars, and used them to scrutinize the valley. On the far end of the lake, a small peninsula held a copse of pine trees, and, past it, trails led off in two directions. "You'd think he'd stick to a trail unless he ran into hikers. He's looking for the compromise between speed and staying off the radar. But making his own path will likely slow him down too much when all he wants is to disappear ASAP."

"Makes sense to me," Carlisle agreed. "More than that, he may not have the stamina or the ability to manage more of a tricky climb than what it took to get to the pass and back down again. He—" She stopped speaking, her body stiffening. "Wait! I have him!"

"You're sure?"

"As sure as I can be from this distance. It has to be him. Wearing all black and definitely struggling." Carlisle's voice carried the edge of determination. "He's within range. This is our chance to close him down, once and for all."

CHAPTER 22

Cliffed Out: When a climber becomes trapped in a location where he or she has no option to proceed in any direction, and technical equipment or a rescue is required.

May 7, 2:26 pm
Pyramid Peak
Aspen, Colorado

"Where?" Meg asked, peering through her binoculars. "I don't see him."

Carlisle dropped her binoculars for a moment. "Look due south of the lake. See the established trail leading into that patchy forest? He's in there. He hit a spot where he broke from the trees long enough that I caught his movement." She lifted the binoculars again, and took about ten seconds to find him. "Got him again. He's not moving quickly. Meg, do you see the stream that feeds the lake, the one running kind of parallel to the path, where it jogs west? On the path, just past there. I'd bet he's at most a half mile in front of us. If he stopped moving, we could catch him inside of twenty or twenty-five minutes on this terrain. Maybe less."

Meg found the spot in the creek and then panned to her left. For a moment she thought she was looking in the wrong location, then movement caught her eye—a figure in black who wove onto the path and then off it again. "I have him. You're right, he's not doing well. He's mobile, but he's possibly staggering. Injury or exhaustion?"

"Could be one or the other, or both, but it could be what ends this for him."

Meg dropped her binoculars to find Newall, his rifle at his shoulder, sighting down the scope. "Corey, do you see him?"

"Yes." Newall didn't move, keeping his eyes fixed on the target.

"You can take him out from here?" Brian asked.

"In perfect conditions, maybe. That's almost nine hundred yards out and partially hidden in the trees. There's no real clear shot to manage at this distance with his bobbing and weaving. Not to mention, any shot I fire that misses will announce our presence to him and he'll rabbit. If I take a shot, it needs to be on target the first time."

Newall lowered his rifle to hang from its sling and scanned the terrain, then pointed an index finger down the valley. "See that spot down there between the two peaks where the valley narrows down? Probably about two miles south of us? I think we can use a pincer movement on him there. We split up—one dog, handler, and agent on each team. One group stays on the scent trail, one loops around in front of him, trapping him in a spot where he can't go back, can't go forward, and, if he's as injured as he looks, won't be able to manage an upward climb. He's carrying a handgun, and we have to assume he's a good shot even exhausted and injured, but he's limited with range. An effective shot will likely only be fifty to one hundred yards max, depending on the gun and ammunition he's carrying. That's assuming he's not injured and can actually shoot with any accuracy. We're safe from him at a distance, and unless he runs into a hiker, he doesn't have anyone to shoot at. He should remain focused on getting away." Newall pointed to the terrain to their right. "There's no trail up there, but the land looks hikeable. Not too steep, minimal scree, lots of trees. I need to go that way. I want to stay in terrain where I can make a long-distance shot with the rifle, if needed. Hopefully, we can box him in, but if anything goes sideways and I need to take a shot, I'll be better set up if I'm above him. There are too many obstacles on the ground—trees, rocks, slopes that angle the wrong way, blocking line of sight. I'll take this upper trail with the goal of lapping him while he's in the forest and can't see a team on the hill above him. Stacey, you stay on the main trail and box him in from behind."

"I like it." Carlisle turned to Meg. "You're with me?"

Meg opened her mouth to respond, but the sight of Brian behind Carlisle stopped her. Brian, who'd been game through this whole deployment, no matter what happened, even after being buried in an avalanche. His body was beaten, bruised, and pushed to the limit. She could do this for him—give him the physically easier path, the one that entered the valley and stayed there, rather than staying hundreds of feet above it. She wouldn't like it, but she'd manage the height for him. "Let's switch it up. I'll go with Corey; Brian, you go with Stacey."

Brian's brows snapped together in confusion. "Does it make sense to mix up the teams? What we did worked before."

Beating around the bush to save his feelings clearly wasn't getting the job done. Not to mention, there was no time for it. "It did. But I think it would be better if I did the more strenuous trail." When he started to interrupt, she held up a hand to forestall him. "You've given your all in the past two days, including from inside an avalanche. We're both exhausted and oxygen starved. But at least I haven't been pummeled down a hill by several hundred tons of snow." She held his gaze, knowing he'd hear what her words really meant. "I can do this. Let me do it for you. Stacey, any issues?"

"None."

Meg handed Brian the bag with Palin's scent. "Safe searching. And keep your sat phone handy. We'll stay in touch often so you know where we are." She turned to Newall. "Let's go. Hawk, come."

This time she led, Hawk at her knee as they descended about a hundred feet and then cut straight across the upper slope of the valley. She slipped the binoculars into her hip pocket to keep her hands free and to keep the lenses from being scratched against rocks if they had to scramble. They kept up as hard a pace as they could manage over the rough terrain. It helped that the slope was reasonable and the footing was secure.

Through the pines on the slope, Meg kept half an eye on Brian's progress as he, Lacey, and Carlisle made their way down to the valley floor without incident, Lacey leading the way. Even from this distance, Meg could see from her speed and single-minded sense of direction the shepherd had the trail.

If they were twenty or twenty-five minutes behind, considering the staggering gait she'd glimpsed through the binoculars, they might be able to catch Palin in about an hour, assuming they were going about twice as fast as he was. There would be no breaks for any of them, but in a few hours' time, they might be making plans to fly home.

The thought of Todd and a sound night's sleep in her own bed gave her a kick of adrenaline.

The end is in sight.

The adrenaline kept her going for the first mile, but soon she started to have to push to keep her pace up. Hawk, too, seemed to be running out of steam. It was little wonder, considering the stress on their bodies from the exertion and the low oxygen concentration, as well as the lack of sleep and the sheer hours of continual activity over the past two days. But if an injured man could do it, so could she.

They pushed on.

Her satellite phone signaled an incoming call and Meg answered it. "Hey."

"Hey." Brian was puffing loudly into his handset. "How's it going up there?"

"I dream of a shower and eight hours solid in my own bed with my partner. You?"

"The same." A tired snicker came down the line. "Well, not your bed and not Todd, but you know what I mean."

It lightened Meg to hear Brian's usual humor, even if run through with exhaustion. "Sure do. Lacey still on the trail?"

"Five by five."

"Excellent. We must be getting close to coming parallel with him, and hope to pass him soon, to give us enough space to get down to the valley floor by the pincer location."

"I'd guess we're about ten or twelve minutes behind him at this point. Definitely gaining on him and will be in position when you need us to be."

"I would expect nothing less. I'll touch base again in ten, unless something changes." Meg ended the call and slipped the phone into her breast pocket, still maintaining the required distance between her avalanche transceiver and her phone. A quick glance above showed her the lower ranges of Precarious Peak were without snow, but she wasn't taking any chances after Brian's experience. Her transceiver would stay on and active with no interference.

About three-quarters of the way to the pincer location,

they left the forest, stepping into an open area running from a plateau above—likely another saddle—all the way down to the river and the pathway below.

It was a long way down, probably seven or eight hundred feet to the path below, far enough down that Meg, even though she was becoming somewhat numbed to the height, felt her stomach roll with apprehension. But then she realized she could see something else and her blood ran cold.

"Corey, wait." Her hand snapped out to grab Newall's arm. "Hawk, stop." She pulled out the binoculars, quickly finding the path below.

She hadn't been wrong. Through the trees at the edge of the forest, she could see Palin down by the trail, but so were two abandoned all-terrain vehicles. And Palin was climbing into one of them.

Meg whipped out her phone and speed-dialed Brian, talking before he could give a salutation. "How close are you to Palin?"

"Hard to tell, because we can't see him ahead. We're still following the path winding through the forest. Why?"

"We're at the point where we're almost parallel to him, probably seven hundred feet up and slightly behind, and I can see him down below. He found two ATVs and he just got in one."

"ATVs? Why would they be out here?"

"Put that on speaker." Carlisle's voice sounded in the distance. "Meg? Repeat what's going on?" Her voice was stronger now.

"We have a clear view of Palin. He's about seven hundred feet down a cleared straightaway downslope, possibly an old avalanche path. He climbed into an abandoned ATV."

"It's not abandoned. Someone has come in to hike. Happens a lot at this time of year when the lowlands are extremely muddy, so they ATV in through the low-lying mud, park off trail, and then climb where it's drier."

"So we have two hikers up here somewhere?"

"Affirmative. We have to stop him. He takes off in one of those ATVs, he's gone. Into the hills, into Crested Butte . . . wherever, we won't catch him. Some of those ATVs can do sixty to ninety miles per hour and can handle extremely tough terrain. He gets one of them going, and we've lost him. Possibly for good."

"Surely, whoever parked those here didn't leave the keys in it," Brian said.

"I'm sure they didn't. But it's not hard to hot-wire an ATV. Even easier, you can start one by jamming a screwdriver or a scissor blade into the ignition and cranking it. It ruins the ignition, but he won't care. He'll run it until he's out of gas and will be far enough away by that time he has options to get free. Corey, be ready to take a shot from where you are. Shoot him, shoot out a tire, whatever it takes. We're not letting this guy go, not after everything he's done. He'll kill whoever he needs to get away. We can't let someone else die because we lost him here. We know he's on the path, so we're coming in at a run. Don't shoot *us*." She ended the call.

"We don't know if he has a screwdriver, or scissors, or a pocketknife, or whatever he'd need to start it," Meg said. "Or if he knows how to hot-wire it."

"No, we don't. But we have to assume he can somehow make it happen. We need to lay low. Keep an eye on him, but not attract his attention by bolting down the slope. Right now, we have the advantage of surprise. He won't expect Stacey and won't see her until she's practically on top of him and within range with a handgun. But it's less than two hundred fifty yards from up here. Child's play with the 700, but I need to line up a shot and I don't have a straight line of sight here." He looked at the couloir thirty feet in front of them running downhill in almost a straight line to the ATVs. "Come on."

Crouching down, trying to stay low and not attract attention, Newall jogged over the grassy verge, holding the rifle close to his chest in both hands.

They stopped dead at the edge of the couloir, looking into the trough below.

"Shit," Newall muttered.

The couloir ran from several hundred feet above them, nearly all the way down to the roadway, and while this area of the slope was nearly tree free, the area down by the road was partially blocked by trees at their current angle. They needed to be farther south for a clear line of sight. That meant getting into the couloir and making the shot from there, or having to climb out and make it from the far side. The problem was the couloir's fifty-degree slope, eighty-foot drop to the bottom, and the field of scree that lay between them and their sweet spot. The other side was significantly shallower, but that didn't help; they were on this side.

"Hawk's going to have trouble here." Meg eyed the tricky slope. "I think *we* might have trouble here."

"I can take the shot solo. You stay here and keep your binoculars on Palin. Tell me what he's doing as I'm getting down there. Just keep your voice as low as possible. We don't want him to hear us and attract his attention. We're enough behind and above him, he'd have to almost turn around to see us, but if he does and spots us, he's out of here."

"Agreed. Be careful on that slope. A wrong step or a slip could send you down to the bottom."

"Definitely don't want to do that." Newall grabbed the rifle stock firmly with his right hand and eased himself over the lip of the couloir, bracing his left hand on the edge. "Going down."

Meg knelt down at the edge of the couloir. "Hawk, come. Down, boy." She stroked a hand down his back as he lay on the grass. "Good boy." A quick glance at Newall—he was moving slowly but steadily down the slope, carefully placing his feet, and stepping down on a sideways angle, keeping his left hand on the scree—then she brought up the binoculars. "Palin's in the ATV still, crouched over, looking under the steering column."

"Likely trying to figure out if he can hot-wire it." Newall's voice floated up to her.

"What are the chances of shooting out a tire?"

"I could do it, but I'm not sure how much difference that would make. He could still get away on just the rim if he stuck to the trail. That could get him out to the trailhead and the road."

Meg lowered her binoculars to check out how far Newall had gone. He was about halfway there, with about forty feet still to go. "We need Stacey to get there, but it could still take a few more—"

Newall let out a guttural cry as one of the rocks beneath his right boot gave way under his weight, tumbling away. His hands already occupied keeping the rifle steady and maintaining his balance against the slope, Newall pitched face forward onto the rocks with nothing to break his fall, then started to roll.

Meg didn't dare call his name and risk attracting attention. "Hawk, stay!" She holstered her Glock and dropped to sit on the edge of the couloir in time to see Newall come to rest, head down at the low point of the couloir.

The way he'd fallen had arrested his downward motion, but he wasn't moving.

Down on her ass, then. Meg would rather bruise her

tailbone than duplicate Newall's fall. She planted both feet out as far as she could, then braced her hands and moved her butt down the slope. Repeating the motion, she worked her way down. *Stare at Corey, don't look down the hill.* Keeping her eyes locked on his unmoving body, Meg slid down the rocky slope as fast as she could. It took minutes, but she got there.

"Corey!" Shifting to her knees beside him, she weighed her options. The rule was never to move someone who might have a spinal injury, but she needed to at least get him on his side to be able to assess his condition. God forbid he'd need CPR; with him wedged facedown into the rock, she couldn't do it. Tucking one hand behind his neck to keep it stable, she carefully rolled him onto his side, as far as the bulk of his backpack would allow.

A quick glance down the couloir showed her Palin was still in the ATV, which remained in place, so she turned her full attention to Newall. He was breathing, but unconscious, his face lax, his cheeks and forehead scraped and already starting to darken with bruising, while blood trickled from under his helmet. Thank God for the helmet, which saved him from a crushed skull under its protection, but hadn't protected his face or his brain from bouncing around in his skull.

At least a grade-two concussion, maybe grade three. Unfortunately, she had the experience to know all about concussions.

"Hey! What are you doing?"

Meg's head snapped up at the roar coming from downhill and across the couloir. She could only see the upper halves of two men, running down the hill as fast as they could without falling, heading straight for the ATVs.

The hikers who left them. The hikers who would have keys to them. He wouldn't need to hot-wire an ATV if he killed the hikers and stole their keys.

Below, Palin's head jerked upright, his eyes finding the hikers closing in on him. They were out of range of his handgun, but wouldn't be for long.

"Stop!" Meg shouted, but if the men heard her outside of their focus on what was going on below, they didn't respond.

Palin would kill them; Meg had no doubt.

Her gaze dropped to the rifle resting against Newall's belly. It looked intact, definitely scratched, but hopefully not so badly it would likely affect its function. And it was a rifle she was familiar with.

Could she do it?

Legally, taking the shot wasn't in question. She may not be a Bureau agent, but she was an FBI consultant authorized to carry a firearm on national deployments. The Glock pressed against her side was proof of that. And there were innocent civilians in imminent danger.

She could take the shot.

But could she make the shot? It had been years since she'd done sniper training.

She had to try or two men would die.

She quickly unclipped the Remington 700 from the two-point sling strap looped around Newall and moved about ten feet downhill.

She had to take the time to check out the rifle. If any small stones had become lodged in the barrel during Newall's fall, there could be a catastrophic failure of the weapon when the bullet got stuck behind the obstruction, and she could die. Moving quickly, she popped out the magazine, then opened the bolt, the round in the chamber ejecting to clatter onto the rocks below. She flipped the gun over to peer down the barrel, relief streaking through her when she could see straight down into the empty chamber. She turned the gun around, rammed the magazine home, and then closed the bolt, loading a new round into the chamber. Now she just had to hope the scope was still accurate or it was game over.

A quick check on her dog to make sure he was still at the edge of the couloir—he was, his eyes locked on her every move—and she turned to the task at hand. The two men were still descending as fast as they could and were probably about 150 yards from the bottom, compared to her roughly 250 yards.

They'd be in range of Palin's handgun within a matter of minutes. Less time if they fell down the steep slope.

She unbuckled and shrugged off her backpack, setting it in the gully as a flat surface on which to brace the rifle, then lay down behind it. It had been more than a decade since her days training with this rifle at the academy, but she fell into the stance like it had been yesterday.

Rifle out, flick the safety off with your thumb, rest the stock of the barrel on the backpack, cheek to the stock, support the buttstock against your shoulder in the V of your left thumb and index finger, both eyes open while sighting down the scope, crosshairs on the target.

She didn't know what distance Newall had dialed the scope into for accuracy, and she certainly couldn't ask him in his current state. She spun the magnification ring to enlarge her target, then adjusted the parallax turret to bring him into focus—Palin was suddenly crystal clear, and she could see his desperate movements to try to get the ATV started before the hikers got too close. He crouched in the driver's seat, his hands hidden from view, but he'd look up every ten or fifteen seconds, judging how much time he had.

Where were Stacey and Brian? She didn't want to take this shot. From this distance there was no way to give Palin a warning and get him to surrender his firearms, like could be done from the hiking trail. But Carlisle, Brian, and Lacey had yet to arrive.

Meg was on her own. One teammate was unconscious, the other two were incoming and she couldn't take the time to call and check their progress. It was all up to her.

She couldn't see how far away the hikers were, but Palin's glances seemed to be coming faster.

Don't do it. Don't make me *do it.*

She knew the next steps—*aim for center mass, squeeze the trigger slowly.*

She blew out a breath and held it on the exhale, tried to calm her galloping heart to quiet her body to the stillness needed to save two lives as she centered the crosshairs on the middle of Palin's chest.

Palin looked up and this time didn't look away as a mask of cold determination slid over his face. He slipped his right hand beneath his jacket and pulled out a matte black handgun.

She took the shot.

Epilogue

Summit: The highest peak of a mountain.

May 18, 3:49 PM
Cold Spring Haven Animal Rescue
Cold Spring Hollow, Virginia

The double knock drew Meg's gaze from the mirror, where Cara was securing her bridal veil with a delicate comb embellished with a spray of crystalline leaves on silver wires, radiating out with clusters of creamy pearls over the simple, smooth chignon wound at the nape of Meg's neck.

"It's me," her father's voice came through the closed door.

"Come on in."

Jake Jennings stepped into the room, his expression going tender at the sight of his oldest seated at her mother's dressing table, while his middle child put the finishing touches on her hair, and his newly adopted youngest daughter hovered beside them, her face glowing with excitement. The sisters wore identical misty blue V-neck gowns, with spaghetti straps and a pleated cascade of chiffon that fell over a long side slit to the floor.

Meg held out her hand, and he crossed the floor to take it. Just short of his fifty-eighth birthday, Jake looked dashing in a black suit, with a silver tie and matching pocket square. His dark hair, so much like his older two daughters', was neatly cut, and the gray threaded through it looked like it had been carefully placed by a stylist to tie into his wedding attire.

She smiled up at him. "Look at you. Take you out of the barn and pastures and you clean up good."

"One could say the same of you." He smiled over at Cara, who stood behind them. "Are you done?"

"She's all yours."

"For a few more minutes." He took Meg's hands and drew her to her feet. "Let me look at you."

She stepped out from the dressing table's padded bench and stayed still as her father dropped her hands to step back and look at her.

She knew what he'd see, from the loose chignon with a few artful curls to frame her face, to his own mother's diamond and sapphire studs in her ears and the matching bracelet that was Jake and Eda's wedding gift to her to complement the cuff links Todd wore, to the simple halter-style wedding dress Meg had chosen once their wedding plans had solidified around the rescue.

The sleeveless dress was a pale ivory chiffon, the strapless under-bodice overlaid with the delicate flowers and swirls of Alençon lace running up to a beaded collar, leaving her toned back and arms bare. The chiffon skirt fell to a hem just brushing the floor, her flat, strappy silver sandals peeking out from beneath.

She was surprised when her father's eyes went a little damp. "Dad?"

He cleared his throat and grinned sheepishly. "Don't mind me. It's not every day my little girl gets married." He held out one hand to Meg, who slipped hers into his, and then one to Cara. "I don't have enough hands."

"That's okay." Cara extended her hand to Emma, who took it in both of hers. "I do."

"It's not every day I get to see my three girls walk down the aisle."

Eda Jennings stepped into the room to find her husband and daughters standing together, holding hands. Her gaze flew up to her husband's face. "Don't you start now, Jake. You know I need to hold it together today." She rolled her eyes at her girls, trying to break a mood tilting toward emotional. "Men. Such delicate flowers."

"That's us," Jake said to Meg with a grin. He released her hand and twirled his finger in the air. "Spin, so I can see all of you."

Meg did a slow spin, the edges of her chiffon skirt twirling out.

"Looks great. And you can't see the little that's left of the bruise on your back."

"Of course it was perfectly placed to be visible," Meg said. "It's not as bad or as big as last week, but there is a decided greenish brown smudge there still."

"Nothing a little concealer and foundation couldn't fix," Cara countered. "You're good as new." Her gaze slipped to the clock on her father's bedside table. "We should probably head downstairs. Don't want the bride to be late."

A sharp triple knock on the doorframe drew everyone's gazes.

Craig Beaumont stood in the doorway, dressed in his usual uniform of a suit and tie, but somehow for once not looking like a Fed, having ditched his typical navy, charcoal, and black for a summer-weight dove-gray suit with a cobalt tie and pocket square. He scanned the family group, his gaze finally settling on Meg. "Sorry to bother you, especially right now. I wanted a quick word with Meg. I won't keep her."

Eda bent to kiss Meg on the cheek. "We'll wait for you downstairs." She straightened and met Craig's eyes. "We start in five."

"Yes, ma'am." Craig stepped back as Eda led Jake, Cara, and Emma out of the bedroom, then closed the door behind them. He turned to find Meg on her feet, staring at him. "It's not bad news. I didn't come here five minutes before your wedding to ruin your day. I actually came to lighten it."

The tension locking Meg's shoulders melted away. "What happened?"

"I just received a text from Carlisle. They've taken Palin off the critical list and moved him out of the ICU. He's going to make it."

Warm relief coursed through Meg's veins, and she sank down onto the padded bench. "Thank God."

Craig stepped closer to lay a hand on Meg's bare shoulder. "You didn't say much about it, but I knew it had to be eating at you."

"I didn't want to take the shot in the first place. I certainly didn't want to kill him."

"You did what you had to do. Newall would have taken the shot if he'd been able."

"Palin would have died then and there if Corey had taken the shot. Between me not being able to calm my heart and breathing from the exertion enough to be truly still, the unknown accuracy of a battered scope, and me being beyond out of practice with that weapon, I'm lucky I didn't miss him entirely."

"You hit him in the shoulder, taking him down. You barely missed the subclavian artery; if you'd hit that, you would have taken him out. He was hundreds of yards away and you were off by only inches. It was enough. Now instead of an easy ticket out for what he did, the justice system will deal with him. For your sake I'm glad this is how it turned out. Newall was prepared to have Palin's death on his conscience. I'm just glad it's not on yours. Especially today."

"I heard from Corey yesterday. He's back on his feet, though he's going to still be off for another week to make sure he doesn't exacerbate the head injury. And Barron is also going to make it, as are the rest of the passengers, though Jon Slaight has a long recovery in front of him."

"Good news all around. Also, Newall and Carlisle supported your actions and have made sure there won't be any blowback. The chance of those two hikers dying was simply too great if you hadn't acted." He gave her shoulder a squeeze and let go. "I wanted you to know about Palin now, so you didn't carry that weight down the aisle with you. Today's a happy day, now for more than one reason." He held out a hand. "Time to go."

Meg smiled, laid her hand in his, and let him help her rise from the bench.

A few minutes later, the family congregated in the kitchen. McCord had just slipped out, having been waiting with Hawk and Lacey—Hawk in a snazzy bow tie and Lacey with a circle of flowers around her neck to match the girls' bouquets.

Meg held her bouquet now, a stunning cascade of peach roses, white lisianthus, creamy calla lilies, baby's breath, and dark green, glossy, trailing Italian ruscus. Cara and Emma held smaller bouquets of the same flowers, with white roses instead of peach.

"All ready?" Jake asked.

"Ready," Meg said.

"Girls?"

"We're ready." Cara linked arms with Emma. "You're going to be great."

Emma's gaze was fixed out the window where an arbor faced eighty chairs. "I didn't realize there'd be so many people. I mean, we talked about it, but now they're . . . there . . . and it feels like there's a lot of them."

Emma's tone was laden with trepidation. For the first time Meg realized how hard this might be for the girl who had found refuge at the rescue with the Jennings family after a horrific life of teenage sex trafficking. Part of her comfort level in healing had involved staying away from the public, and most certainly staying out of the limelight. Now she would be facing both. Sometimes Meg needed to remember that it was less than two years since Emma had left the life that had destroyed much of her most formative growth.

Meg laid her hand on Emma's wrist above where she clutched her bouquet. Emma's arm trembled under her fingertips. "If this makes you uncomfortable, you know I won't think any less of you if you'd rather sit this one out."

Emma's eyes shot wide with horror. "No! I can do this. It's just . . ."

"Scary. I get it." Meg's gaze fell to where Hawk sat next to Lacey. "We were going to send Hawk and Lacey down the aisle to Brian in front of you, but how about Hawk walks with you, and Lacey with Cara? Would that make you feel better? To not do the walk alone?"

Emma smiled down at Hawk. "It would. He'd stay with me?"

"All the way to the front of the aisle, then you'll be with Cara. You tell him to heel and he'll heel. I'll make sure you're set from here." Emma relaxed under Meg's touch. "Hawk, come." Hawk immediately came to stand beside Meg, staying well clear of her floor-length skirt. "Tell him to come, then when you start to walk, tell him to heel. Give him the command once again, just as you're about to walk through the chairs. He'll go at your pace and will look to you for instructions. And you're always safe with

Hawk by your side. Trust me on this one. Now call him to you."

"Hawk, come." Emma's voice already sounded steadier. Hawk moved to stand at her left side.

"That's it. Ready?"

Emma nodded.

Jake opened the back door and music began to play.

"Tell him to come, and off you go. He'll be with you the whole way."

"Hawk, come. Heel." Emma went out the door, her back straight, holding her bouquet in front of her, the black Lab at her side.

Cara squeezed her arm. "Good thinking."

"I should have thought about how this would affect her. All those strange men."

"*We* should have thought. I'll make sure she's okay through this." She hugged Meg, then pulled away with a brilliant smile. "Let's go get you hitched. Lacey, come. Heel." She went out the door, down the steps, and slowly walked toward the arbor, Lacey keeping perfect pace.

Meg looked at her parents, at her father's beaming smile and her mother's damp eyes. "We're up next."

"We're so proud of you." Eda kissed her cheek. "For the woman you've become, the life you're leading, and the man you've chosen as your partner. Your dad and I have over thirty years' experience, and we can tell you, we can see the same kind of longevity for you and Todd. We love you."

Meg blinked back the moisture in her own eyes.

"Now, now, you two, didn't we say we weren't going to start that? Though every word is gospel." Jake held out a cocked left elbow to his eldest daughter. "Come on. He's waiting."

Meg threaded her hand through her father's arm, transferred her bouquet, and then did the same with her mother to her left. She took a deep breath. "Here we go."

Everyone stood at the first sight of the bride, and Meg felt all eyes lock on her as she went down the back porch steps to the strains of Pachelbel's Canon. She walked with her parents across the lawn and then to the aisle between the rows of wooden chairs. In the white fenced paddocks beyond, Auria, their old bay mare, stood with her head over the fence, watching the proceedings like every other wedding guest, while Jeeves, their long-term resident emu, ignored everything going on around him, happily sprinting through the grass on his long legs, his head held high on his long, curved neck.

They couldn't have asked for a better day. Brilliant sun shone through the wisps of clouds riding on gentle breezes across the blue sky. And while spring in Virginia could be variable, it had been a stellar week with temps in the high seventies, or, as it was today, the low eighties. As a result, Eda's spring flowers were in full bloom, her carefully tended gardens a riot of scent and color.

The rows of chairs facing the arbor were packed full, and a quick scan of the crowd showed familiar faces, both human and canine: Todd's parents—Todd and Luke, younger carbon copies of their father, and Josh, of his mother—Lauren Wycliffe and Scott Park, both with their dogs, Rocco and Theo, standing with Craig and his wife; Special Agent Kate Moore; Greg Patrick, with his dog, Ryder; Supervisory Special Agent Carl Rutherford; Executive Assistant Director Adam Peters and his wife; Brian's husband, Ryan; Martin Sykes from the *Washington Post*; as well as Chuck Smaill, Chief Niles Koenig, and a large number of firefighters from Todd's firehouse and throughout DCFEMS. And so many more.

At the front of the crowd, Todd stood slightly off to the

right, his brothers on his left. Brian presided over the ceremony from the center of an arbor draped and wound with a filmy, trailing white fabric and bordered with stunning peach-and-white flower arrangements, Lacey sitting quietly on his left, Hawk on his right. Cara and Emma, with matching brilliant smiles, stood to Brian's right.

But her eyes were really only for Todd, who wore a charcoal-gray three-piece tuxedo with a snow-white shirt and a black satin necktie to match his black satin lapels. He stood, hands clasped in front of him, looking entirely at ease, and, as he met her gaze, gave her a broad smile.

The walk up the aisle was blessedly quick, then her parents kissed her on the cheek and stepped away to take their places beside McCord, who stood with Saki, Cara's therapy dog. Both Blink and Cody had been deemed either too anxious or too energetic for the ceremony itself, and were happily enjoying new dog chews inside the house.

Meg turned to the front, and Todd stepped forward to take her hand, bringing it to his lips and whispering, "You look amazing," before they walked to Brian together.

Brian—one of the few times she'd ever seen him in a suit and tie—grinned at them and gave Meg a wink. Then he opened the black leather folio in his hands. "Please be seated." He waited as the wedding guests took their seats. "Thank you. Friends, family, and loved ones, we come together today to join Megan Jennings and Todd Webb in marriage. We gather around them now in this wonderful place, and we look on with love and hope as these two begin their new life together as one."

As if to punctuate Brian's words, Auria let out a high-pitched, drawn-out whinny, her head thrown high.

"Auria apparently agrees," Brian quipped as everyone laughed.

Her laughter shattering whatever few nerves she had—pointless nerves, as she had no doubt this was her path and her partner on it—Meg met Todd's eyes, seeing the same certainty and commitment there, and answered the squeeze of his hand with one of her own.

"We hold marriage up as a sacred union between two people who are committed to loving one another and spending the rest of their lives together," Brian continued, "faithful to each other, and to their journey together. But we also know as a society that marriage is a serious institution. It requires deep commitment, faith and trust in your spouse, and a lot of patience to make it work."

The ceremony continued with vows given and received, rings—both carried in a small pouch behind Hawk's bow tie—exchanged, and the promises sealed with a kiss. Then, before Meg knew it, she and Todd were walking down the aisle together to the cheers and claps of those around them. Walking into their new lives as husband and wife.

The rest of the afternoon passed in a blur of congratulations and photographs, and then finally they gathered under the tent hung with chandeliers and twinkle lights twined with gauzy fabric, at white draped tables loaded with flowers, china, silver, and crystal. Dinner was a happy affair, full of chatting, humorous anecdotes from McCord as the master of ceremonies, with some help from Cara, as well as numerous toasts.

During one of McCord's breaks, when he had gone back to sit down with Meg's parents, Meg caught McCord and her sister mouthing something to each other, complete with broad smiles. Meg leaned into Cara. "What's going on with you two? Getting a little wedding fever?"

Cara laughed. "Not yet. Though that may happen sooner rather than later. Right now, we're just happy to share in your wedding bells."

"I know you. You have some kind of secret. And McCord is subtle as a tank. What gives?"

Cara's gaze shot around the room, taking in the guests

eating and drinking, clearly having a good time. "It's not the time."

"You're pregnant!"

Cara's laugh came out as a snort and she slapped her hand over her mouth, causing Todd to stare at them both curiously. Cara dropped her hand and leaned in closer to her sister. "Definitely not. Again, that may happen sooner rather than later, but later than a wedding."

"Then what is it?"

Cara's gaze shot to McCord, where he sat beside Jake. "I'll tell you, but just you for now. We don't want to make a big deal of it on your special day." She whispered in Meg's ear.

Meg's eyes flew open and her jaw actually dropped. *"Really?"*

"Yes. The official announcement is Monday, but they let those involved know yester . . ." She trailed off as Meg pushed back from the table and stood. "Where are you going?"

"I have an announcement to make."

Cara grabbed her wrist, aware they were attracting attention. "Don't announce it. It's your day."

"A day he's a part of." Meg lay her hand on Todd's shoulder. "Come with me to the mic. We have an announcement."

Todd's gaze darted from Cara, to the hand Cara held on Meg's wrist, to Meg. "We do?"

"We do." She looked down at her sister. "I'm so damned proud of him. This is the perfect time to announce it, here among friends, especially those who know exactly what he went through to get there."

Pain shadowed Cara's eyes at the memory as she released Meg's wrist.

"Everything okay?" Josh asked from the other side of Todd.

Todd shrugged. "Got me. I'm just going with the flow." He followed Meg to the mic.

Meg flipped the mic on and tapped it lightly twice to get the crowd's attention. "Hi, all, hope you're enjoying dinner." She smiled at the appreciative response. "We're going to take a few minutes of your time because I just learned something I have to share." Her eyes met McCord's and she smiled when they flared wide and he shook his head. "It's right to share this now. Yes, it's our wedding day, but there's enough love and joy to go around for this too. Cara told me something McCord learned yesterday. The official announcement will come on Monday, but McCord is this year's Pulitzer Prize winner in Journalism, Investigative Reporting, for his story on the Philadelphia crime family racket in blood diamonds and his personal experience throughout his investigation." Meg's grin widened at Todd's whoop behind her and as McCord flushed a ruddy red when her father enthusiastically slapped him on the back.

The crowd broke into cheers and applause, and, for once in his life, McCord was speechless.

Meg leaned closer to Todd. "Grab our glasses?"

"Great idea. Hang on." Todd strode to their places, grabbed their champagne flutes, and returned, handing her one.

Meg raised her glass in the air. "I know it's McCord's job as MC to do the toasts, but as bride, I'm claiming a shot at one as well. McCord, we couldn't have been more suspicious of you when fate threw you into our lives two years ago. But since then, you've not just become a friend, you've become family. When you disappeared during the Giraldi case, we went after you because family takes care of its own." Her voice grew a bit husky, and she felt Todd lay a warm hand against the exposed skin of her back to bolster her. "You scared the hell out of us, but we should have known you wouldn't go down easy." She held Mc-Cord's gaze. "We're so proud of you, for the outstanding work you do, for how you put so much effort into becoming a part of our team when we weren't initially as welcoming as we could have been, and for how you're now a crucial part of that team and are instrumental in our ability to close many of our cases. I'm beyond thrilled the rest of the world will know it as well." She raised her glass higher. "To Clay McCord."

"*To Clay McCord!*" The call thundered through the tent while McCord laid a hand over his heart and bowed his head in acknowledgment.

After taking a sip of her champagne, Meg waited for him to look up again. "Don't let this go to your head, McCord. Come Tuesday, you're back on the clock. I'm sure we'll have another case to drive you crazy with before you know it." Laughter broke out and Meg took the opportunity to step away from the mic.

Todd led Meg to her chair and seated her. The moment she put her glass down, Cara grabbed her in a tight hug. "Thank you," she whispered.

"You're welcome. He deserves all the accolades he's going to get tonight." She glanced sideways to where Todd watched them both, smiling. "We have more than enough spotlight to share."

"We sure do." Todd tapped his glass to hers one more time.

After dinner was over and the tables cleared, except for the flowers, one end of the tent was open for dancing. Todd leaned over to Meg, where she and Cara were talking to a smiling Emma. "Hey, I think we're up."

"Up?"

"First dance, we're up." He stood and held out his hand. "Dance with me."

Meg went to put her hand in his, and then, just as her

fingertips brushed his palm, she drew back, earning a puzzled look.

"Problem?"

"Not really." She pulled up her chiffon skirt and quickly unbuckled her sandals, slipped them off, and slid them out of the way under the table. She ran her toes through the grass underfoot. "I remember a particular request from you. Our first dance, barefoot in the grass. You said it would be sexy. Still in for that?"

His grin answered for him before he replied. "All in." He toed off his shoes, then stripped off his socks and jammed them in his shoes, which he tossed next to Meg's. "Good thing it's a warm evening." He held out his hand again, and this time she took it.

People were clustering around the dance floor when Todd shot an index finger at the DJ who picked up his mic. "Ladies and gentlemen, we're going to gather for the happy couple's first dance." The first notes of Ed Sheeran's "Perfect" filled the warm night air.

But Todd led her past the wooden dance floor laid out over the lawn for the evening, out the open-sided tent, and into the grass beyond. Overhead, stars twinkled in a glorious light show they were never able to see through the light pollution surrounding DC. Fireflies flitted over the surrounding pastures, transient sparks in the dark, and in the distance a Chuck-will's-widow nightjar sang.

Todd opened his arms and Meg stepped into them, his left hand taking her right and his right hand coming around her waist to snug her in tight as her hand found its place on his shoulder.

"Happy?" he asked.

"So happy. We've waited long enough for this. And Craig brought some great news just before the wedding that really took some pressure off. Rod Palin is out of the ICU. He's going to make it."

"That's amazing!" He gave her a squeeze and pulled her in closer. "You did what you had to do, but I didn't want it weighing on you."

"And now it isn't. It's been a wonderful day. And then McCord's news on top of it? Pretty perfect."

"Can't disagree. Maybe all of it is a good omen. The beginning of some smooth sailing for us."

"Nothing I'd like more. And I'm looking forward to that luck holding over our honeymoon. I'm really looking forward to getting away with you. Two weeks, no fires, no cases, just you and me . . . and Hawk. You're sure you don't mind bringing him along?"

"I'd expect nothing less. We can't leave him behind. I know how your bond works. And nothing can get in the way of you guys being ready to jump back in as soon as we're home."

Curling her hand behind his neck, she pulled his head down for a soft kiss. "I love you. It never fails to astonish me how much you get me."

"I love you too. And it's not so different from how you get me. It's why we work. Now and always."

"Now and always."

She pressed her cheek against his, tipping her head back slightly so she could see the stars twinkling overhead as he spun her into the dance.

Acknowledgments

Writing *Summit's Edge* took me to new territory—not only an area of the United States I'd never personally visited, but straight up a fourteener, when I've never climbed anything higher than Mount Norwottuck in Massachusetts, a mere 1,110 feet tall. I was extremely fortunate to have several experts to assist me in ensuring my details were correct:

Judi Simecek—for being my primary boots-on-the-ground consultant for Aspen and greater Colorado. Your knowledge of the region allowed me to find the perfect location for my planned plane crash; thank you for humoring my many questions about the Maroon Bells area. Your early read of the manuscript also ensured all local details were correct, and your recommendations strengthened that aspect of the manuscript. Your willingness to assist allowed me to bring this beautiful area to vibrant life.

Jerome Simecek—for sharing his knowledge of airplanes and flying, especially the specific and significant challenges of flight in the Aspen area.

Tom Irwin—for our initial discussion on how to stage the hijacking, including airplanes and airports of all sizes, which specific type of plane to use in this scenario, aspects of airplane security and how to legitimately circumvent it, and how to make a plane disappear from radar. It was Tom's knowledge as a retired commercial airline pilot that allowed me to set up a believable situation so the rest of the story could unfold.

Shane Vandevalk—for what is becoming his typical invaluable help on any manuscript. Shane and I spent a long time brainstorming the hijacking in great detail, as well as methods of taking down a suspect to ensure Meg's final shot was legally indisputable. Shane is also my weapons consultant and was instrumental in all weapons and ammunition details. On top of all that, Shane was, as always, an enthusiastic title-brainstorming partner, including proposing *Summit's Edge* for this novel.

Matt Vandevalk—for his specific assistance with the Remington 700.

Jordan Newton—for additional help on title and plot brainstorming, as well as for veterinary advice on canine physiology and how to prevent high-altitude illness in dogs.

My critique team—Jessica Newton, Rick Newton, Judi Simecek, and Sharon Taylor—for once again jumping in enthusiastically for another excellent and in-depth edit. Your combined hundreds of comments and thousands of corrections collectively make for one heck of an edit, but they work to produce a very polished manuscript, and I'm so appreciative of your efforts. (I bet James is as well; he just doesn't know what he's missing!)

Nicole Resciniti—for not just being my agent, but a partner in my career, and for always having my back and for being ready to assist in any aspect of publishing.

The Kensington team—Louis Malcangi and his art team, Jesse Cruz, Larissa Ackerman, Lauren Jernigan, Robin Cook, Susanna Gruninger, Vida Engstrand, Kait Johnson, Alexandra Nicolajsen, Kristin McLaughlin, Sarah Beck, and Andi Paris. From an author's perspective, your support is invaluable as we work together to make the best possible book, and to launch it into the world. Many thanks for all you do.

James Abbate—for your enthusiastic assistance with all aspects of the project, from plot selection, to cover brainstorming, to always keeping me in the loop on production dates, to lightning-fast and very helpful edits, to being available at seemingly any time day or night, despite our time difference. Most importantly, you help me manage an overloaded writing schedule and are as flexible as possible in making sure all deadlines are met with my sanity intact. I appreciate every bit of what you do to help smooth my way, but special thanks particularly for that last aspect!

Jen J. Danna, writing as Sara Driscoll